W9-BQW-793

Her gaze drifted down his bare back and up again, lingering on his shoulders

Nate froze. He didn't know what to do, what to think. *How* to think.

Okay, Claire checking him out had nothing to do with him and everything to do with her being celibate for two years. But that didn't explain the sudden leap of his pulse.

He had to put an end to this.

He turned, deliberately catching her in the act, his gaze challenging.

She met his eyes with a "got me" smile…and something else, which years of friendship made easy to interpret. An invitation.

Nate felt as if he had been punched.

For a moment that seemed to go on forever he saw possibilities. Saw everything he'd ever wanted, everything he'd believed beyond his reach.

And then the moment passed.

Dear Reader,

Bring Him Home, is the third book in a series exploring the impact of an ambush in Afghanistan on the lives of its survivors—three Special Forces soldiers plus the widow and bereaved fiancée of the two men killed.

Back in civilian life, each hero deals with the aftermath differently, but needs the right woman's love to truly move on. In *Bring Him Home,* Nathan Wyatt's right woman is the widow of his best friend. To make things even tougher for him, I gave Nate a catch-22 situation during the ambush, which means Claire is the *last* woman he should fall in love with. In fact, it's the story of a love triangle, a man trying to reconcile a woman to her husband's fateful choice, a choice she's having trouble forgiving. In the process Nate finds both love and redemption.

I lost a dear friend, Harlequin Desire author Sandra Hyatt, while writing this book. A decade ago Sandra, Abby Gaines, Tessa Radley and I formed a writing support group, the Writegals. The job description for a Writegal was critique partner, cheerleader, sympathy giver, partner in crime, info exchanger and kick-in-the-pantser. We all struggled through our journey to publication together, one by one getting The Call and each achieving our dream of being published with Harlequin Books.

Sandra was a wonderful person and a gifted writer, and her passing reconfirmed one of the themes inherent in this series, and in particular *Bring Him Home.* Love can transcend death. And if grief must be the price of having extraordinary people in our lives, then pay it, and pay it gladly.

Karina Bliss

Bring Him Home

KARINA BLISS

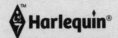

TORONTO NEW YORK LONDON
AMSTERDAM PARIS SYDNEY HAMBURG
STOCKHOLM ATHENS TOKYO MILAN MADRID
PRAGUE WARSAW BUDAPEST AUCKLAND

If you purchased this book without a cover you should be aware that this book is stolen property. It was reported as "unsold and destroyed" to the publisher, and neither the author nor the publisher has received any payment for this "stripped book."

Recycling programs
for this product may
not exist in your area.

ISBN-13: 978-0-373-60708-2

BRING HIM HOME

Copyright © 2012 by Karina Bliss

All rights reserved. Except for use in any review, the reproduction or utilization of this work in whole or in part in any form by any electronic, mechanical or other means, now known or hereafter invented, including xerography, photocopying and recording, or in any information storage or retrieval system, is forbidden without the written permission of the publisher, Harlequin Enterprises Limited, 225 Duncan Mill Road, Don Mills, Ontario, Canada M3B 3K9.

This is a work of fiction. Names, characters, places and incidents are either the product of the author's imagination or are used fictitiously, and any resemblance to actual persons, living or dead, business establishments, events or locales is entirely coincidental.

This edition published by arrangement with Harlequin Books S.A.

For questions and comments about the quality of this book please contact us at Customer_eCare@Harlequin.ca.

® and TM are trademarks of the publisher. Trademarks indicated with ® are registered in the United States Patent and Trademark Office, the Canadian Trade Marks Office and in other countries.

www.Harlequin.com

Printed in U.S.A.

ABOUT THE AUTHOR

On average, romance authors take five years and write four and a half manuscripts before they get their first book contract. Despite her willingness to be the exception, New Zealander Karina Bliss ended up fitting that statistic almost exactly. En route, she became the first Australasian to win a Golden Heart from the Romance Writers of America.

Bring Him Home is her tenth romance book for Harlequin Superromance and the third of a series around Special Forces heroes. The former journalist lives with her husband and son north of Auckland. Visit her on the web at www.karinabliss.com or drop her an email at karina@karinabliss.com. She loves to hear from readers.

Books by Karina Bliss

HARLEQUIN SUPERROMANCE

1373—MR. IMPERFECT
1426—MR. IRRESISTIBLE
1475—MR. UNFORGETTABLE
1524—SECOND-CHANCE FAMILY
1596—LIKE FATHER, LIKE SON
1622—WHAT THE LIBRARIAN DID
1668—THAT CHRISTMAS FEELING
        "Kiss Me, Santa"
1682—HERE COMES THE GROOM
1722—STAND-IN WIFE

Other titles by this author available in ebook format.

All backlist available in ebook. Don't miss any of our special offers. Write to us at the following address for information on our newest releases.

Harlequin Reader Service
U.S.: 3010 Walden Ave., P.O. Box 1325, Buffalo, NY 14269
Canadian: P.O. Box 609, Fort Erie, Ont. L2A 5X3

This book is dedicated to all those
who have lost someone.
And to the memory of my friend,
Sandra Hyatt. It was a privilege.

CHAPTER ONE

Northeastern Afghanistan

EARS RINGING FROM the explosion, Nathan Wyatt struggled to retain consciousness, one hand instinctively closing on his weapon, while he flung the other forward to find a brace as the Humvee spun one hundred and eighty degrees. His nose hurt like a bastard.

The vehicle ground to a halt on its destroyed front tires with a slamming jolt, facing the second of the four-vehicle convoy they'd been leading.

From the backseat, Nate blinked, trying to process what he was seeing.

The road mine had blown in the hood, twisting their custom-fitted bull bars into a kids' climbing frame and sending shrapnel tearing into the interior. Groaning, Ross slumped over the steering wheel, blood soaking his lower body. Beside him, Steve raised shaky hands to a head wound.

The roar of an accelerator dragged his attention through the shattered windscreen. The second convoy vehicle was reversing at high speed, its occupants—local allies—firing wildly. Bullets whizzed past the mangled Humvee. *C'mon, guys, we taught you better than—*

Boom!

The truck imploded in a blinding flash of light and the Humvee shuddered under a percussion shock. Gravel, rock and flaming debris showered the roof. Nate's brain engaged. Fast. The first improvised explosive device had been weight triggered. The second, timer detonated. Someone had waited to set it off when the truck backed up to find cover.

He jerked upright, wiped a hand over his rapidly swelling nose. "Ambush!" he hollered at Lee. No response. For the first time he realized the gunner's legs weren't dangling from the turret. Seizing a link of ammo for the .50 machine gun bolted to the Humvee's roof, he yelled at Steve, "We've lost Lee!"

Boom!

The jerry cans of fuel exploded in the burning truck, spewing flaming material in every direction and belching clouds of black smoke. It swirled through their doorless vehicle, making him cough.

"Need help!" Steve shouted. Grabbing the comms unit with one hand, he used the other to press down on an arterial wound in Ross's thigh that was pumping blood like an oil well, thick and viscous.

Nate dropped the ammo link and scrambled for the medic kit.

"Contact, contact!" Steve shouted, giving the coordinates for backup as Nate ripped the packaging on an elastic latex band and jerked it tight a couple inches above the wound. A third explosion from the burning truck rocked their vehicle, and Nate cursed as one of the two steel S-hooks caught Ross's flesh. Good thing he was unconscious.

Steve dropped the mic and took over with Ross. "Got it. Recon!"

Reshouldering the link of ammo and his weapon, Nate swung up through the hole in the Humvee's roof, emerging into fierce heat and choking clouds of noxious black smoke. Even through a broken nose he could distinguish the obscene note of barbecuing flesh.

The blazing truck was providing temporary cover. But it only needed a shift in the hot desert wind to expose them. To show the enemy their job wasn't done.

It took one glance to ascertain the machine gun was inoperable. As he armed his M4A1 with a grenade launcher, he strained to see through the stinging smoke. Trying to locate the enemy, sight Lee, discover an LUP—laying-up position. The fumes coated his throat, already tight with emotion he couldn't afford. *Stay alive, mate. We'll come for you.*

But first they had to save themselves.

The ringing in his ears gone, he could hear exploding rocket-propelled grenades, bursts of 40mm grenade fire and the steady stream of small arms and machine guns. Through the billowing smoke he caught glimpses of tracer rounds, and could see that the convoy's two remaining vehicles were under attack and returning fire. Nate ducked back into the Humvee.

His body twisted at an awkward angle, Steve was applying a QuikClot sponge to Ross's wound. "Our guys engaging." Nate handed him a pressure bandage and started collecting extra weapons and ammo. "No sign of Lee, but visibility's shit, which is buying us time. Can't see an LUP. We'll have to take our chances with the ditch alongside the road. Now let's get the hell out of here before the insurgents discover we're not dead yet."

"My foot's trapped." Steve tied off a bandage. "Leave me a crowbar and a GPMG. I'll catch up to you two."

Nate dropped his armful on the ground outside the Humvee, fetched the crowbar and set to work, cutting off Steve's protest. "You can waste time arguing or you can plug Ross into a saline/morphine drip."

Steve bent over Ross. Blood from his head wound dripped onto the unconscious man and he paused to wipe it with his sleeve. It was shredded and bloody with shrapnel, but the Kevlar vest had protected his chest. "Smoke starts thinning, you go," he barked.

Nate began levering the jagged metal away from Steve's calf. "Don't distract a one-eyed man." The left was swelling shut and his nose had clotted, forcing him to breathe through his mouth, which drew the acrid smoke farther into his lungs. Every cough made him feel as if his face was being hit by a two-by-four.

In the midst of the chaos, both men worked with glacial calm. Steve stuck a needle in Ross's arm. "Stay alive, Ice."

Ross stirred. "Hey, we're the Indestructibles," he muttered. He opened his eyes. "Where's Lee?"

His hands slippery with blood and sweat and a fear he wouldn't give in to, Nate redoubled his efforts. "Expecting him any minute, leading the U.S. frickin' cavalry."

Ross lapsed back into unconsciousness.

"Smoke's thinning," warned Steve.

"Got it." With a grunt, Nate levered the last of the tangled metal away from Steve's calf, then swore. The ankle was securely clamped in place by the twisted bull bars.

For a moment Steve stilled, then calmly finished taping the IV to Ross's body. "Pass me some hardware and get outta here."

Nate dropped the crowbar. "I'll get a hacksaw. Cut off your foot if I have to."

"There's no time, mate." Steve's voice was shaky but determined.

As if substantiating his argument, they heard the whine of an RPG. Twenty meters in front of them the road exploded. They'd been spotted.

Steve picked up Ross's weapon. "Take Ice and find cover. I'll keep them busy."

"No man left behind." Scrambling to his feet, Nate hauled out a machine gun and lay on the ground beside the Humvee. Wiping the sweat from his battered face, he took aim and fired. A burst of rounds kicked up the hill.

"I said go. We're not all dying today."

Ignoring Steve, Nate lined up another shot.

A second RPG imploded, fifteen meters to the left of the vehicle, igniting a small pool of fuel. "Get Ross the hell out of here and save his life." Viciously, Steve kicked Nate in the ribs with his free foot. "That's an order, soldier!"

With a roar of frustration, Nate scrambled to his feet and hoisted Ross onto his shoulder. Steve loaded him up with munitions. "Tell my family I love them. And tell my wife—" His voice broke. "Tell Claire I'm sorry."

Nate set his jaw. "I'll drop Ross and come back."

His best friend's gaze met his. "Goodbye, mate."

"I'm coming back, goddamn it!"

Steadying Ross, Nate ran. Lungs pumping, stomach sour, heart breaking. He ran.

The blast flung him forward on a surge of heat and power. He landed winded, staring into a blue Sunday sky with Ross on top of him. Rolling them both into the ditch, he elbowed up the shallow bank with desperate speed. The Humvee was burning, Steve, a silhouette amidst the flames. Half a dozen insurgents descended from the wadi, opening fire.

On a sob, Nate raised his weapon to his good eye, aimed and pulled the trigger.

And then the fighting started.

CHAPTER TWO

Eighteen months later

NATE MARKED THE BLONDE as a potential stalker the moment she walked poolside on Hotel Hollywood's rooftop garden where rocker Zander Freedman's party raged with its usual excess.

For a start she wasn't conscious of being observed—not a trait of any of the celebrity guests here. And she was nervous. Despite the cool way she lifted her chin as she walked through the throng, she clutched her purse tightly. Damn it, the bag was large enough to conceal a weapon.

He couldn't read her eyes. She wore shades that dwarfed her face, but her exposed arms were too pale for a local and the simple blue halter sundress was department store, not designer. After a year in the service of the rich and famous Nate could tell the difference. And though she seemed as pretty—and as skinny— as any anorexic starlet, the boobs were real.

His gaze dropped to her feet. Serviceable sandals and unpainted toenails in a place where everyone was buffed, polished, gleaming, manicured, pedicured, tautened…hell…a couple even had butt implants.

He glanced at the other security detail to see if she'd triggered their radar. Luther and Jake were doing a perimeter check; Andrew had been waylaid by an older movie actress, known for her penchant for muscle. And judging by the twenty-two-year-old's starstruck expression, he wasn't unhappy about it. With a pang, Nate remembered a time when he'd been part of a team he could rely on. "Don't party with clients," he growled into his mouthpiece and Andrew jumped guiltily.

As a line of waiters simultaneously popped the corks on twelve bottles of Krug champagne, the blonde paused by the ice sculpture of an electric guitar, its strings dripping in the Los Angeles heat. Waving away the waitress who approached her with a tray of hors d'oeuvres, she scanned the crowd with the single-minded intensity Nate recognized as that of a rabid fan.

Casually he stepped closer to his employer, currently holding court by the guardrail, a cigar in one hand, a tumbler of Grey Goose vodka in the other. A rock icon with a genius for market-ing, Zander was fresh off a season of a hit reality show where Rage's lead singer had cast new band members for his comeback tour.

Unfortunately the show had also increased his quota of crazies.

Swinging his attention back to the blonde, Nate caught her staring in their direction. Probably harmless, just wanted to ask Zander to father her babies. Or hear her sing.

Or she could be like the fan who'd shot John Lennon.

She swallowed hard, tucked a loose strand of long hair behind her ear then started walking toward them. He strode forward to intercept her through the olfactory blanket of expensive perfumes, lotions and liquor, today leavened with chlorine and… Nate took another whiff. Surely even Zander's crowd wasn't arrogant enough to smoke marijuana at a public event? He'd check that out next.

"Ma'am?" With a polite smile, Nate stopped in front of the blonde and lifted his mirrored aviator shades so she could read in his eyes that he meant business. "Can I see your invitation?" Instead, she reached out a hand. Lightning fast he caught her slender wrist, registering the rapid beat of her pulse under his fingers.

"Nate," she said in a New Zealand accent. "Don't you recognize me?"

Shocked, he dropped her wrist as if he'd been

burned. "Claire," he croaked then took a deep breath to steady his voice. "What are you doing here?"

But he knew. With Steve dead, they needed to appoint a third trustee for her family trust. Nate thought of the papers sitting in his study while he psyched himself up into finally dealing with them and cursed his procrastination.

His best friend's widow lifted her sunglasses, and he braced himself for the accusation he knew was coming. But her blue eyes held only affection…and empathy. He forced himself not to flinch. "Can I have a hug first?" she said.

"Of course." His arms were leaden as he embraced her. "How are you?"

"Jet-lagged." If Claire noticed his reluctance she was ignoring it. "I dumped my bags off at your condo. Or, rather, your neighbor's. She was in her garden, fortunately. I tracked your location through that celebrity-locator website. Technology must really make your job harder."

"Yeah." She was expecting to stay with him? He broke into a cold sweat under his black Burberry suit. "But how the hell did you talk your way in?"

"I said you were my brother," Claire confessed cheerfully, "and that we had a family emergency. And I showed them this." She opened her handbag and retrieved a snapshot.

He glanced at it, unprepared for the pain that swept over him. It had been taken three years earlier, shortly after Nate and Claire had gone halves in *Heaven Sent*.

In the photo, the three of them stood in front of the dilapidated fishing vessel, Claire in the middle. Steve had just suggested renaming the boat *They Saw Us Coming* and they were all laughing into the camera.

Nate dropped it back into her bag. "You should never have got through security," he rasped.

"You could at least pretend to be pleased to see me. I've come halfway across the world to get you."

"Get me?"

"Only for a few days."

He had to nip this in the bud right now. "Claire, Zander's going on tour next week. I can't come home right now."

"*Rolling Stone* magazine said it doesn't kick off until next month."

"Yeah, but we fly out early to set up," he lied. "I'd lose my job. Look, I'll sign those papers you sent through a while back. You can take them home with you. And of course I'll reimburse you for your flights."

"Unfortunately it's no longer that simple." There was a hint of desperation in her voice.

"Hang on…Luther?" He spoke into his mic. "Cover Zander for me for a couple minutes."

The receiver crackled. "Got it."

Cupping Claire's elbow, he steered her into the shade, away from the curious glances of the polished and indiscreet guests mingling nearby. "Fill me in."

"I have a buyer for the house."

"You're selling?"

She nodded. "And I need you to sign the transfer of ownership. If you come home for a few days then we can complete the documentation very quickly. I can't afford the sale to fall through."

His frown deepened. "Are you in financial trouble?"

"No, but I need more capital to fast-track the boat upgrade so she's ready for November."

"Okay, now you've really lost me."

"Before the broadbill and striped marlin arrive? And the snapper numbers take a leap." She smiled. "So to speak."

He looked at her blankly.

"My new fishing charter venture?" she prompted. "It was all in my offer for your share of the boat, Nate."

He hadn't even opened the last envelope. His face heated.

Her smile grew a little tight. "Just as well I jumped on a plane, huh?"

"Claire, I'm sorry. Things are so busy here." Lame, even to his ears.

"You don't have to make excuses," she said quietly. "Not to me. Everyone has their own method of grieving and if yours is avoiding your friends for a while…I get that." She took a deep breath. "But I can't keep sitting in limbo. With Steve dead and you living overseas, the trust isn't working anymore. I want to break it, put everything back in my name. All I need is a few days. Can't you spare me that?"

His Italian tie suddenly felt too tight. "We'll find another way," he said, loosening it.

"There isn't another way." For the first time she sounded impatient. "If I lose the buyer I won't have the money to upgrade *Heaven Sent*. Without the upgrade I'll miss this sports-fishing season. I've given up my job—"

"You've already quit your job?" Claire was marketing manager for a boutique hotel in Whangarei. She was diving into a risky prospect without a lifeline.

But she was looking past him with an expression that told him exactly who was behind him. His boss had a shark's instinct for drama. Nate turned. Pushing forty, Zander Freedman looked ten years younger, which was no surprise since Nate knew he spent most mornings at treatment clinics.

His famous face was tanned and taut with cosmetic surgery under a full head of implant-enhanced hair. His silk T-shirt had been custom made to hang loose over his slight paunch and cling to the biceps he was inordinately proud of.

"Claire, this is—"

"I know who he is." Smiling warmly, Claire held out her hand, and Nate sensed Zander's interest. Great, just great. "I'm Claire Langford from New Zealand, an old friend of Nate's. I have to apologize for crashing your party, but I wanted to surprise him."

Nate narrowed his eyes, instantly suspicious. She'd known he'd have made excuses if she'd given him warning.

"Langford?" Zander's forehead wrinkled as much as the Botox would allow. "Nate, isn't that the name of an army buddy from the ambush?" The rocker was a military-history nut and Nate's Special Forces background, specifically the heroism award at the end of his career, had cinched this job.

"My husband, Steve, was one of the two men who died," Claire answered.

"Shit," Zander said. "Then you'll need a drink." Claire blinked and he added, "It works a whole lot better than sympathy."

For all his skewed worldview, the rocker got some things right.

She smiled. "Thank you, I do want to move on." Her gaze returned to Nate's. "Which is why I'm here."

"Then let's toast to new beginnings." Zander snapped his fingers and a waiter materialized with a tray. A crystal tumbler of Grey Goose stood out from the tall flutes of Krug, the champagne's straw-colored bubbles sparkling in the sun's last blaze before sunset. Zander dumped his empty tumbler and picked up the full one. Then handing Claire a flute, he gestured for Nate to take a glass. "C'mon, buddy, break your bodyguard code for once, hey? This is a special occasion."

Grimly, Nate accepted a drink, hoping Claire didn't read this as a concession. They all chinked glasses. "You know my brother, Devin, married a New Zealander," Zander told Claire. "A frickin' librarian. That woman can give you a paper cut just by looking at you. All you Kiwi chicks that tough?" He chuckled because she looked as fragile as bone china.

Until you noticed her eyes—Viking blue.

Lowering her lashes, she inquired politely, "Is your brother rejoining Rage?" The rocker paused midswig. He expected everyone to know everything about him. "I've been out of circulation," Claire added, obviously realizing her mistake.

"Oh, sure." Zander grew magnanimous. "Let me bring you up to date with what I've been doing." As he expanded on his favorite subject, Nate watched Claire. When had she gotten Hollywood thin? And her smile was overcast with a fatigue that went beyond jet lag. He drained his champagne.

"How's Lewis?" he asked abruptly, interrupting Zander midflow.

"He's become a troublemaker," she said.

"Excellent." Zander glanced between them. "Now, who the hell is Lewis?"

"My thirteen-year-old son."

"I lost my virginity at thirteen." Zander savored his vodka. "She was seventeen, worked at Dairy Queen, which was pretty apt, because she was stacked. The sex was all over in seconds, of course." He grinned at Claire. "I've improved since then."

She laughed.

Nate frowned. Even married women weren't safe around Zander. Widows. She was widowed. His earpiece crackled into life. "Nate, got some trouble quadrant four," Luther rumbled. "I've sent Andrew to cover Zander."

"I'll be right there. I'm wanted," he said to

Claire. "Let's organize a driver to take you to my house."

"No hurry." Zander put an arm around her shoulders. "I'll look after her."

Nate hesitated. Telling the rocker to behave would only make him act more outrageously. He nodded to Claire. "I won't be long." Then he strode over to the far corner of the deck where Luther towered over the skinny self-proclaimed successor to Eminem.

JT Trigga held a joint in one hand and his date's booty in the other. Behind them, the rapper's bodyguards—all tatts, glares and bling—jostled like linebackers. "If you give it to me, sir," Luther was saying in his deep, calm voice, "I'll dispose of it for you."

"Yeah, I bet you will." JT Trigga blew a smoke ring in Luther's face. "Chill, cuz, it's only Mary Jane." He spotted Nate. "Tell your boy, here, to turn a blind eye."

"We can't do that today, JT." Nate summoned a regretful look. "Not in public. I'm sorry." Before the rapper could argue, he flicked the joint out of the man's fingers and ground it out under the heel of his shoe.

"This ain't no party," JT complained. "It's a suck-up to the press.... Zee's sellin' out. Where is he…? I'm gonna tell him."

This son of a bitch wasn't going anywhere

near Claire. Nate glanced at the rapper's body-guards, all thugs, not an ounce of professional-ism amongst them and probably carrying more metal than they were licensed for. And the girl-friend was clearly underage. "Zander's tied up right now," he said smoothly, "but he asked me to introduce you to Vince Rutledge." Ruth-lessly, he sacrificed the renowned music jour-nalist from *Rolling Stone*.

JT brightened. He had a new album pend-ing. "Yeah?"

"Except your entourage will have to stay here. We don't want to crowd him. Your daugh-ter, too."

"My what?"

Nate returned a blank look. "Not your daugh-ter?" He hesitated. "Okay, maybe we'll tee up another time. You know how Zander feels about jailbait."

The rapper stiffened, and inwardly Nate cursed his slipup. Claire's presence had unset-tled him. He winked. "He'll be jealous."

JT relaxed. "Give her cab money," he said to his boys.

The teenager started to complain, but Luther took her by the arm. "Let me organize that for you, ma'am."

"You boys relax, enjoy yourselves," Nate suggested to the entourage. He and Luther had rescuing underage damsels down to a fine art. "We'll cover your boss.... Follow me, JT."

He foisted the rapper onto a reluctant Vince, then organized a ride for Claire and went to fetch her. He needed time to come up with a fix that would get him off the hook. He'd do anything for her—except go home.

She and Zander were standing where he'd left them, blond heads close, talking intently. To his astonishment, as he closed the gap, Claire reached up and gave the rocker a hug. Never a man to miss an opportunity, Zander enthusiastically returned the embrace, his hands creeping down her back to rest on the upper curve of her bottom. Nate's fist curled involuntarily. If Steve were here...

But Steve wasn't here.

Zander caught Nate glaring at him and offered his irrepressible grin, the one that charmed him out of trouble with men and women alike. Nate scowled. Not this time, mate. His employer's grin broadened, but he released Claire. When she saw Nate, a curious mix of anger and apology crossed her face.

His survival instincts kicked in. "What's going on?"

"Zee." Dimity, Zander's personal assistant, teetered over on heels so high she had to take tiny steps. "We need you for photographs with the new band members."

"Jeez, I'm sick of them already," Zander complained, but dumped his glass. "Goodbye, Claire, next time I'm visiting my mom and brother you can take me fishing."

"It's a date," she said.

"Then we'll definitely leave your chaperone ashore," said Zander, kissing Claire's cheeks in the French style. As he left with his PA, Nate gestured Andrew to follow.

"Chaperone?" Claire asked.

"Don't worry about it.… I've organized you a ride to my condo."

"I should tell you something first."

"Later," he said. "When I'm off duty. I can't look after you and do my job." Dusk was falling, along with inhibitions, as alcohol took effect on the guests. And the civility of this crowd was tenuous at best.

She hesitated. "Of course." They walked through the crowd. A young woman had stripped to her bra and thong and was frolicking in the pool in front of a geriatric rocker. He had his hand in the halter of his young date's top. Shocked, Claire glanced at Nate.

"Think of it as a bazaar," he advised. "Everyone here wants something—sex, money, fame, contracts."

She shook her head. "That doesn't make him less of a creep."

"The exploitation is mutual," he said dryly. "You think she wants him for his looks?"

"Hey, Nathan!" An old girlfriend of Zander's caught him by the lapels. She was drunk, swaying on her stilettos. "Has Zee replaced me yet?" Stormy asked in her sex-kitten voice.

He steadied her, smiling his reassurance. "You know you're one of a kind." She'd really loved the son of a bitch and Nate knew first-hand she had taken the breakup badly. He'd been there when Zander dumped her. Sometimes he hated his job.

She dropped his arm for that of Zander's English tour manager, Bill, who looked as if he couldn't believe his luck. "We need some privacy, mate. Where can we go?"

"The top floor of suites has been reserved for guests."

"Yeah, but is it guarded?" Bill pressed a nostril on his beaky nose closed and feigned a snort, too drunk to be cautious. Stormy giggled.

"You'll be given a warning," Nate said evenly. He could feel Claire's gaze on him.

But she didn't say anything until they were in the elevator heading down to the lobby. "They're doing coke," she said. "And you're okay with that?"

"If they're consenting adults, my policy is hear no evil, speak no evil, see no evil...and think of the dollar bills."

A frown creased her brow. She searched his face. The Nate she was looking for didn't exist anymore.

The elevator doors opened and he ushered her into the bustling lobby and then out to the courtyard where a limo waited.

"Do you like your job?" she asked.

He shrugged. "Twelve hundred a day. What's not to like?" Handing her his house key, Nate opened the limo door. She didn't get in.

"You won't do another runner on me, will you?" When he'd left New Zealand, he hadn't said goodbye.

"Where else would I go?" he said, trying to keep the sharpness out of his voice.

"Promise me, Nate."

He gave a curt nod. Still, she hesitated. "Just remember," she said, "I'm not here to make your life harder. Only to make mine easier."

Nate nodded again, fighting the guilt kindled by her appeal. "Go back to my place, catch some sleep, we'll talk in the morning."

"I'll wait up," she said.

His mouth tightened. "Fine...but I'll be late."

"It's good to see you, Nate." She smiled wryly. "Even if you can't say the same."

The door clicked shut, the limo drove away and he could breathe again. Think again, without the pressure of those clear blue eyes on him. There was a flight to New Zealand tomorrow night. He'd make sure she was on it.

On the rooftop, he relieved Andrew and sent him to keep an eye on JT's entourage. Surrounded by TV cameras, Zander was putting on his gloves in preparation for his big gesture—smashing the guitar ice sculpture to signal the official launch of his tour. He gestured Nate over.

"I told the gorgeous widow she could have you for three days," he said. "You can thank me by getting rid of JT. That prick's really starting to annoy me."

CHAPTER THREE

N<small>ATE DIDN'T HAVE MUCH</small> in his fridge. Starving, Claire surveyed the contents. Long-life milk. A cantaloupe. One block of cream cheese. Greek yogurt. Each sitting on its own shelf. She checked the freezer. A packet of bagels. He must eat breakfast here and nothing else.

When in Rome. She cubed the cantaloupe and added it to the muesli she'd discovered in the pantry, eschewing the milk in favor of yogurt. She'd been too nervous about seeing Nate to eat on the plane. Or at the party.

Thinking about their encounter, she nearly let her appetite desert her again. But she was determined to regain the weight she'd lost after Steve's death, so she found a spoon in one of the many empty drawers in the kitchen.

The only thing this house had plenty of was space.

Her footsteps echoed across the flagstone floor as she took her bowl of muesli into the dining room where an eight-seater dining table sat in solitary splendor. Heavy drapes of a hideous salmon pink clashed with the golden wood. The place was obviously a rental, because it held no personal touches at all.

Claire put her bowl on the table, picked it up again. She didn't want to eat here, or in the living room that had a river-rock fireplace that Fred and Wilma Flintstone could have broiled a brontosaurus in, one enormous couch, a slab of coffee table and a high-tech entertainment system. The only place in this mausoleum that looked lived in was Nate's office.

She'd found her lawyer's unopened envelopes there.

On impulse she opened the French doors leading off the kitchen and took her breakfast onto the patio that overlooked the canal. The balmy air carried a sea breeze from Venice Beach, one block north, which simultaneously made her homesick and reminded her why she was doing this. For a new start.

As she ate, Claire worried about Nate. He'd looked so different, impeccably groomed, clean shaven, expensive haircut. For a moment when he'd recognized her, she'd thought with relief, Ross and Dan were wrong. He hadn't changed.

He was still Nate, loyal and caring, who valued people above everything. Nate, who always remembered birthdays and Christmas and organized get-togethers because as he'd once told her, he was replacing every bad memory of his foster childhood with a good one.

The muesli caught in her throat. Putting down the spoon, she stared out across the canal, to the brightly lit houses. Their refracted light on the black water made it glisten like oil. How many good memories did it take to cancel out having one of his best friends dying in his arms?

She'd been so sure he'd open up to her. She knew how to be sensitive, unlike Ross and Dan, who'd told him bluntly that it was time to re-engage with the people who cared about him. Though equally frustrated and hurt by Nate's withdrawal, Claire empathized with his need to distance himself from well-meaning friends and relatives. Hell, she understood it.

Except, as soon as the shock wore off, he'd become remote, cynical, jaded...at home in a world he once would have laughed at, condoning behavior he once would have scorned. She'd never seen a man so disconnected from his old self.

That's when she knew even an emotional appeal wouldn't work.

So she'd gone out of her way to be understanding and conciliatory. And he'd lied to her. Outright lied to her. Claire pushed the bowl away. Zander had told her they weren't flying out for another couple weeks.

Anger rose in her and she quashed it, the way she'd quashed other emotions over the last eighteen months. Because they didn't serve her. She'd learned that when Steve died. It didn't matter how much you wept or raged or begged God for things to be different. You couldn't change reality. So you had to work with it. Her son and Steve's mother needed her to be strong. She needed to see herself as strong.

Claire pressed the light button on her wristwatch: 1:00 a.m. She'd wait up all night if necessary. However reluctant he was to see her, Nate wouldn't break his promise. She might not be able to rewrite the past, but she would direct her future.

Taking her half-eaten meal to the counter, Claire did a mental time-zone conversion, then retrieved her cell from her tote bag and dialed a New Zealand number. Along with Nate, Lee and Ross, Dan had been her husband's troopmate in the SAS, but he hadn't been in the convoy during the ambush. It had taken him a long time to come to terms with that.

He was also Steve's cousin. As a kid, Steve had spent most school holidays at the Jansens' family farm, and Lewis, who wasn't happy about moving, had recently expressed a desire to do the same.

For the next two weeks he was staying with

Dan and his wife, Jo, while Claire made the Stingray Bay beach house more suited to permanent residency and got the boat renovations under way. She and her son could both do with the break.

"Lewis is in bed," Dan said after they'd exchanged greetings.

"Did I get the time wrong? I thought it was only 9:00 p.m. there."

He laughed. "I worked him into the ground… poor kid. We're docking lambs."

"I hope he's not giving you any trouble." *Because he's been giving his mother a lot of trouble lately,* she thought wryly.

"Occasional moments of teen angst, but we're ignoring them. Is our other boy giving you trouble?" Claire had asked Dan to keep her flying visit to L.A. a secret from Lewis because she didn't want to get her son's hopes up. Nate had dashed them enough times already.

"I'll get back to you. Currently I'm cautiously optimistic." With Zander in her corner, surely Nate had run out of excuses. A phone started ringing somewhere. "Listen, I've got to go. Give Lewis my love and tell him I'll phone tomorrow."

She reached the hall after the answering service had kicked in. "Hi, Nate, it's Marcie. Left a message on your cell too, but just to confirm…

Roberta doesn't need an escort to court tomorrow. Her husband's back in jail. On an unrelated charge, thank God. Talk soon. Bye."

Claire stared at the phone. Did all her old friend's associates break the law?

She wondered if Zander had broken the news yet or if she'd have to. Once she could have predicted Nate's reaction. Now...

Claire hugged herself as she heard the front door open. Now she didn't know him anymore.

"YOU'RE STILL UP." Catching sight of her as he opened the front door Nate smiled, but his brown eyes radiated a cold anger.

Zander had told him.

Claire returned a conciliatory smile. Then he shouldn't have lied to her. "I said I'd wait up." She noticed that his dark hair was disheveled, his tie hung loose and his immaculate white shirt was half undone. "Are you...drunk?"

"I don't get drunk." Nate slipped the suit jacket off, threw it at the coat stand and missed. He wore a gun holster. "More like comfortably numb."

"I hope you didn't drive."

"No, we caught a cab." Half turning, Nate held out his hand. "Pia, come meet my stalker."

"Mia," corrected a female voice. Disbelieving, Claire stared at the tipsy goddess, all curves and collagen lips, who grabbed Nate's hand and stumbled inside.

Knowing how important it was to settle this, he'd brought a pick-up home?

"Mia, meet Claire. Claire, meet Mia."

"I don't do threesomes," Mia said flatly.

Nate laughed. "You've gotta love Hollywood," he said. "It's okay, babe, Claire's a friend… married to my best friend." Freeing his holster, he removed the cartridge from the gun, then opened the hall cupboard, revealing a small safe. "I know in this town that doesn't mean much, but in our circle it's a very big deal. Well, maybe not too big a deal since Claire has screwed me…metaphorically speaking." Depositing the weapon, he slammed the metal door shut. Hard.

Claire took a deep breath. "Nate."

He smiled and wagged a finger at her. "All this talk of understanding, when you intended playing Zander's heartstrings all along. He says I have to do my dooty…that's how Americans pronounce it, dooty. There's some irony in being lectured on doing the right thing by a guy notorious for putting himself first."

Mia laughed. "That is funny." She fondled his chest, clearly oblivious to his real mood.

"Almost as funny as you lying to me about tour dates," Claire said evenly.

"I promised Mia a private party, so we'll discuss this tomorrow. C'mon, babe, let's find a drink."

"I've been hitting on this guy for months," Mia confided happily to Claire as Nate ushered her past. "Talk about hard to get."

"You're telling me." Claire followed them to the kitchen. "You could have avoided this, Nate," she pointed out. "I sent letters, my lawyer sent letters.… You're not the only one struggling with Steve's and Lee's deaths."

He had his back to her, opening cupboard doors. "All due respect, Claire, you have no friggin' idea what I feel." He passed Mia a couple of glasses.

She wanted to shout, *Steve was my husband.* But that would crack her self-control and she needed those shields. "You agreed to be a trustee," she reminded him quietly. "All I'm asking is that you do your job."

"Here it is," he said, holding up a Jack Daniel's bottle.

"You guys aren't acting much like friends," Mia ventured.

"Sure we are." Nate flashed Claire a hard smile. "Here's what we're going to do. I'll lend you whatever money you need to bring the boat up to spec. That will take the pressure off selling the house. And I'll sign any papers your lawyer sends me. But no one pushes me into doing what I don't want to, Claire. Not even you."

Her throat tightened. "That's not good enough." She needed to make her own way, follow new dreams, since following the ones she and Steve had shared was no longer an option.

"That's my best offer." One arm hooked around Mia's waist, the other hand clutching a bottle of JD, he headed for the stairs.

Mia glanced over her shoulder with a worried frown. "Are you all right?" she said to Claire.

Her mouth started forming an automatic yes. "No. The last six months have been hell. My son's been getting into trouble and I've had to move him away from his deadbeat friends." She hated resorting to emotional blackmail, but Nate had left her no choice. "And I really need Nate to talk to him about Steve's death."

Shocked, Mia stopped. "Your husband's dead?"

Dropping his hand from her waist, Nate turned and looked at her. "He died almost immediately after impact," he said harshly. "There's nothing to add."

"And I've told Lewis that. We all have. But Dan wasn't on patrol and Ross can't remember a thing. You are the only eyewitness. I understand it's difficult for you, but he needs to talk to you about his father's last hours."

"No." His hand tightened on the balustrade. "I'll pay for counseling."

"What?" Unable to believe his callousness, Claire stared at him.

His gaze fell from hers. "And you can have my share of *Heaven Sent,*" he added. "Consider it an apology for your wild-goose chase."

She didn't think he could hurt her more. He'd rather buy her off than spare a measly few days helping get her and Lewis's lives back on track. He was going to ignore the emotional welfare of a thirteen-year-old boy, a kid who'd idolized him.

Mia kissed Nate's cheek approvingly. "Aren't you sweet."

Something broke in Claire. "You selfish, insensitive son of a bitch! For months I've been making excuses for you to my son and stopping your mates from coming over here and dragging you home. 'Give him time,' I said. 'He'll come back to us.' You think it doesn't hurt that our friendship died with Steve?"

Nate stood perfectly still, his face white under his tan, Mia wide-eyed beside him.

"Do you think I enjoy having to swallow my pride and chase you halfway across the world?" The dam had broken; she couldn't stop the deluge of words even if she'd wanted to. "It's been a year and a half since the ambush, and you're telling me that I can't move on with my life because *you're* grieving? He was my husband, Nate."

"Claire." He took a step toward her and she held up a hand.

"*My* husband. All I want to do is take control of my finances and protect my son." Tears prickling her eyes, she turned to Mia. "Can't you see he's only using you to avoid dealing with me? The war hero is a goddamn coward!"

Mia opened her mouth, closed it. Nate stood frozen to the spot.

She had to get out of here. Holding tight to her anger, Claire stormed out of the house, remembering too late her bag was still in the kitchen. She'd walk along the beach until they went to bed, then sneak back and gather her stuff, because she wasn't going to spend one night under her former friend's roof. At least she still had Nate's spare key.

She heard hurried footsteps behind her. "Claire!"

Blindly she kept marching along the canal path. "Go to hell."

"Come home, Claire." Nate tried to take her arm and she shook him off.

"Not until I'm good and ready.... Go exploit poor Mia."

"We decided she could do better than me.... And you can't go walking around here at night," he added patiently. "It's not safe."

She hadn't even considered that. Her anger deflated, leaving only a bone-deep weariness. What was she going to do now? Her footsteps slowed and then stopped. She looked at him, but the streetlight was behind him and his face was in shadow.

"I've been selfish," he said. "I'm sorry."

"Too little, too late." Claire returned the way she'd come. This time he knew not to take her arm.

"How many days are we talking about?" he asked as they reached his house.

Relief was a lump in her throat. "I figure two, maybe three at most."

"I don't want anyone to know I'm in the country."

Her heart sank.

"That means Lewis too," he said, spelling it out.

She'd had to rip a scab off a wound to make him do this. She wouldn't show vulnerability again. "You're in luck. He's at Dan's for the school holidays."

"I can't tell him anything he hasn't already heard from you."

"Any other conditions?" she said coldly.

"No." The exterior light illuminated a stranger's face. "That about covers it."

CHAPTER FOUR

"If you're not going to eat that..."

Nate handed Claire the bread roll and cheese from his barely touched airline tray. Under different circumstances he might be amused by her appetite. She'd already eaten his complimentary cashew nuts, along with her own.

"Anything else you want?" It had been a long time since he'd flown cattle class, but she'd refused to let him upgrade her to first, telling him to go ahead and book for himself.

Much as Nate needed the space, he couldn't bring himself to enjoy Air New Zealand's premier service while she sat in economy.

Accepting the roll, she eyed his dessert—a slice of blackberry cheesecake. He drained his glass of wine and indicated her unopened 187 ml bottle of merlot. "Swap you," he suggested.

Claire passed it over. "Hair of the dog?" Her tone was carefully neutral.

"It'll help me sleep."

"I have a homeopathic remedy."

"Hell, no," he said feelingly and they shared

an involuntary smile. Claire had once given Steve a sleeping tincture for the unit. The smell of the stuff alone—a cross between a decomposing rat and a flatulent elephant—had made everyone gag. The pilot of the Hercules had dropped altitude solely to jettison the bottles into the Pacific.

"It's odorless," she promised.

Nate unscrewed the cap on her wine and refilled his glass. "This will do fine." Her lips tightened. Good. A buffer of disapproval made this whole thing easier. After the ambush, alcohol had helped counter his chronic insomnia, but since moving to the States he'd only needed it on the first anniversary of the ambush. And when his old life collided with his new life.

"You didn't used to drink so much."

"You didn't used to eat so much," he countered. "Though God knows you need to."

She concentrated on digging a spoon into the creamy filling.

Nate wanted to kick himself. "Sorry. I can't see a slender woman now without worrying she's got an eating disorder."

Claire glanced at his tray. "Give me your mint chocolate and I'll forgive you."

He surrendered it, holding on to the silver wrapper until she looked at him. "You're still beautiful, Claire," he said awkwardly.

She shrugged as if to say it wasn't important now, and Nate changed the subject. "If you're going to be a skipper you must have renewed your qualification?"

"Yes, I'm certified again. Do you remember Dad's fishing partner, Uncle Dave in Northland? Lewis and I holidayed with him and Aunt Sally last Christmas and I skippered on his charter to bring my hours up."

"So Lewis is keen to be involved?"

"Heck, no!" She gave that deep-throated chuckle that always made Nate smile because it came from such a slight frame. "He already thinks I'm a slave driver for making him clean his room occasionally, let alone swab decks and handle bait. No, Lewis is concentrating on improving his grades."

"He's having problems with his grades?" The kid had always done so well in school.

"His old friends placed a low value on education— they decided it was cooler to skip classes. But the headmistress of his new private school is confident that between us, we've got him back on track with his studies."

She'd put down her spoon. Casually, Nate said, "How's the cheesecake?"

Claire refocused on her plate. "Excellent." She picked up her spoon again. "So there's no point regretting the swap now."

"Did you apply to the SAS trust for Lewis's school fees?" The unit had a support system for bereaved families.

"I'll see how it goes," she said vaguely.

Nate frowned. "That's what the trust's for, Claire."

"And I'll get them involved if I have to," she said with finality.

Claire finished his dessert, and shot him a sidelong glance as she peeled the plastic off the cheese. "You probably wouldn't recognize Lewis, he's grown so tall over the last year. I have a few photos on my phone."

Resisting the urge to tell her that trying to draw him into the family circle wouldn't work, Nate accepted her cell. For a moment he didn't recognize the gangly youth standing next to her in the picture. "He's as tall as you." The child had been replaced by a teenager, with the half smile of someone embroiled in the desperate battle between cool and shy. His blond hair was Claire's, but he had his dad's hazel eyes. Nate couldn't meet them.

"It was taken at Dan and Jo's wedding," she said. "There are a few shots there. Flick through," she invited.

He did so reluctantly. Jo was the picture of a radiant bride; her groom a bedraggled, bruised mess with a beaming smile.

"What the hell?"

"Jo had Dan dropped in the wilderness with twenty-four hours to get to the wedding." Claire munched her crackers. "She wanted to convince him of her faith in him. I don't entirely understand her logic, but Dan did, so that's all that matters. He'd been beating himself up about not being with you guys through the ambush. But he's better now."

And just like that she'd tricked him into caring. *Why wasn't I told Dan was in trouble?* Biting back the question, Nate blanked his expression and returned the cell.

Because he'd never asked.

"You were missed at the wedding, Nate," she said. "You and Jules."

Lee's fiancée. Searchers had found their missing gunner's remains the next day, spread-eagle over a boulder. The insurgents had packed explosives under his corpse and the approach of the retrieval crew detonated a trip wire. Two more men died. There was nothing to retrieve of Lee except one of his boots, found a few meters away. One of the local allies picked up a fingertip, which confirmed his DNA.

He refilled his plastic wine goblet, then pushed the call button. "How is she?" he heard himself ask. The hostess arrived before Claire could answer. "Another bottle of red, please."

The brunette hostess glanced at the two empty bottles on his tray and then instinctively at Claire.

She shrugged. "I wish I had some influence, but I don't."

Flustered, the other woman murmured, "Let me get that for you, sir," and left.

Claire speared him with those Viking blues. "Jules is struggling—like all the survivors. But we're a support group for each other. Maybe you should try it."

Nate scowled. "Remember our deal. No one knows I'm home."

"Jules is my lawyer, Nate. You'd know that if you'd opened her mail."

Shit.

"But don't worry." Claire bit into her cheese and cracker with a snap. "I'll be sure to tell her we can't care about you anymore."

"I'd appreciate that."

The hostess reappeared with a third bottle. Claire turned her attention to the in-flight romantic comedy, leaving Nate alone with the drink and his thoughts.

No man left behind.

He'd intended to carry Ross to relative safety and return. But in his heart he'd known there'd be no second chances. Risking his own life was one thing; risking Ross's another. Steve had played on that and Nate had let him. And left him.

Now all he remembered was the spark of relief when the decision was taken out of his hands. He didn't want to die. *I was only obeying orders.* How many times through history had culpable men said that?

The day he'd been awarded a valor medal was the second-worst day of his life. Thank God he'd resigned from the service before it was approved, otherwise he'd have been stuck with the military's highest honor, the Victoria Cross. As a civilian, he'd escaped with the New Zealand Cross. A bravery medal for a coward. And even if he wasn't a coward, he hadn't deserved recognition.

A hero would have found a way to save both.

The rattle of a service cart pulled him out of his dark reverie and he realized the air hostesses were clearing dinner. Nate put up his tray table and settled his thin pillow against the window after a fruitless attempt to get more incline from his seat. Claire glanced at him, but didn't try to reengage him in conversation. She was learning.

Closing weary eyes, Nate tried to rest. He'd had a busy morning briefing his stand-in. Fortunately, he job shared Zander...no one could handle that ego 24-7...and it had been relatively easy to talk his counterpart into covering him for a few days. It had been much harder to find a volunteer bodyguard for his women's-shelter work. He fell asleep to the soothing hum of the B747 engines.

The dream was always the same. He was behind the wheel of the Humvee, trying to outdrive a pursuing foe, bumping and jolting through pitch-dark terrain, terrified and straining to see. Everyone was there.… Dan, Lee, Ross and Steve, unconscious and bloody. Only he could save them…except he was driving blind. He felt the vehicle lose terra firma.…

Nate woke with a low groan, his temple pounding, and struggled to reorient himself. The cabin lay in darkness. Here and there the dim flash of screens indicated the insomniacs watching in-flight movies. Nate tensed as the cabin rattled under another pocket of turbulence. No wonder this dream had felt so real. A blanket lay over his legs. About to push it off, he realized his hand was intertwined with Claire's.

Turning his head, he saw her curled beside him, watching him anxiously. That someone had witnessed his distress hit him like an electric shock. Dismay must have shown in his face, because she closed her eyes, giving him privacy.

But her fingers tightened on his.

Nate suffered her comforting clasp a couple of minutes before he freed his hand. By then, his forehead was beaded with sweat.

ARRIVING IN HIS HOMELAND at dawn was another torture. The Kiwi accents in passport control stabbed Nate with nostalgia.

"G'day, mate," said the Maori customs official. "How was Paris when you left?"

"I got off the flight from Los Angeles."

"Yeah, mate. I'm talking about Paris Hilton."

"Nice one, bro."

Adding to the unwanted twinge of wistfulness was the fresh coolness of spring rain after L.A.'s dry heat and the scent of green pasture as Claire drove three hours north in Steve's pink 1959 Cadillac Coupe DeVille. "Something else I can't sell without your signature," she commented above the rumble of the V8 engine.

"Do you want to?"

"Yes." Expertly, she manipulated the gear lever mounted on the steering column. "It's time she went to a collector who'll cherish her like Steve did."

There was an edge in her voice that in any other woman he would have called bitterness. He must be mistaken. Steve and Claire had had the perfect marriage. "You drive her much?"

"Only on special occasions. She sits in storage mostly. But I thought you'd enjoy a ride in her if I talked you into coming home."

He caressed the brown leather. He and the guys had shared some great road trips in this Caddy. Steve had meant to repaint her when he'd bought her in a never-to-be-repeated deal, but somehow the pink had become part of her charm. "If you want to nap, I'm happy to drive."

"I'm fine for now." She glanced over. "Did you get any sleep?" And it was between them again, that moment she'd seen him unguarded.

Nate lowered the window, let the cold breeze play over his face. "Yeah," he lied. "So fill me in on what I need to know about the trust." She'd promised to cram appointments to facilitate his return to the States.

Over the next hour she outlined her business plan, the negotiations over the house, and brought him up to date on the mechanics of dissolving the trust.

"Sounds like it's been in the planning for a while," he commented as they pulled into a gas station at Wellsford.

"I started the ball rolling six months after Steve died."

Nate unbuckled his seat belt. "Aren't you supposed to wait two years before making life-changing decisions?"

"One year," she corrected. "It's now closer to

two." She got out of the Caddy and crossed to the pump. Except all the delays had been due to him.

He got out to help, removing the petrol cap and positioning the nozzle while Claire keyed in a dollar amount. "So, what feedback are you getting from Ross, Dan and Jo about all this?"

"Not much. I've been drip-feeding information until it's all signed and sealed." She pulled a credit card out of her purse. "Obviously, they're aware my house is on the market and I intend moving to Stingray Bay. Dan and Jo know I went to L.A. to fetch you, because they're looking after Lewis."

"Why the secrecy? And put your wallet away. I'm paying for the gas."

"Because I don't want anyone talking me out of it," she said frankly. "And I'm paying for this.... Want a Kiwi meat pie to remind you you're home?"

"Sure." With a frown, he watched her walk into the service station. These were big decisions she was making. You'd think she'd have run them by close friends.

"You okay to drive now?" Claire said on her return. Was she deliberately trying to distract him? Nate accepted the keys, the pie and the hint.

"Happy to."

They had the same goal, break the trust. Three days tops and he was out of here. Everything else was her business.

She'd fallen asleep by the time they'd reached Whangarei, where he bypassed the city to take the turnoff to Stingray Bay, forty-five minutes east. She was curled up like a kid in the passenger seat, blond hair falling across her cheek. Undoing his seat belt, Nate shrugged off his Italian-leather jacket and covered her, keeping a hand on the steering wheel.

As the Caddy ate up the miles the road changed with the rural landscape, becoming narrow and winding. Nate pulled over at a one-lane bridge to give way to a lumbering dairy tanker, letting the dust of the unsealed road settle behind it before he accelerated. How many times had he traveled this way, heading to the bach—beach house—of his favorite couple? Usually with Lee, Ross and Dan, sometimes alone. Looking forward to R & R—diving for crays and scallops, fishing off the bridge, surfing when there was a swell.

His pulse started to beat faster as the car bypassed the mangrove swamps. They were close. Nate wound down the driver's window, inhaled the swampy-salty odor of mudflats exposed by low tide. Some of the happiest times in his life had been spent here. Glancing at Claire, he wondered how she could stand returning now. Except her memories predated Steve's arrival in her life. Her family had holidayed in Stingray Bay for four generations, and she'd inherited the bach from her father. That probably offset the deep sadness making him grip the steering wheel.

"Are we here already?" Opening her eyes, Claire yawned and sat up.

He blinked hard. "Just about." The Caddy swung left onto the thumb of land that ended at the mouth of an estuary that divided Stingray Bay North and South.

Amidst the rush of coastal development, the sleepy settlement remained a nostalgic relic. Though the outhouses had been superseded by indoor plumbing, most of the four hundred dwellings were the original baches clad with fiber cement board. The permanent population of a few hundred swelled to four times that in summer, which coincided with the opening of the only store at the campground.

It was a place where inhabitants measured their day by the tides.... Collecting shellfish in the estuary when it was low, launching the aluminum dinghy—tinny—when it was high, and in-between times sitting in deck chairs and watching its slow ebb and flow.

A place where you got out of your vehicle on

arrival and didn't climb in it until departure, where nightlife was a game of Monopoly or cards and the only way to reach the store was to walk across the footbridge separating Stingray North and South or kayak across the estuary. There was no direct road access between the halves. To reach one from the other by car you had to drive for forty-five minutes around the mainland.

Toward the end of the tiny peninsula, the road became gravel driveway and Nate steered the Caddy into the communal grass yard behind a row of old baches. No one put up fences here. Claire's bach sat at the end, freshly painted blue fiber cement board siding with white trim, patio doors at both ends and a corrugated-iron roof.

The bathroom was a lean-to accessed from the front deck, which stepped down to a lawn of hardy kikuyu grass and overlooked the wide estuary and the baches of Stingray South, five hundred meters across the water. The rear deck gave a peep of the ocean beach, which lay below a rise some twelve feet from the rear boundary. It had always been a spectacular location.

Claire handed him the house key, sliding over to the driver's seat as he got out of the car. "I'll be back around nine tonight." She was going home to Whangarei to change vehicles, catch up with Steve's mother and gather the paperwork for Nate to read over before their appointments tomorrow. "Help yourself to what's in the freezer. I'll bring fresh supplies with me."

She waited while Nate retrieved his weekend bag from the trunk. "And if you feel like taking a look at *Heaven Sent,* she's in the boat shed near the footbridge. There's a key for it on a hook beside the fridge."

With a nod, he went to close her door, but she reached out and held it open. "Are you sure you're okay…being here?"

"Drive carefully," he said and clicked it shut.

When the Caddy had rumbled out of sight, he sat at the sturdy wooden picnic table on the deck looking out to the estuary, his bag beside him. It was a typical September day, the wind a brisk spring-cleaner full of bustle and blow.

It still took thirty minutes to get cold enough to go inside.

The whole living space was about the size of his kitchen in L.A. Open-plan lounge/dining took up most of it, with a pocket-size kitchen barely large enough for a couple to stand at an L-shaped counter, holding the stove and sink. Off the kitchen a curtain partition led to a bedroom so small there was barely room to walk between two single beds. Another curtain off the living room led to a bunk room and master bedroom. When he and the guys stayed, they'd

pitched a tent on the lawn, invariably comman-
deered by Lewis and the neighborhood's kids
through the day for use as a fort.

The covered rear deck had a railing that doubled as a clothesline for towels. In summer all
the living was outdoors on the decks, all cook-
ing done on the barbecue, and space was never
an issue. As a winter residence it seemed way
too small for a woman and her teenage son.

Don't get involved.

He gravitated to a large corkboard in the living room. It held a tide calendar and decades of
faded snapshots of sunburned laughing holiday-
makers, himself among them. His gaze shied
away.

He'd bought a bottle of scotch duty free, but
he couldn't open it. It seemed irreverent somehow, though God knows they'd had some parties here in their time. But this was a happy
place, morbid drinking had no place here.

Nate dumped his bag in the small bedroom,
changed into running gear and headed for the
ocean beach where he pounded up and down
the soft white sand of its three-kilometer length
until his legs were jelly and he could barely put
one foot in front of the other. Then he returned
to the bach and took a shower, making a mental note to improve the water pressure. Donning

a pair of boxers, he fell exhausted into one of the single beds.

Already the walls were closing in.

CHAPTER FIVE

CLAIRE VISITED HER mother-in-law first because she hated lying. Unfortunately, her deal with Nate meant she had to, and not just to Ellie.

Dan and Ross couldn't know her mission to fetch Nate was successful, either. So in typical fashion she seized the bull by the horns and got the hard part over first. She found Ellie sorting through a pile of crotchless panties.

"Claire, I wasn't expecting you until tomorrow!" Dropping the lacy scraps on the shop's counter, she came round and embraced her in a rattle of silver bangles and Red Door perfume. Up until a year and a half ago, Ellie Langford would have won a red ribbon for best preserved against any jam or jelly at the county fair.

She still looked younger than her sixty years, but Steve's death had aged her. When her face was in repose, there was an extra droop of her eyes and mouth. "So how was your break? Who were you staying with again?"

"An old friend… You wouldn't know him." At least not anymore. She hadn't told Ellie where she was going for the same reason she hadn't told Lewis.

"Him?" Smiling, Ellie pulled away. "Honey, are you dating again?"

Claire suffered a moment's panic that Steve's mother might consider it time. Then she saw the dread behind the smile and breathed again. "Don't scare me like that," she chided. "It's bad enough fending off inquiries from acquaintances."

"I'm trying to be impartial about this…. Steve would want you to be happy."

Then he shouldn't have gone and died on me. "Let's settle for cheerful," Claire suggested. "We can manage cheerful…right?"

"Absolutely." Ellie returned to sorting crotchless panties into sizes. "What people don't understand is how impossible it is to replace a perfect husband."

Claire hid a smile. Steve used to say he barely recognized his father on his mom's lips. Since his death, seven years earlier, Robert had been sainted, knighted and given a million-dollar makeover.

The reality had been very different.

Ellie had been a homemaker, perfectly content to let her workaholic husband rule the roost while she flitted between her garden, lunch with girlfriends, beauty appointments, the tennis club and volunteer work. Her comfortable life had ended abruptly with Robert's early retirement. He'd become a grumpy old man whose primary purpose became hunting on the internet for facts to support his view that the world was going to hell in a handbasket. A regular caller to talkback radio, he also spent many hours formulating letters to the editor and his local M.P., which his wife had to type as he refused to learn keyboard skills.

It wasn't as if she had anything better to do.

In desperation, Ellie had accepted a part-time job in a friend's lingerie store and discovered a previously untapped genius for retail. Supported by Steve and Claire as guarantors, she bought the business a year after Robert dropped dead of a heart attack while arguing with his insurance company that he was "perfectly healthy, goddamn it, and they shouldn't charge him higher premiums just because he'd turned sixty-five."

Until her only child's death, the Merry Widow couldn't have been happier.

Ellie finished her sorting. "When Steve was a boy staying at the Jansen farm, he rang me every day."

Claire doubted that, but she said soothingly, "I'll remind him next time we talk." She'd tried to protect Ellie from Lewis's exploits—sassing teachers, egging houses, graffitiing bus stops—but being in the shop, his grandmother had heard all the gossip eventually.

And her solution—telling Lewis his father would be turning in his grave and what did he think he was doing, worrying his poor mother?—hadn't helped. Claire adored her mother-in-law, but her constant referencing to what Steve would do or say to fix the situation—unsurprisingly filtered through Ellie's value system—made her crazy.

More important, it made Lewis crazy.

A customer approached the counter with a bundle of lingerie and she stepped back, marveling as her mother-in-law talked the giggling middle-aged woman into adding a pair of crimson crotchless panties to her sensible double-D bras.

"Because it's never too late to add fun to a marriage," Ellie said. "Hang these in the new playwear section for me, Claire?" She handed her daughter-in-law two bundles of panties.

Hooking them to the railing, Claire smiled as she glimpsed naughty-nurse and French-maid costumes amidst the sheer gowns, open-bust teddies and corsets.

Steve would have liked this section, she thought, and tears prickled her eyes. Their wedding anniversary would have been in a couple of months. Just twenty and twenty-one when they got married, they'd conceived Lewis on the honeymoon.

She fingered the lace, satin and bows as wistfully as an old woman with all her sensual years behind her. *You're only thirty-four,* she reminded herself. Steve had been her one and only. What would it even be like to sleep with another man? Damn you, Steve Langford, for leaving me in the position of having to think about it.

"Claire, honey, you want to come to dinner tonight?"

She turned, smiling. "I'm heading to the bach for the rest of the week to assess what needs doing for a move. Because it looks like I have a buyer for the house. Touch wood, we'll finalize a sale this week."

"That's great," said Ellie, but her tone held dismay. Fortunately, Steve—channeled through his mother—thought a transfer to Willingham School was an excellent idea, even though it involved a permanent move to Stingray Bay when the Whangarei house sold, to avoid a ninety-minute commute.

But approving the move and having it happen were two different things.

"It's only forty-five minutes away," Claire reminded her. "We'll still see plenty of each other."

"It's just, you and Steve built that place."

"And it's another link broken." Claire picked up Ellie's hand and squeezed it. "But this is the one that matters."

The older woman's eyes filled. "Oh, honey!"

"We're not crying," Claire warned. "Think about how much you hated the window frames instead."

Her mother-in-law rallied. "Mustard! What were you two thinking?"

"It's not mustard, it's Golden Dream and it looks wonderful against the silvered wood."

"Personally, I always thought you should have painted the clapboard instead of letting it weather."

Claire widened her eyes. "No! Really?"

Ellie laughed. Her bangles rattled as she pushed Claire toward the door. "Get out of here! I've got lingerie to sell."

Unfortunately Claire's phone conversation with Dan was harder. "You're kidding me," he said when she told him Nate hadn't returned with her. "I can't believe he turned you down."

"Only because it wasn't necessary," she replied hastily, parking the pink Caddy in the garage of her Whangarei home. Was lying as bad when you crossed your fingers behind your back? "He gave me all the authorizations I need to sell the house and dissolve the trust."

"I thought doing it remotely would take weeks of to-ing and fro-ing with documents?"

Collecting her belongings, she nudged the door shut with her butt, dumping some of them into the five-year-old BMW station wagon that was her usual transport.

"Nate has a smart lawyer.… I'm unsure of the exact details, but he's assured us he can work something out quickly and in the meantime I can progress the sale with documents he signed while I was there."

"It would have been easier if he'd come home though, wouldn't it?"

She started to sweat. "His boss wasn't happy about him taking time off."

"Claire, you don't need to make excuses for him. I've known for a while he doesn't want us in his life anymore. But I thought you'd break through."

The house was musty from being closed up for three days and she opened windows. "Because I'm the poor widow, you mean," she said lightly, hearing in his voice the pity she so hated.

"Partly," he returned. Bless Dan and his new honesty. His bride Jo's influence. "But also because he always dropped his guard with you."

"There are still vestiges of the old Nate," she said, heading straight to her bedroom to repack.

"He's doing some volunteer work for a women's shelter on his day off. Providing a security escort if the women need one when they do a school drop-off or pick-up…attending court." She'd overheard him arranging a replacement. "Don't give up on him, Dan." The way Claire had—at least until she'd seen him waking from a nightmare. She wouldn't make that mistake again. He needed his friends, people who understood the hell he'd been through.

"I never give up on family," he said. "And Nate's like a brother. But I'm through with this touchy-feely hands-off approach—and yeah, I appreciate the contradiction. Soon as we're done docking lambs, I'm heading over there with Ross to deal with this once and for all."

Oh, Lord. Gathering a pile of laundry, she tried to keep the panic out of her voice. "He'll be on tour with Zander."

"I don't care if he's in Paris or Pretoria.… If it takes an intervention then—" He stopped. "Hey, Lewis." All frustration disappeared from his voice. "I'm talking to your mother.… No, we're not discussing an intervention for you.… Sheesh, teenagers, it's all me, me, me. I'm suggesting your uncle Nate update his Facebook page.… Yeah, okay, smart mouth, so I'm not on Facebook either, but trust me, you won't be friended when I am."

Claire grinned. Lewis would be loving Dan's teasing. She loaded the washing machine, set it going.

"Here's your son," Dan said. "Whatever he tells you about daily beatings is a lie."

"Mum?"

"Hey, how're you doing?"

"Good."

In the kitchen, she filled a jug with water. "I hear you've been docking lambs. Is that as gruesome as it sounds?" The herbs on the kitchen windowsill drooped forlornly, so she watered the parsley and mint.

"Not really. We put a rubber ring around their tail and that stops the blood circulation and then falls off around eight to ten days later." He dispensed his new knowledge with a farmer's casualness. "It makes them easier to shear, plus if you don't then sh—poop builds up—"

"Ugh, okay, stop there." The coriander was beyond saving; Claire dumped it in the bin.

Glee entered his voice. "…and that can lead to fly strike… That's wool maggots, Mum."

"And that's too much information. Seriously you'd rather dag lambs than spend quality time with your mother?"

"This is way more fun."

"Well, I'm glad to know where I stand." Poor peace plant in the hall, it soaked up half a jugful. "Listen, hon, I think we'll finalize a sale of the house this week."

"So we can move to Dullsville even sooner." There was a scowl in his voice. "Great."

"It means less traveling." Willingham was thirty minutes from Stingray Bay, and a seventy-five-minute commute from Whangarei. Since Lewis had changed schools, Claire had been making the drive until the property sold. Anything to get Lewis away from his former crowd.

"Yeah, and weekends with no one to hang out with."

Returning to the bedroom, she started to refill her suitcase, replacing summer dresses with practical jeans, tees and sweaters.

"Invite your new friends from school."

"Like they'll want to hang out in Stingray Bay."

"Hon, we've been over this so often—"

"And you never listen to what I want! So there's no point talking about it."

What could she say? You'll thank me one day. I'm doing this for your own good. Claire sat on the bed. "We'll make this work," she promised.

"I have to go," he said sullenly. "Uncle Dan's waiting."

Her hand tightened on the receiver. "I'll phone tomorrow."

"Uh-huh."

"I love you, Lewie."

"Bye."

Claire hung up with a sigh. When he'd been a little boy, he'd said it back. Until a few months ago, when she'd started practicing tough love, he'd say, "Me, too." When she'd made him move schools, he'd changed it to "Bye." Emotionally, it was a very effective punishment. But it wouldn't make her change course.

THE BACH WAS IN DARKNESS when she pulled in, earlier than she'd expected at eight-thirty, and for a moment Claire panicked that Nate had left the moment her back was turned. Talking herself down, she got out of her station wagon, walked into the bach and switched on a light. "Nate?"

No response.

Dumping a bag of groceries in the kitchen, she wondered if he'd gone to the boat shed. Then she glimpsed him through the open curtain of the spare bedroom. He was sprawled on the bed, out cold. She glanced at the bottle of scotch on the countertop. Unopened. Exhaustion, then.

He lay uncovered, one arm flung over his face as though warding off a foe. She tiptoed into the room, grabbed a duvet off the other bed and placed it over his lower body, then stood quietly for a moment, watching him in slumber.

He'd grown his dark hair longer over the past eighteen months and a lock fell across his closed lids. Instinctively she reached out to smooth it, pulling away from the intimacy with her hand inches from his face. He wasn't Lewis, though she felt equally protective of him in this moment.

Nate groaned in his sleep and turned over, exposing a muscular back. Tentatively, Claire touched his shoulder, the skin surprisingly warm given the chilly room. "It's okay," she said firmly. "Everything's going to be okay." His shoulder relaxed, he settled more deeply into sleep. She had an impulse to crawl onto the bed with him. Like Hansel and Gretel in the forest, with only each other for comfort.

Silly.

Claire crept out and pulled the curtain across the door, stifling a yawn. She'd barely slept in the previous seventy-two hours, since she first chased Nate across the world. Deciding to follow his example, she dumped the perishables in the fridge, left the rest of the shopping on the counter and went to bed.

Crawling into the middle because it stopped the bed feeling so empty, she lay in the dark and mentally went over tomorrow's tasks, until she fell asleep and dreamed of lambs gamboling across fields while she chased them with rubber bands.

Her first thought on waking was, Freud would have a field day with that one. Her second was that the house was burning down… She could smell smoke. In a panic, Claire fell out of bed and stumbled into the living room.

The patio slider was open onto the deck, where Nate, dressed in jeans and a navy sweater, was barbecuing. "Good morning! Breakfast is in ten minutes. We have to leave in forty if we're going to make our first appointment in Whangarei by nine-thirty."

Dazed, Claire checked her wrist, but her watch was still on the bedside table. "What time is it?" The aroma hit her now, the sweet sizzle of bacon and sausages. Her stomach growled.

"Seven-ten. It's cold out, you might need a sweater." Nate returned to the grill and something in his comment made Claire look down. Her nipples pushed against the skimpy pajama tank. Refusing to feel self-conscious in front of an old friend, she returned to the bedroom where she pulled on a sweater and dragged her hair into a ponytail. When she came out, Nate was breaking eggs on the barbecue plate. Seeing him, a sudden blush touched her cheeks and she detoured. "I'll make toast and coffee."

He didn't look up. "Good idea."

Bless him, he'd unpacked the rest of the food she brought last night. Plugging the kettle in, Claire glanced over to the dining table and saw her business plan was open. "You've been up for a while?" she called.

"Since five." Spatula in hand, he leaned against the doorjamb, keeping an eye on the barbecue. His jaw was unshaven and the morning breeze ruffled his hair. "I've read enough for today's meetings."

Claire measured three scoops of coffee into the plunger. "No need. All you'll have to do is sign papers."

"It was a cursory glance.… I've got a couple of questions."

She wasn't sure how she felt about that. "If my brain works…" Claire poured boiling water over the grounds. "I'm not a morning person."

"That's why I lured you awake with bacon. I didn't want my head snapped off."

She saw a glint of amusement in his expression. So he'd guessed she was prickly about this. "I'm not that bad." Nate raised a brow. "Okay," she conceded. "On holidays I'm that bad." When the SAS buddies were together they'd be up at dawn, clomping around the bach gathering fishing tackle and impatiently waiting for her to rise. Steve knew all the same spots, but the fish only showed when Claire was there.

She poured coffee, added cream and took him a mug. Standing alongside the barbecue, she cradled her own and instinctively checked wind direction and tide. "Did you see *Heaven Sent* yesterday?"

"Not yet." Because he didn't want to feel the pull of her, she suspected. He'd loved that boat as much as she had. She'd already told him she wouldn't accept his half as a gift, she'd buy him out as planned. Unless… Claire took a sip of coffee, savoring the caffeine hit. Maybe after seeing *Heaven Sent,* he'd be open to retaining a shareholding? The boat could be an anchor to his old life.

"So you've already started the overhaul?" Nate asked.

"Not me. Between work and Lewis I've barely had time to eat." Claire inhaled deeply and her mouth started to water. "I paid a local contractor to scrape the hull and sand her down. As soon as the house sells, I'll order a new shade canopy. And I've got my eye on a new engine that's on sale."

"I guess you already know that even with a new engine she'll never match the modern charter boats for speed."

She handed him a plate from the two stacked beside the barbecue. "You guessed right!"

He wasn't deterred. "Which also boast sunken cleats, modern fittings, in-floor live-bait tanks—"

"I'm not competing with the luxury end. My prices will be midrange and I'll target those anglers who value polished wood and history in their charter experience."

"Sixty years of history, in fact." One dish filled, Nate picked up the other.

"And the advantage of more space," she argued. "Even with a full complement of fifteen clients on board, there's easily five feet between anglers.... Let me go set the table." Claire escaped inside.

He'd made a sacrifice in coming home. She'd glimpsed the measure of it on the plane, but that didn't mean she was going to encourage the third degree.

Still, as Claire cleared the table of reports and replaced them with cutlery, she acknowledged he'd raised some good points. The magnitude of her new project was daunting, but a "one day at a time" mentality had served her well since Steve's death. There was no reason to pull a Chicken Little now. And this day was plenty busy enough with multiple appointments with the estate agent, lawyer and bank. At least, she thought as Nate placed a laden plate in front of her, they'd be working on a full stomach.

She pulled out a chair and sat down. "This looks delicious."

Dumping his plate, Nate picked up the marketing report from the pile of documents she'd stacked on the couch and opened it.

"Don't let breakfast get cold," she warned.

"You're looking at a four-passenger minimum.... Will that cover costs?"

No prickles. Claire speared a piece of sausage and added a wedge of barbecued tomato. "Mooring fees here are minimal compared to the usual charter bases. I'll do pick-ups from Whangarei if necessary. And I've got support from my former boss at the hotel." She paused to eat, savoring the tomato-beef combination. "Mmm, this is so good.... We'll be putting together taster packages for guests and targeting family groups." She cut into the egg, watched the golden yolk ooze over the toast. "I'm conscious that being a female skipper will work against me with some anglers. But I'm confident I'll find a niche within the tourist, family and female market. A lot of women game fish.... I'm one of them."

His expression eased. "You've put a lot of effort into this."

"I had a lot of sleepless nights to fill." Claire snatched the report out of his hand. "Eat."

Nate sat down and picked up his cutlery. "I am aware of the irony," he said. "Showing interest after months of avoiding any involvement. But my absence didn't mean I stopped caring about you…or Lewis."

It was an olive branch and Claire took it. No matter what Nate thought, there were some bonds that couldn't be broken. His concern only confirmed that.

"I know it'll take time to build up the business," she admitted. "For the first couple of years I'm only expecting to make enough to cover the boat's running costs and meet basic living expenses. I'm fully prepared to dip into what's left from the sale of the house to supplement that. Maybe I'll have to do a little freelance marketing. Or sublease the boat to another skipper occasionally. I have a lot of options, but the most important thing is to begin."

She glanced at her watch and started eating faster. "And that means selling the family home in Whangarei, today, if possible."

He waved his fork. "Have you considered selling this place instead?"

"Absolutely not. It's been in my family for four generations. It passes to Lewis and Lewis's kids eventually."

Nate refilled her coffee mug. "What if you rented out the Whangarei house for a year, see how it goes?"

She shook her head. "I need too much capital, Nate."

"I could—"

"No, I'm not accepting a loan from you. If the bank won't lend me the money, I'm hardly going to borrow from a friend."

He'd been tucking into his breakfast, now he paused. "The bank's against it?"

Damn. She smiled. "The only way to get the business off the ground was to quit my job. Banks have to be conservative. Without an income, I can't apply for a loan, despite having substantial collateral."

"Uh-huh." He returned his attention to his breakfast. She waited for more, but he said nothing.

"What are you thinking?" It occurred to her that she hadn't needed that question in over a year and a half.

His gaze lifted. "I'm thinking I'd like to read all those reports thoroughly."

Her knife clattered onto the china. "I knew it! It's too late to get involved now, Nate. I'm too far down the road."

"I'm aware of that," he said dryly.

Claire ended the conversation by pushing to

her feet. "I'll grab a shower, dress and we'll go." She threw out a lure. "We've got to keep to schedule if you want to be home in L.A. within a couple of days."

CHAPTER SIX

CLAIRE WAS RIGHT. It was too late to start second-guessing her decision.

As he cleared the table, Nate reminded himself that he was here to sign documents, break the trust and leave with the minimum of involvement. It was a covert op—in and out and no harm done to himself or anyone else.

Their first appointment was with the estate agent negotiating the sale of Claire's home.

"So, Nate, it's great to have you home at last." Adam Scott pumped Nate's arm in an enthusiastic handshake. "I'm sure we're all keen to play our part in delivering Claire's dream."

Politely, Nate freed his grip. "And how's your part progressing, Adam?" They were here to view a formal offer from the buyers.

"I'm glad you asked that, Nate." Gesturing to a seat in the client's private meeting room, the young agent refocused his inclusive smile on Claire and some of the phoniness went out of it. She'd dressed in a smoky-gray pantsuit and looked beautiful even though Nate's new expertise suggested the style was at least four seasons out of date. He wondered when she'd last bought herself new clothes…and whether she could afford to.

Adam opened a manila folder and steepled his hands over it. Nate half expected him to say, "For what we're about to receive, make us truly thankful." "The offer's a little lower than we were expecting, Claire," he said earnestly, "and I accept full responsibility for raising your hopes too high. But they were so enthusiastic when they viewed…what was it, three times?" He passed her the document.

She looked at it and grimaced. "A little? This is twenty thousand under the asking price."

"I'm sure they're expecting a counter." Adam included Nate in his reassurances. "Another five or six grand and I think we've got them."

"Five or six," she echoed, dismayed.

"For a quick sale and a cash buyer in a stagnant market."

As she eyed the figure again, Nate pictured Venice Beach, fixed it firmly in his mind and kept his mouth shut.

"My price already reflected the fact that we're at the bottom of a housing slump." Closing the folder, Claire returned it to Adam. "You said yourself, the market's picking up again.

Which means if I wait another six months then I'm bound to receive a better offer?"

Good call. Nate relaxed his shoulders. Even if it was a bluff.

Adam smiled, knowing it too. "But no one can forecast these things with any surety, Claire," he cautioned. "And you need the money now, don't you?"

Never give a commission-driven salesman too much information. It became emotional ammo. Nate tensed for Claire's reply.

"Which is why it's so important," she countered, "that I decide my bottom line." She turned to Nate. "I'm beginning to warm to your idea." She didn't mean it; the glint in her eyes told him it was a tactical move, but he answered her seriously.

"You know that's my preference."

The agent's nostrils flared. "What idea?"

"Nate suggested I rent out the property and accept an interim loan from him until the business starts turning a profit."

Adam was on his feet before she'd finished the sentence and pulling his cell out of his jacket. "Hey, let's not write off these buyers just yet," he suggested with a pained smile. "I'm sure there's more fat in this. I'll go call them."

Nate waited until the agent left the meeting room. "Maybe this is a sign." There was a lot on the line here. Her financial future. Lewis's. She was sinking everything into the project. And if the charter business failed in two, three years? Then what? No assets, except the boat and the bach, which Claire had admitted she'd never sell. Steve had spent years chipping away at the mortgage to make sure his wife had equity in the house to fall back on if anything happened to him. "Rent out the house. Keep an escape route open. It's what Steve would do."

"In case you haven't noticed, Steve's not here."

"That wasn't his choice, Claire."

"Every time a soldier's deployed, he implicitly accepts the possibility of death."

What was he missing here? Nate swallowed. "Believe me, our entire focus is on completing our mission and coming home alive."

"But the choice to risk your life is yours. The people who love you can only choose to wait."

She turned her attention to the documents in her lap. Her long hair swung forward, obscuring her profile. "Do you understand how much that passivity costs us?"

As he stared at her, baffled, Adam bustled into the room. "They'll go up to five hundred and ninety thousand, final offer. That leaves you only ten short of the asking price."

"Minus your commission," Nate said before Claire could react. "What is that exactly, Adam?"

"Industry average, Nate."

"Three percent on the first three thousand dollars," Claire read from the document in her lap. "Two percent on amounts above that."

"So we're talking around fifteen thousand," Nate told her, "which leaves you five hundred and seventy-five thousand. Then you have to deduct the mortgage…" He waited for her to do the math. "My interest on a loan would be at mate's rates."

She saw where he was going with this and obligingly pulled a face.

Adam glanced between them. "Let me ask my boss if there's wiggle room on our commission," he suggested.

"Thanks," she said when the door closed behind him. "Every dollar counts."

"Which is why you need to be sure about this, Claire."

"Hey, what's the worst that can happen?" she said lightly. "If I spend all my savings and the venture fails I'll just sell the boat and get a real job."

He frowned. "Is that supposed to be reassuring?"

"It's only money, Nate. Compared with losing Steve…" She forced a smile. "I need to do something a little scary, something that excites me. I feel like I've simply been existing since Steve's death. And frankly it's time my son had a better role model. I want Lewis to remember how we used to be before his father died."

His misgivings grew, but the door flew open before he could articulate them.

"Good news," Adam announced. "We'll knock four grand off the commission."

"That's great." Delighted, Clare stood to hug him. "Thank you."

Adam ducked his head. "Hey, that's why we're here, Claire, to deliver the dream."

Shit, thought Nate. *Shit. Shit. Shit.*

Claire bent to hug him too, her hair a fragrant fall against his cheek. "Kudos, partner," she murmured.

Adam picked up the discarded folder and sat at his desk, his gold-plated pen slashing through the text as he made amendments. He misread Nate's disquiet.

"Don't worry, it's still legal as long as you initial the changes. So give me your autographs, guys, and I'll it rush over to the buyers for countersigning."

Claire scrawled her signature with a flourish, and then handed the pen to Nate. He leaned forward. Hesitated. "Why aren't you using the education fund provided by the SAS?"

She blinked. "What's that got to do with anything?"

"The fund's specifically set up to assist the families of its fallen. Why aren't you asking for help with Lewis's private-school fees?" Claire had pride but, she was also a pragmatist—unless she wasn't thinking clearly.

"Nate, can we concentrate on the matter at hand and talk about this later?"

He returned his gaze to the document. He'd always felt protective of her, ever since he'd caught her in a private moment of anguish after farewelling Steve. It had been years earlier. He and the guys had been staying at the Langfords' bach when they'd got an urgent call-up. Piling into Dan's ute, Nate realized he'd left some trainers behind. When he'd returned to the bach, Claire had been in the living room sobbing over her sleeping son's cot. He'd stood transfixed. Claire—who'd hugged her husband goodbye so calmly minutes earlier—in bits. And become crashingly aware that war wasn't an adventure to everybody.

That some people had more to lose than he did.

Nate had backed away unseen and returned to the ute. As it accelerated away, he looked at Steve, grim and taciturn beside him, while Ross and Dan traded jokes in the front. Their gazes met and his mate had shrugged, a curious helplessness in his eyes that Nate never saw again.

Until the moment Steve realized he was about to die.

Nate stared at the pen, immobile on the white paper. *Just do it. Sign and get the hell out of here. Save yourself. Yeah, you're good at that.*

"Something wrong, Nate?" said Adam.

"I'm reading the fine print."

"No need," Claire reassured him. "I did that on the original sales agreement."

Of course she had. She was a smart woman who'd done her homework. Even a cursory glance at the reports told him that. But…Nate hadn't seen the boat, hadn't ensured *Heaven Sent* was fit for her new purpose. This morning, before Claire had woken, he'd taken the boat shed key off its hook then thought, *Why put yourself through this? You don't need to be involved. Claire knows what she's doing.*

His grip tightened on the pen.

Except, she'd said she wanted to feel again. Sometimes you did things you shouldn't to escape the numbness.

He put down the pen. "I can't do this."

"Why not?" she said, sounding bewildered.

"Because Steve would want me to ensure this is in your best interests first."

"But your involvement as a trustee was nominal when Steve was alive." She was trying to be reasonable, but her eyes were flinty…the Viking close to the surface. "It was only ever a way to protect our assets while Ellie established her lingerie business."

"You didn't just pull my name out of a hat, either," Nate reminded Claire. "You chose me.… Not Ross, not Dan or any of your other friends. You trusted me."

"And you've been AWOL for months!" she cried, losing patience. "Why poke your nose in now?"

"Because you've got no one else looking out for you." *You haven't let anyone else in.* "Because taking a risk to feel something again isn't the basis for a business decision."

"Would a cappuccino help?" Adam asked nervously.

"That was a throwaway comment," Claire said to Nate.

"The most revealing ones are. Why aren't you accepting support from the SAS trust?"

She ignored the question. "The reports are sound, aren't they?"

"From the little I've read, yes."

"The forecasts, the risk analysis."

"Again, from the little I've read—yes. But you haven't talked about this to anyone outside the people with vested interests. No offence,

Adam, I appreciate your generosity in taking a drop in commission."

"You're welco—"

Claire slammed her hand on the desk. "You can't do this!"

"Actually, I can. Give me the trust document."

Reluctantly she passed it over.

He'd scanned it on the drive to Whangarei and put it aside, blaming his nausea on reading in a moving car. Now Nate flicked through the pages to the text he'd tried to block from his mind. "'The trustee must act in the best interests of the beneficiaries,'" he read out. "'Before making decisions, the trustee must acquaint themselves with all the relevant facts and consider expert advice.'" Nate held up a hand as Adam started to interject. "'Then the trustee must turn their own minds to the question in hand, acting honestly and in good faith.'" Steve could have been looking over his shoulder as he read, his presence was so powerful. "'The trustee is not permitted to delegate their decision-making power.'"

He raised his head and looked at Claire's furious face. She hated him right now but that couldn't matter. Nate's need to protect her countered even his own deep desire to run. Who said atonement was easy? *Thou shalt not walk away....* Not this time.

"I'm a selfish, inconsiderate asshole who let you down for months," he said, "then added insult to injury by dragging my heels all the way home." He took a deep breath. "But Steve would haunt me even more than he does now, if I don't do my job, Claire. All we're talking is another week at most, that—"

She cut him off. "I wish to God I'd left you in L.A." By the agent's expression, Adam wished she had, too.

"Give us a minute to talk privately, will you, mate?"

"But don't go far," Claire reassured him, glaring at Nate. "I'll sort this."

Once Adam left the room. Claire paced the floor. Nate waited, hands held loosely in his lap, his mind resolved. She swung to face him.

"For a decade I shared my husband with the SAS. Whenever he wasn't with his family, he was with his unit. You and the guys probably spent as much quality time with him as Lewie and I did."

He had no idea where she was going with this.

"I never stood in Steve's way once, Nate, and you know why? Because the SAS was his dream. Because he believed in duty and service and honor and so did I." Her tortured gaze pinned his. "Did you know he wasn't even supposed to be on that tour?"

His stunned shock must have answered her question.

"So he didn't tell you about our agreement." Her mouth twisting, Claire sat down again. "When Steve was selected for the SAS, he made me a promise. 'Ten years, Claire, and then it's our time—yours, mine and Lewis's. We'll have the other baby you want. We'll be a normal family. I'll be around weekends.'" Her voice cracked. "'I'll be safe.'"

Ah, God, he began to understand.

Claire's eyes filled with tears; impatiently she knuckled them away. "He promised me, Nate. And I'm so angry at him for not honoring his side of the deal. I'm angry at him for leaving his son to grow up without a father. I'm angry because I want to say all this to my husband and I can't. I want to forgive him, but all the good feelings are tangled up with the bad feelings and I have no clarity on my life with Steve anymore. In some ways that's the worst loss of all."

Nate found his voice. "You had a great marriage."

"Did we?" Claire dropped her head in her hands. "Or did we have a marriage in waiting?"

"He loved you," he said passionately. "It tore him up to leave you and Lewis."

She raised her head. "You asked why I didn't accept a stipend from the SAS trust. Because I'd rather hate them than hate Steve."

"Claire," he croaked.

"You asked me to be honest," she reminded him. "Deal with it. I don't want to be Steve's widow. I don't want to be a single parent. I don't want to plan a future without him. But I have to, for Lewis's sake. And mine. Don't drag this out. Sign the papers. For God's sake, let me get on with my life."

"You might not feel like you were his first priority, but you were. I swear, as soon I've assessed the risks—"

"Go to hell." Pale with anger, she opened the door, and Adam nearly fell in. "Don't listen to this man," she instructed. "I'm going to the lawyer's to get him fired. Then I'm coming back."

She glared at Nate. "Don't be here. In fact, I want your stuff out of the bach when I return."

"I have no transport," he reminded her, though he suspected she was beyond reasoning with. Her next words confirmed it.

"So walk!"

CLAIRE STORMED OUT of the estate agency and into the high street, eighteen months of unexpressed rage boiling through her veins. And God, it felt so good. So good to rip off the mantle of long-suffering widow, meekly accepting her husband's fate because he'd died for his country. A good cause. Ha!

Well, what about my cause? What about Lewis's cause? Did you ever think of how your son would suffer if you died, you selfish bastard?

It was freeing to have this anger in the open, anger she'd suppressed for so long because it was wrong to speak ill of the dead, wrong to rail at the man she'd so loved.

But as she stabbed the unlock button on her car-key remote, Claire experienced the righteousness of rage. To hell with acceptance, to hell with stoicism, she wanted to slash and burn. Some tiny part of her brain knew this would wear off, but for now the brutal honesty was liberating, heady.

She got in the driver's seat and slammed the door. "At least you made it easy," she yelled in the confines of her car. "I spent half our married life alone while you were on deployment." It was like having a boil lanced; all the poison releasing in one toxic ooze.

Claire revved the engine, made an illegal U-turn and accelerated in the direction of her lawyer's office. She would never tie her life to a man's again. Never. They only let you down.

The lights turned red and she slammed on her brakes.

As for Nate…

She couldn't even articulate her thoughts where Nate was concerned, there was just a welling of murderous impulses. If she saw him again, she'd hit him. Swear to God. When the lights turned green, Claire burned rubber. "Now he has a conscience," she sneered. "Now he's concerned about our well-being."

Ahead, a young woman with a pram waited at a pedestrian crossing. Reluctantly Claire pulled to a stop. Different if Nate had been there for her, after Steve died, when she needed him. Needed his empathy, needing that mutual understanding they'd always shared. Of all the times to resurrect *that* Nate, he had to choose now. "And after helping me get the best price for the house, too. I mean, what the heck was that?" The crossing clear, she accelerated again. Some imagined command from on high from his dead buddy and never mind her wishes. Claire could have screamed.

"I don't forgive you," she said aloud to Steve. "You hear me? I don't forgive you. Live with it." She registered her words and suffered a pang of loss so sharp that she had to drop one hand from the steering wheel and press it against her breast.

You did say you wanted to feel.

CHAPTER SEVEN

HER LAWYER TOOK Claire's white-hot rage and doused it under dust-dry reality.

"Ideally, a trust deed is a lengthy, precise document—" Jules Browne held up three flimsy pages "—containing detailed provisions on the trustee's powers and responsibilities with a protector clause that would allow you to hire and fire, or limit what Nate can do." She paused to tuck a strand of shoulder-length brown hair behind her ear. "As I've mentioned previously, honey, yours isn't one of them."

"Unfortunately, you weren't in our circle of friends then," Claire said bleakly. The curse of accepting the cheapest quote. At the time the deed had been drawn up, Lewis had been a baby, Claire hadn't been working and money was tight. "To be honest, we probably wouldn't have included that clause anyway. We trusted Nate."

"And now you don't?"

"He shouldn't have the power to throw his weight around when he's spent over a year resisting every attempt I made to get him to do his damn job!"

"Having had every single legal letter ignored through that period, I completely agree." Jules laid the document on her neat desk. "But if Nate refuses to step down, the only way to get rid of him is to take him to court."

Claire stared at her friend in dismay.

"And scheduling a hearing depends on the backlog.... We could be talking months."

"Argh!" Claire started pacing the office. "I haven't got that kind of time."

"Calm down." Jules gently pushed her into a leather armchair, then poured a glass of water from the jug on her desk. "Here...let's talk this through. It's possible I can pull strings for an early hearing."

Accepting the glass, Claire noticed Jules's bare left hand. "Where's your engagement ring?"

Jules hid her hand behind her back. "At the jeweler's.... The...ah...stone was loose."

Claire said carefully, "Okay."

Jules sighed. "I'm lying," she admitted. "I've stopped wearing it at work. It only draws questions from clients who don't know about Lee. 'Oh, what a lovely engagement ring. When's the big day?' That kind of thing." Unlocking her desk drawer, she pulled out a large diamond solitaire, and slid the platinum band onto her finger. Even on an overcast morning, it seized all the room's ambient light and dazzled, exactly like the man who'd bought it for her.

"It's not a ring that goes unnoticed," agreed Claire.

Jules was looking at the diamond. "Do you think it's awful of me?" she said in a low voice.

"Of course not." Momentarily, Claire forgot her own troubles. "Look, there's no standard operating procedures for getting on with your life. We each muddle through as best we can." Jules and Lee had only a six-week whirlwind romance before he deployed. Some might think that should have made it easier for her to get over him. Having grown closer through their mutual bereavement, Claire knew different.

"You caught me by surprise, coming early." Jules adjusted the ring on her finger. "I would have been wearing it to see Nate."

"No one doubts your love for Lee," Claire said.

Clearing her throat, Jules retreated behind her desk, saying briskly, "Let's return to business, shall we?"

Claire took the hint. "If legal action's the only way to keep Nate out—" she steeled herself "—then let's start that ball rolling."

"Grounds usually include one of the following. The trustee has acted outside their powers…"

"Strike one." Her anger began to rise again.

"Or has acted capriciously…"

"Strike two."

"Or has taken into account irrelevant or improper factors—"

Claire stood up and began pacing again. "He thinks this is a knee-jerk reaction to Steve's death, which it bloody isn't."

Jules continued calmly. "Or has made a decision that no reasonable trustee could make."

"Strike three and he's out. How can we not win?"

"Because he'll claim he's acting in your best interests and however angry you are, Nate thinks he is, doesn't he?"

Claire scowled.

"You're a beneficiary as well as a trustee," Jules added, "which means your motives for firing him would be questioned."

"My motives are that he's been useless.… We have good records for that."

"He could argue that having witnessed Steve's death, he's been incapable of fulfilling his duties until this point. Certainly, prior to the ambush he was exemplary in fulfilling his role as trustee."

Claire snorted. "All he did was sign an annual account document and a trust tax return. All token stuff to meet minimal legal requirements."

"The law is what this will be judged on, Claire."

"And he wasn't incapable, he was unwilling!" She met her friend's unwavering gaze and sighed. "Like I'm unwilling to hear what you're going to say next."

"Talk to him, try to negotiate a solution that works for both of you. You'll get a lot further, a lot faster than taking him to court."

"Argh!"

"You're welcome." Jules smiled. "Maybe Nate's changed into the badass you describe, but sounds like his heart's still in the right place...at least where you're concerned. Use that as your starting point."

"Except I told him to go," Claire confessed. "Pack his bags and leave."

What if he had? "Oh, hell." She fumbled for her cell and rang his. It was switched off. Her next call was to the estate agent, who reported Nate had left shortly after she had. When Adam started talking about the buyers, she cut him short. If Nate was leaving, the sale was dead in the water. "I'll phone you later...and you, Jules."

As she cut the connection, she was already halfway out the door.

Claire drove home to Stingray Bay at breakneck speed using a local's knowledge to cut corners and accelerating on every straight. She scanned the roadside for the sight of Nate's rangy frame, as well as the drivers of oncoming vehicles in case he'd organized a rental.

He had fifty minutes' head start, which wasn't much for a normal person, but was way too much for an ex–Special Services soldier bent on leaving. The station wagon bounced over the grassy knolls that made up the communal yard behind the baches, all empty at this season. As she found the key on its nail under the deck and slotted it into the patio door, she peered inside. "Nate?"

The place looked the same way they'd left it, breakfast dishes stacked in the kitchen sink. Claire swept aside the curtain to the spare room and her heart sank. Bed neatly made, bag gone. Without hope, she searched the bach, but there was no note, no message of farewell. And why would there be? Her husband's best friend was already struggling emotionally and she'd spewed all her shameful, darkest thoughts onto him.

Still, Claire went onto the deck, staring along the curve of peninsula she'd just driven, desperately searching what she could see of the road through the pohutukawa trees. Empty. Half a kilometer along the estuary a solitary figure walked the strip of beach exposed by an outgoing tide. An overnight bag hung from one shoulder and Claire straightened. "Nate!" He was too far away to hear.

She tore down the wide steps cut into the clay bank, her high heels sinking into the wet sand as she hit the estuary beach. Impatiently she kicked them off and tossed them up the hill. "Nate!" In bare feet, she broke into a run, the broken shells sharp against her winter-soft soles. A shard lodged between her toes and panting, she stopped to dislodge it. When she looked up, Nate was gone. Claire ran faster, but there was no sign of him. "Nate!"

He couldn't have just disappeared. On the thought, her panic dissipated. She knew where he was heading. Pinching the stitch in her side, she dropped to a walk and caught her breath.

Between the footbridge and the concrete boat ramp three boat sheds sat in varying degrees of dilapidation. Two had been built half on land, half on wooden piles, which were encrusted with generations of oysters. The largest, grounded on a concrete slab was an enormous A-frame constructed entirely of corrugated iron, with roller doors both ends. Age had faded its paint to an oxidized red. The clear sheets of corrugate that acted as skylights were an opaque yellow, and rust had scalloped some of its edges at ground level. But it was sound enough to house a forty-foot vessel with a twelve-foot beam and four-foot draft.

As she'd suspected, the side door was open. Claire stopped to gather composure then stepped inside. *Heaven Sent* was propped on a jerry-rigged hard stand, which Nate was inspecting carefully.

She cleared her throat. "It doesn't look much, but it's solid…and cheaper than hiring a boat cradle." She hated the nervousness in her voice. Nate was the one in the wrong. But she felt as good as naked when his gaze lifted to hers.

She couldn't help what she felt about Steve. God knows she'd spent months trying to talk herself out of these feelings because they'd had a good marriage, she'd loved her husband with all her heart, and it was crazy to hold him responsible for dying on his last tour.

A better woman would have been able to battle through these unworthy emotions and forgive him. A lesser woman would have been selfish, demanded he honor his promise and kept him alive. Instead, Steve was dead and Claire swung between regret and resentment. And now Nate knew her dirty little secret.

"I'm out of the house," he said. "I'll sleep in my half of the boat until I've done what I need to."

She forgot her awkwardness. "Nate, if I lose my sale, I lose my chance at having *Heaven Sent* ready for this season. And if I miss the season I have to wait another year. You've already killed the project by default."

"I bribed your buyers with a week's holiday on the Gold Coast to wait for an answer."

"What?"

"And I'll work on the boat so you don't lose momentum on the upgrade. Lewis is due home in what, ten days? Let's make eight our deadline."

She hadn't expected such a quick concession, but it wasn't enough.

"And at the end of that time if you decide this isn't a good idea…?" Jules had told her to be conciliatory, but she couldn't be, Claire realized, not on this. "I'd rather pull the plug now than put my fate in someone else's hands again."

Some emotion she couldn't identify crossed his face. "I understand," he said. "So here's my offer. I assess your business plan, double-check all your figures on the refit. If I think you're taking too big a risk I'll try to talk you out of it. But if I can't, I sign the deed of sale regardless. This isn't about a power trip, Claire. It's about getting you to pause, take a deep breath. That's all."

"And I'm supposed to just believe you?"

"If you don't trust my word anymore, I'll sign something."

She looked at him. "I'll have Jules put something together."

His jaw tightened, but he nodded. "I guess I deserve that."

"You've been AWOL for well over a year. I'm not the only person with something to prove here, Nate."

"Never said you were, Claire," he replied quietly. Picking up his bag, he slung it up and onto *Heaven Sent*'s deck, where it kicked up a puff of dust.

"You can't sleep here," she said.

"I thought we'd reached an agreement?"

"The cabin's a mess. Come back to the house."

"I could rent one of the empty baches.… I've seen a couple of signs."

"Don't be silly…unless…" She broke eye contact, recalling her earlier confession. "Unless you feel uncomfortable staying now, after what I said about Steve."

"I'm hardly in a position to judge you."

There was a lump in her throat. "Still, I shouldn't have unloaded on you, it wasn't fair. Steve was your best friend."

He walked over and put his arms around her in the first hug he'd given freely. "You're my friend, too," he said. "You'll get past this. You'll love him again."

Hot tears burned. Claire buried her face in his shoulder, borrowing his warmth. "How can you be so sure?" she said. "All I do is play with the same old puzzle pieces of our life together, over and over. There are no new pieces, Nate."

She felt him tense, under her cheek his heart-beat picked up. "Yeah, there are," he said. "You said I spent as much time with Steve as you did. Maybe I can fill in the gaps."

NATE COULDN'T BELIEVE he'd just blurted that. But something in him went crazy at the idea that Steve had lost Claire as well as his life. He'd screwed up, no question, but their marriage had been the bedrock of his mate's life. And the backdrop of their "tight five" unit. Didn't matter how much he, Dan, Ross and Lee stuffed up in their personal relationships, Claire and Steve—Steve and Claire—were the constant. The gold standard.

She pulled free of the hug to look at him.

"You'll talk about your deployments? I thought that wasn't allowed."

"I'm not giving away troop movements, or strategy, just giving you an idea what was going on with Steve while we were away." He'd need to think this through carefully. What he told her, what he didn't. Couldn't. Nate realized what he'd let himself in for.

She must have seen his sudden reserve. "Nate, I've heard censored versions my whole married life, they won't help me.… But I appreciate the thought."

A swallow fluttered under the rafters, drawing their attention. "There's a pair nesting here," Claire said. "They come back every spring." But he watched her, the pale line of throat, the curve of her cheek as she lifted her face.

Did he have the guts to try to help? Maybe. His foster childhood hadn't produced a conversationalist, and a career in the SAS sure as hell hadn't given him any practice articulating emotions. Though the bonds forged were unbreakable, they were never discussed. Knowing your brother would take a bullet for you reduced the necessity to talk about feelings.

Guilt was a lump permanently located in his chest. Give it attention and it throbbed. It throbbed now. Ah, God, did he have the guts for this? "Steve nearly got us killed once," he said before he chickened out.

Claire crossed her arms. "What!"

"I'll tell you tonight. Right now, let's see what you've been doing to our boat."

"You can't drop that bombshell and leave it!"

"Come to think of it, there are other stories I should tell first, but daylight hours are for pulling my weight as a trustee." He looked at his watch. "It's 11:00 a.m. After I've checked her over, how about taking me to see that engine you've got your eye on?"

"Eleven? I must call Adam back." She fumbled in her jacket pocket. "Damn, I left my cell at the bach with his number. I'll meet you there.… But you tell me that story as soon as we have a free hour, Nate, you hear me?"

"Remember to phone Jules, get her to draw something up."

At the door, she paused. "Did you really bribe my buyers?"

"I prefer the term *incentivize*." He repeated the words she'd said to him in L.A. "I'm not here to make your life harder."

Claire looked at him for a long time and he tried not to flinch.

Sometimes he wondered if, like a superhero, this woman could see through walls. "Maybe we can keep Jules out of it," she said.

Nate shook his head. "Don't give me wiggle room. If I find something I don't approve of, neither of us want my conscience free to kick in again."

She smiled. "That's the first joke I've heard you try to make since L.A."

"It wasn't a joke." He tried not to return her smile and failed.

But it faded pretty quickly after she left and Nate took his first good look at *Heaven Sent*. Hull scoured, covered in fine dust, with a narrow canopy that only emphasized her wide bottom, she was nothing like the sleek cruisers he'd grown accustomed to in L.A.

Her charm had always lain in her price. Claire had found her on eBay under classic crafts, where all the derelicts were listed. She'd been looking at boats ever since Nate met her, and had been trying to talk Steve into buying *Heaven Sent* when they'd met one night for dinner.

Nate didn't know much about boats other than how to board them covertly in antiterrorist drills, but Claire had made a good case for "the bargain of a lifetime." After hearing Steve inform his wife for the twentieth time that, bargain or not, they couldn't afford the outlay with their mortgage, he heard himself saying to Claire, "I'll go halves with you."

Everyone at the table stopped eating and looked at him. He shrugged. "I fancy a project, and I've got the money." He lived in the SAS single men's quarters at Rennie Lines. On leave, he helped Ross build his house and joined Dan as an extra hand on his parents' farm when they weren't all at Stingray Bay. He was an active relaxer and sitting around wasn't his style.

Now Nate climbed the ladder to the deck and walked into the small wheelhouse, taking in the antiquated black switchboard and control panel, all dials and spewing wires with an on/off lever more commonly used to animate Frankenstein. Had Claire included rewiring in the upgrade? He couldn't remember.

The small cabin belowdecks proved to be in the best shape. When they'd bought it they'd concentrated their initial efforts here so Nate could be self-sufficient on longer stays at Stingray Bay. His gaze swept beyond the tiny galley and two divans either side of a fixed table to the bespoke double bed curved into the prow.

All the soft furnishings had been swathed in plastic and every surface was thickly covered in dust. He'd fitted the galley's countertop last time he was here. The small sink still sat on the floor waiting to be fitted next.

Nothing had changed; everything had changed.

It was a strange feeling, going through the boat, bittersweet. Like revisiting a lover, abandoned midaffair, he felt guilt, some remorse and a flutter of the old excitement. Two years since he'd last walked her deck, run his palm over the kauri railing and told her she'd soon be beautiful. He found the antifoul paint he'd bought on special stacked in a cupboard, cans of it. A bright kingfisher blue.

He was almost glad Claire had turned down his offer of his half share, except he wasn't comfortable taking money from her, either. He wasn't sure that they'd work that out, but currently he had more pressing concerns than *Heaven Sent*'s ownership. He reached in his jeans pocket for his cell.

The most important concern was telling his egocentric employer that his personal bodyguard wasn't coming home tomorrow.

Zander wasn't happy. "I have as much sympathy as the next guy, Nate, but get your priorities straight. I pay your salary and with the tour coming up, I don't need any additional stress. Set up an electronic signature, it's how I work with Devin." Devin was Zander's New Zealand–based brother and former band member.

"It's not as simple as that. I have to suss out if the business is a starter and I can't do that remotely. And if I skip town, I kill any chance of talking Claire out of it."

"Hang on… That wax is too hot, you want to give me third-degree burns? Jeez, my chest looks like a friggin' barber's pole.… Listen, Nate, do you think you're irreplaceable?" Zander's ill humor with his beautician spilled into his tone.

"This is important," Nate said patiently. "I wouldn't ask otherwise."

"I've already given you three days." Petulance crept into the famous voice. "I'm not happy, Nate. If I let you start laying down terms, then I'm setting a precedent for everyone else."

"Tell them I haven't taken a break in a year," Nate suggested.

"I never thought you'd let me down over a piece of tail."

"You're breaking up…I'll try…better reception." Pissed, Nate rang off before he told the rocker to stick his head up his own tail. Everything came down to sex for Zander and explaining otherwise would be as effective as telling Hefner that some bunnies came without boobs. He wished to hell the guy would grow up, but he'd been pandered to for twenty years and wouldn't transform into a Boy Scout anytime soon.

His employer might cool down, he might

not. Shit. This was getting harder and harder. But right now his bigger concern was helping Claire. Job security was the least of Nate's worries.

CHAPTER EIGHT

"YOU'RE RIGHT, it's a hulluva good price," Nate said, reading the specs poster taped to the new diesel engine in one of Whangarei's premier marine showrooms. Waving aside a salesman, he bent to look underneath. "Installation costs will add another thirty or forty percent to your bill, though."

Claire's smugness evaporated. "As much as that, why?"

"*Heaven Sent*'s existing engine beds would need to be modified."

She stared at him in dismay. "And here I was thinking I'd covered all bases with exhaustive questions on parts availability, nautical miles per gallon and warranty."

"All important," he said. "But you have to look at how a new engine will work with existing components. On an old boat like ours, there's no room to fit a larger propeller, and a lighter engine won't generate the high torque needed to drive *Heaven Sent*."

She dragged up her knowledge on torque.

The force needed to make the propeller rotate. "I know the theory, but I'm still a novice on practical maintenance, which is why I figured buying new would be the best way to go." Too late she realized she was giving him ammunition.

"Is that why you discounted reconditioning the Leyland 680?"

Cautiously, Claire nodded. "I need reliability, not an engine that requires coaxing."

"The work I did on the Leyland after we purchased was Band-Aid stuff." There was no superiority in his tone. "A professional overhaul will yield much better results. I think it's worth getting a quote from a reconditioning specialist."

Claire waved away another salesman. "I thought I'd nailed this."

Nate dropped a hand on her shoulder. "Don't beat yourself up, I know this stuff backward." He and Steve had been in Mobility Troop, patrolling a thousand square kilometers of southern Afghanistan's rugged plains and foothills. Engine maintenance was an essential part of their skill set, she recalled. It made her feel better.

She was conscious of the warmth of his palm on her shoulder, conscious of a thaw between them. "I guess you've saved me from making an expensive mistake." She added grudgingly, "It almost makes up for you being such a pain in the ass about this trustee business."

Nate removed his hand. "Hey, make me suffer, I deserve it." There was that note in his voice again, bitter as medicine.

Why does Steve haunt you, Nate? He wasn't a man who confided easily, but she had a week to pry it out of him. "I won't, but Jules may," she cautioned as they left the store. They were meeting her in a café to sign the minicontract Jules had hastily put together after Claire's phone call. "Lawyers dislike being given the runaround, too."

JULES WAS ALREADY SITTING at a table at the busy inner-city café when they arrived. It was covered with papers, and the debris of an early lunch. Giving her a wave, Claire pushed Nate in her direction. "Go make your peace while I order. Espresso, right?"

He approached the table slowly, unsure how to greet her. With a handshake? With a hug? Lee had been one of his closest friends, but his mate's whirlwind courtship meant Nate had met Jules only once before his death.

At the time she'd simply represented yet another in a long line of Lee's girlfriends and h cool reserve, combined with a noisy bar, h fostered a rapport. Later, when he'd quizzed Lee about "Miss Congeniality," he'd said, "Watch it, Wyatt. You're talking about my future wife."

Nate had cracked up. "You making a commitment is as delusional as Lady Gaga trying to give up makeup for Lent."

"Much you know. I'm proposing after this deployment."

None of the guys had taken him seriously and his unresponsiveness to their ribbing through the tour—like I'm giving you jackasses more ammo on my love life—only confirmed their view that their resident Romeo had got cold feet.

Dan found the engagement ring, packing up Lee's personal effects, and brought it to the hospital where Nate sat with Ross in critical care. The three of them had stared at it for a long time.

"If we give it to her, it'll only make things worse," Ross croaked from the bed. "I say, we sell it and find a way to give the money to his family."

"She *is* his family…or was meant to be," Dan said. "Shit, I can't believe we didn't believe him. We're idiots." For a moment, they'd fallen silent, remembering their buddy. "I think it will be a comfort, a confirmation of how important she was to him. I say we give it to her."

"I disagree," Ross said. "It's salt in the wound."

He turned his head on the pillow. "Nate, you've got the deciding vote."

He'd already begun his withdrawal and shrugged. "It's not like she can suffer any more, is it? And if it strikes her as too morbid she can always sell it."

They gave her the ring. She'd blanched white, and then stared at them with stricken eyes. Even in his numbness, Nate was moved. There was no doubting her love for Lee. From that moment she'd been adopted by Lee's circle. A natural loner, she'd resisted being taken into the fold, but she wasn't given a choice. Another reason Nate had left the country. It was the only way to escape.

But he was glad she'd found somewhere to belong.

He reached the table, still undecided on a greeting. She made the decision for him by thrusting out her hand. "Hello, Jules." He shook it, returning her polite smile. They could have been strangers meeting, instead of two people inextricably bound by a common tragedy. But his move to the States immediately after the memorial service meant they were strangers and God knows his indifference since had done nothing to endear him to her.

"Well, we haven't seen you for a while, but you're certainly making your presence felt n aren't you?" she said pleasantly as they took their seats.

"I've been ignoring your lawyer's letters for what…over a year? Feel free to call me an asshole."

She gave him an assessing look, then dropped her gaze to the papers in front of her. "As Claire's lawyer, it's important to retain an impartial professionalism."

"Let's step outside that magic circle a moment."

Her gaze lifted. "You're an asshole."

"The facts point to it," he agreed.

Jules waved reassurance to Claire, who was watching them anxiously from the line at the counter. "She's wasted a hell of a lot of money over that period trying to get you to fulfill your role as trustee," she said through a big smile. "You might want to think about reimbursing. I kept records."

"I was going to ask about that."

"Uh-huh." She looked skeptical. "This better not be another way of messing her around."

"All I want is a week to assess the risks. Steve was my best friend and it's time I did right by his wife and son."

"She said this was your idea?" Her tone less hostile, Jules waved the new contract.

"The final decision on selling the house has to be hers."

"Okay then," she said grudgingly, and handed him a pen. He resisted the urge to touch the rock on her finger, like some kind of talisman.

"How are you, Jules?" he said awkwardly. Last time he'd seen her, she'd been a frozen figure at the memorial service. She'd let him hug her then.

"Fine," she said shortly. There was a brief silence. "You?"

"Fine," he replied in kind.

Both of them looked instinctively toward Claire for rescue, noticed and pretended not to. God, this was uncomfortable. Nate thought he'd learned to talk to anybody working for Zander, but somehow small talk failed him.

Jules cleared her throat. "So," she said. "Zander Freedman."

It was so unexpected Nate laughed. "You're kidding."

She smiled sheepishly. "The crushes you have when you're thirteen tend to stay with you."

It also explained her attraction to Lee. She liked the wild ones. "If I've still got a job, I'll get him to autograph a picture."

"Has staying longer put your job under threat?"

"Keep your voice down." Nate glanced at

Claire; she was at the cashier. "He's still learning to share his toys…he'll come round."

"And if he doesn't?"

"Then I'll pimp my services somewhere else."

"Who's pimping what?" Claire said behind him.

Jules didn't miss a beat. "Nate is my pimp for Zander Freedman's autograph," she said. "Tell him to make the inscription tasteful," she told Nate. "Something like, 'Juliet Browne, you were the best I ever had.'" She proffered her pen. "Maybe you should write that down."

"I think I can commit that one to memory." For the first time Nate understood Lee's attraction to this woman. He'd never know where he was with her.

Claire put down the tray. "Don't tell her Zander hugged me," she advised Nate. "She'll never get over it."

"Wait, you met him and haven't told me? My God, our friendship is hanging by a thread! Unless that éclair's for me."

With an exaggerated sigh, Claire handed it over, along with another coffee. "Now I'm stuck with your oatmeal slice. Nate, I got you a sausage roll for Kiwi nostalgia."

Instinctively his eyes met Jules's. Lee had been a sausage-roll connoisseur, but maybe she hadn't had time to discover that. Judging by the way she was biting her lip, she had. He spoke to mitigate the grief. "Did you know Lee's sister used to post sausage rolls to Afghanistan?"

"No," she rallied. "That's impossible."

"They'd arrive all vacuum packed. He could have sold them a dozen times over, but he never did—even his buddies only got one. The rest he inhaled. It was probably the oddest thing that got posted."

Jules hesitated, and then reached in her handbag. "Speaking of posting…" She pulled out a colored envelope and slid it across the table. "I was too annoyed to send it," she confessed. "But even though I'm not a superstitious person I couldn't bring myself to throw it out. Happy belated birthday."

He accepted it because he didn't want to hurt her, and then realized this was an opportunity. "Do you know how this birthday card tradition started?" he said.

"No, tell me."

"I don't have family," he explained. "Our first tour everyone was getting mail except me. It didn't bother me, I was used to it. But on my birthday I got a card from Claire and baby Lewis, from Ross's brother, Dan's sisters and parents, from Lee's family. Most of these people I hadn't even met."

"Steve mentioned it in a phone call," Claire said. "It wasn't hard to coordinate."

He looked at her, startled. "It was you? I always thought Steve had organized it." He added softly, "Hey, thank you."

"You're welcome."

"I still get cards," he told Jules.

"Because you wrote back," Claire said. "We were all surprised by that."

"The guys told me I had to," he admitted. "I didn't know any different." They all laughed.

He hadn't replied last year and still got cards from everyone this one. Forcing himself to open Jules's card, Nate read the standard message carefully, then smiled at his dead mate's fiancée. "Thanks," he said. And meant it.

"Okay, enough hedging," Claire said. "Tell me something I don't know about my husband."

Reluctantly, Nate put down the report he'd said he wanted to finish.

It was late evening and he'd been reviewing all the quotes Claire had collected on the boat upgrade while she sat opposite on her laptop, tweaking the website for the new business.

"Nice design." He bought time by glancing at the screen. Marketing wasn't his area of expertise, but he appreciated how she'd integrated the theme colors—teal and navy—into the site. "It's not active, though, is it?"

"It will be as soon as I'm sure of making the proposed launch date."

He frowned. "You're not even pretending to keep an open mind."

"Or maybe I'm supremely confident you'll come to support this project the way I do," she countered. "Because of your open mind."

Such a smart woman.

He looked down at the report. She'd negotiated some great deals, no question.

"If you've had second thoughts," she said, "about talking about Steve..."

"Steve once committed credit-card fraud," he said, feeling the first lash of memory and ignoring it. He'd decided he could manage this by being selective about the stories he recounted.

She blinked at him over her laptop, the screen light giving her face an angel's glow. "I don't believe it."

"Shut that thing down and I'll tell you." He'd already suggested she get an early night—she'd been yawning ever since dinner—but although she kept saying, "Great idea," she hadn't moved.

"Blackmail," she complained, but closed the lid and stretched in her chair, looking at him expectantly. It would take a while to go through the reports and assess Claire's state of mind, so he'd said the incident in which Steve nearly got the unit killed needed to come chronologically. That was bullshit.

He couldn't tell that story. If the ambush was a fire, that story involved sitting close enough to have your eyebrows singed. On the other hand, Claire wasn't going to be a soft sell. Nate needed to work out how to present his mate in the best light, with the least collateral damage.

Why hadn't Steve told the guys about his deal with Claire?

"First I knew of it was when I received a letter from some kid in Indonesia thanking me for becoming his Child Fund sponsor," he began. "Steve admitted he'd stolen my credit-card details and signed me up."

Another lash, through flesh to bone. Revisiting the good times only accentuated what he'd lost.

Claire's eyes brightened with amusement. "Why would he do such a thing?"

"We'd been talking about him being married so young. I was pretty feral then—a hard-ass who mocked what he couldn't understand. I'd said something on the lines of, 'Who needs a dependent? I'd hate someone leaning on me, tying me down and cramping my style.'"

She was still smiling, but the expression was fixed.

Closing the report, Nate sat back. If he focused on orchestrating Claire's reactions, his own became bearable. "When I asked him what the hell he was doing forging my signature on a World Vision application, Steve said I needed to lose the chip on my shoulder and understand that mine wasn't the only sad story in the world. That he and the other guys relied on me for their lives and I needed to start caring about someone other than myself. I lost my temper, told him to keep his preachiness for the little wife who I was sure obeyed his every command."

"What!"

"I'd only met you once," he reminded her. Yeah, if he concentrated on Claire, it became easier. "We were both on our best behavior."

She snorted. "I don't remember you being on your best behavior. You checked me out, informed Steve I had a nice ass, kept choking back cusswords and spent the whole evening ignoring me."

"I didn't know how to talk to a pretty woman I wasn't trying to hit on," he admitted. "I watched, though…how Steve treated you, how you treated him. Waiting for one of you to slip up on the lovey-dovey respectful-partnership scam." He shrugged. "As I said—feral."

"So that's why you were staring?"

"Well, that, and as I've already mentioned,

your ass," he said. "At least until your husband told me to quit." How had they wandered so far off track? "You have to remember, I had very basic socialization skills for the civilized world."

Nate looked out through the patio doors to the night and refocused. Once, normal life had been as far away to him as the few lights twinkling across the estuary. He swallowed hard. "Without Steve, I'd never dreamed of applying to the SAS. For me, the army was a cheap way of learning a trade. But I found I liked it.… The camaraderie, the professionalism, the structure." For the first time in his life, he'd had security.

"I assumed you and Steve met at selection."

"No, six months before. We were in separate units brought in to make up numbers for an SAS training exercise." He cleared his throat. This was getting hard again. "The pair of us had been captured, trussed up and tossed in the back of a truck. As we were jolting to base, your husband said, 'I'm going to be SAS one day.'" Nate desperately wanted to stop, but Claire was captured now, leaning forward with a riveted expression.

"Of course, I said not to talk crazy," Nate continued. "SAS troopers were gods, we were mere foot soldiers. Steve said, 'You're just afraid of failing.' That pissed me off. I pointed out that I stood more chance of success than he did, I was a better tracker, a better shot.… One of my foster dads was a keen hunter. 'The next selection's in six months,' he said. 'My troop-mate Ross's old neighbor is ex-SAS. He says he'll give us a training program.'"

"And you all passed."

Nate shook his head. "The golden boy failed. Lee reapplied next intake, alongside Dan. By then we could tell them that selection was a walk in the park compared to the training cycle." It killed him reliving these poignant memories, but he forced himself to continue. "I didn't have the habit of study and Steve's extra tutorials were the only thing that got me through."

"Steve always said he'd have failed if you hadn't sorted out his fear of heights on his initial parachute jump." She added curiously, "What did you do?"

A reluctant smile broke through. "A simple technique, heavily reliant on the element of surprise."

She studied his grin, then comprehension dawned. "You pushed him?"

"I had help. Ross distracted the instructor."

"That's terrible!" But she was trying not to laugh. Every smile Nate won was a victory for Steve. "What did my husband do after you landed? Hit you?"

"Hell, no… I had to duck a kiss, he was so grateful. Steve would have been kicked off the course if he hadn't jumped and returned to the regulars." And he'd still be alive.

He stood, unable to sit still. But there was nowhere to go. He put the report on the table.

"So you cured his acrophobia," Claire marveled. She hadn't made a similar connection.

Nate forced himself to sit down again. "Let's just say his fear of heights paled in comparison to his fear of being pushed."

He waited until she'd stopped laughing before he added gruffly, "The army gave me an education, but Steve gave me a role model. When I met him, I only knew who I didn't want to be. Suddenly I was around men who'd learned how to govern their tempers, who had principles and goals. Who saw honor as a way of life and not something you won on a battlefield."

The knife in his gut turned sharply, eviscerating him from the inside out. He'd thought he'd become one of them. "Drink?" Nate bought himself a recovery minute by going into the kitchen.

"Thanks."

Tough it out, he told himself as he filled the kettle, *she needs this.* "Seeing how you and

Steve treated each other, I started seeing relationships differently." He barely registered what he was saying now, random thoughts spilling into words while he struggled for composure.

Hand trembling slightly, he flicked the outlet switch. "I started wanting more than one-night stands." Returning to the living room, Nate resettled on the couch, well away from the overhead light above the dining table. "But making a relationship work didn't come naturally."

"Bree got over you eventually." Claire rose and turned up the thermostat on the convection heater, then curled up at the other end of the couch, pulling a mohair throw over her legs. "Nate, I always wondered.... Did the fact that Steve and I were going through a bad patch for a couple of years scare you off matrimony? Is that why you got cold feet?"

"Partly," he admitted. Talking about something else calmed him. "Seeing how deployment could rock a strong marriage like yours, I figured I didn't stand a shit-show of making one work. But there was something missing with Bree." He shrugged. "An easiness, maybe. We both had to try too hard."

Okay, he was in control now. Time to shut up with the confidences.

"If it's any consolation, she's happy now, married to a great guy."

He'd shut up after saying one more thing. "I'm sorry it affected your friendship with her."

"She didn't understand SAS brotherhood," she said. "I could hardly bar you from our house."

That stung him into a reply. "What are you talking about? You frosted me for at least a year."

"Well, you deserved it! Breaking off an engagement over the phone. What were you thinking, Nate?"

"That if I knew I couldn't marry her, I should tell her right away." He still saw nothing wrong with that. Nate waited for Claire to explain it to him.

"Hopeless," she said, which was no help at all. "Next time you want to break someone's heart, run tactics by me first, will you?"

He folded his arms. "There won't be a next time. I've decided I'm not marriage material."

"But you wanted a family."

What he wanted and what he deserved had split irrevocably. Nate deflected. "What was it with you and Steve? You had a new baby, a new house.… Everything should have been terrific."

Claire looked skeptical. "You mean he didn't tell you?"

"Only that you were unreasonable, irrational and bossy as hell."

She laughed. He'd always been able to make her laugh. "In those early years it felt as if Steve had four other wives, all of whom could read him better than I could. It's easy to get insecure when you're knee deep in nappies and your big advantage over the buddies—sex—gets jumbled in with housework and mortgages. All the exciting, adventurous stuff happened with his unit."

"Not true. Most of our patrols were monotonous as hell." Long days spent in a blistering-hot truck, lurching over featureless desert and everyone stinking to high heaven because they hadn't washed in a month. Each man's quirks magnified by weeks of living in each other's pockets.

As the boiling kettle whistled and shut off, he said, "The only drama came if you were taking a shift as a motorcycle outrider and had to outrun an Afghan dog.... Those things are a cross between a hyena and a mule. Or an axle breaking and having to reweld it in forty-degree heat."

"C'mon, Nate," she challenged. "Steve said there was no rush that matched the rush after combat."

"It's what we were trained for, Claire. We wanted to use our skills." He fell silent a moment. "And an IED can nullify all that. Anyone can fill a pressure cooker with fertilizer and diesel and wire it to a couple of AA batteries. They're one of a terrorist's most effective weapons because they pin life or death to a roulette wheel of random luck…. They're frickin' perfect."

Nate became aware of Claire as she hugged her knees, and was stricken. "God, I'm sorry." He should have quit while he was ahead.

"And you go half-crazy reimagining a different outcome," she said quietly. "If it exploded a few meters to the left, maybe the injuries wouldn't have been fatal. If only there'd been someone else's truck in the lead, because in the initial grief you're willing to sacrifice a stranger's loved ones for your own."

She smoothed out the mohair over her knees. "If the convoy had left earlier, or later, taken a different route. If the batteries on the IED were flat. I've rewritten it a thousand ways. But you can't change history, Nate." Her eyes met his. "You can only try to accept it."

Except some things were beyond making peace with.

Abruptly he stood, feigning a yawn. "Jet lag's kicking in. I'm skipping a hot drink and turning in."

She rose to give him a hug that held way too much reassurance and Nate tried to relax his tense muscles. Why the hell had he ever thought he could be some kind of Dr. Phil for Claire when he was so screwed up himself? He'd back right off before he caused even more damage.

"Sleep well," she said.

"You too." He kissed her cheek, satin smooth and cool under his lips, and went to bed feeling like Judas Iscariot.

CHAPTER NINE

Claire woke to the sound of Nate moving around the bach. "Turn on a light if you want to," she called. "I'm awake."

Rolling to the window beside the bed, she drew the curtain, startling a rabbit nibbling the dew-tipped kikuyu grass. It bolted across the shared driveway and disappeared among the sand dunes with a blur of cottontail. Though the animals were a pest here, she smiled.

Above the three Norfolk pines that bordered the communal yard, dawn streaked rain clouds pink. She undid the window latch and pushed it open to breathe in the salty sharp air, leavened with pine needles. The scent always made her think "summer holidays," even when a glimpse of sea through the dunes was a choppy, stormy gray. Nate tapped on the doorjamb. "Coffee?"

"Wonderful." As he pulled open the doorway curtain and appeared with a steaming mug, she sat up. "What time is it?"

"Just gone six." Yet he was already showered, clean shaven, dressed in designer jeans and a formfitting sweater. "I want to get as much done as possible while I'm here, so I figured I'd make a start on stripping the old canopy today, keep you company while you're sanding handrails."

Claire accepted the mug. Assess her, he meant. "What about reading reports?"

"I'll do that at night. There's plenty to do on *Heaven Sent* without spending money and my help will stop you falling behind."

"And you can tell me more stories about Steve."

He didn't look at her. He'd withdrawn again, "new" Nate evident in his shuttered expression. Well, she'd expected that. "I'm not sure I'm doing Steve any favors and—" his gaze met hers "—I upset you last night."

"I think they'll really help," she stated.

He shifted, uncomfortable. Claire sipped her coffee. "Okay," he said at last. "I'll think about it."

After he'd left, Claire settled against the pillows, thinking hard. Witnessing Nate's distress last night had shaken her; somehow she had to get him past this self-destructive grief. And there was only one chink in the armor he used to keep her at arm's length.

Steve.

It felt as if Nate was trying to convince her that Steve was a great guy…as if he wanted to help her forgive him. But Claire already knew her husband was a great guy. That wasn't the problem.

Steve being dead was the problem.

Steve dragging his heels on their agreement and getting himself killed was the problem.

Steve breaking their son's heart was the problem.

And it wasn't going to be solved by heroic stories or a mysterious incident involving her husband nearly getting his troopmates killed.

Claire took another hit of caffeine. But she wouldn't tell Nate that. However misguided, his attempt to find the magic words last night was deeply touching. And endearing. And, she suspected, therapeutic for him. His stories wouldn't help her forgive Steve, but they might help Nate accept his buddies' deaths.

And through his anecdotes she might learn, not in what he wanted to tell her, but what he didn't.

Though it was a short walk, they drove to the boat shed after breakfast. Rain pelted down and Claire had a trunkload of gear—sanding boards, an orbital sander, extra gloves and an old vacuum cleaner. "Another couple of days and I can start cleaning up, ready for painting," she said as she unlocked the shed and they hurriedly unloaded the gear.

The interior was cold, rain beat down on the tin roof and she switched on the lights to lift the gloom. Reaching for the coveralls she left on a hook beside the door, she cast a doubtful look at Nate's good clothes.

"They'll wash clean," he said. "And if they don't, I'll buy replacements." He turned to assess the canopy.

"I have a better idea. Follow me." Claire climbed to the deck and went into the cabin, where she opened a drawer. "You left these here." She handed him a folded pair of paint-splattered jeans and a plaid shirt, soft with wear. "I washed and stowed them for when you came back."

It was a couple of seconds before he took them. "Thanks."

He stripped off his sweater, and as the T-shirt under it lifted, Claire glimpsed the taut and tanned muscles of his abdomen. "I'll get started," she said, and left before he unbuttoned his jeans. *Idiot for getting flustered,* she told herself as she pulled on her coveralls and tied her hair back with a scrunchie. *Nothing's changed.*

When Nate emerged from the cabin, she was using the orbital sander on the last length of kauri handrail. The plaid shirt was tighter across the shoulders and he'd slashed the jeans across the thighs for a better fit. She'd already noticed he'd bulked up over the past year and a half.

"Did you turn into the Incredible Hulk in L.A.?" she teased over the buzz of the machine because it was easier making fun than gawking.

Nate shrugged. "Zander's into weights, we do a lot of workouts together."

He climbed the small stepladder that gave him access to the weatherworn canvas canopy, and she averted her gaze from his perfect butt and distracted herself from this uncomfortable awareness with thoughts about her son. It was 7:15 a.m. Was Lewis up mustering lambs or still in bed?

She was trying not to be a helicopter mom by phoning every day. At thirteen, he needed male role models and Dan fit the bill perfectly. But Nate was her son's favorite. Methodically, she moved the motorized sander over the handrail, careful not to gouge the wood. Claire hadn't given up on him seeing Lewis; she was simply biding her time.

Ninety minutes later Claire called a coffee break. Her hands still tingled from the vibration of the machine and her fingers were sweaty in the rough chamois gloves as she peeled them off, removed her dust mask and admired Nate's handiwork as he removed the last of the rotting canopy.

"The boat feels so much bigger without it."

"What are you replacing it with?"

"Aluminum and some kind of wonder fabric… There's a quote and spec brochure at the bach. All they need is the go-ahead, but they need cash in advance." She told him the figure. "It'll have to wait until the house sale's confirmed."

He was silent as she poured coffee from the thermos and brought out the chocolate-banana muffins she'd taken from the freezer that morning. "Are you withholding comment in case I read it as encouragement?" she challenged.

Amusement sparked in his eyes—russet brown flecked with gold. "Being stroppy work for you very often? Just curious."

Claire bit her lip to keep from smiling. "These muffins are cold but defrosted, I hope." She passed one over. "Dip it in your coffee."

Dusting the central slatted bench that doubled as seating and a storage bin with the tail of his flannel shirt, Nate sat. He'd rolled up the sleeves and with his strong tanned forearms looked like any other tradesman, except for those manicured Hollywood hands.

He caught her looking at them and grimaced. "That's why I'm not wearing gloves…. I need a few calluses or the locals will drive me out of Stingray Bay." Adding sugar to his coffee, he said too casually, "The place is deserted this time of year. Aren't you going to find it lonely outside the summer influx?"

Claire bit into her chilly muffin. "I know a few locals. You'll see more people when the weather fines up. And any peep of sun and you're in paradise again." Settling beside him, she looked up to the roof. "Sounds like the rain has stopped now."

It was isolated here without the summer crowds, but settling Lewis close to his new school was paramount. They could always move again if it didn't work out. But she wasn't expressing any doubt to Nate. He didn't need more grounds for questioning her decision. "About Steve," she said, changing the agenda to hers.

He stiffened, then casually added more sugar. "Yeah?"

"What was his view on that rough patch in our marriage?" Nate said nothing. She stopped chewing. "You will talk about him, won't you?" Just a trace of plaintive in her tone, like a berley trail used to draw a big fish closer to the bait. Speaking of bait… "He and I worked through those problems, remember?"

Nate's frown cleared and Claire knew what

he was thinking. If they'd got through tough times once…

He took the hook. "How much paternity leave did Steve have when Lewis was born?"

"Ten days before you were deployed to Timor. The next time he came home, Lewis was four months old." How desperate she'd been to see him, how quickly things had started going wrong.

Nate bit into the muffin. "He said you and the baby had become your own little unit," he said between chews. "You had a routine, a support group of new mums and he felt like he wasn't needed."

Her tongue touched a frozen spot on the muffin, and Claire paused to dig out the muffin core and threw it onto the dry dirt floor for the resident swallow, wishing she'd chosen another lead-in.

"I think we both had such high expectations of how that leave would play out, and reality just didn't live up to it," she admitted. "I was exhausted and Steve's tentativeness around the baby made me so nervous I'd take over. He'd get defensive and leave me to it."

The bird flew down from the rafters, keeping a wary eye on them as it darted forward for the frozen crumbs then flew back to its aerie. "Having a baby made me more sensitive to the dangers of deployment, but Steve dismissed my concerns."

Talk about back to the future. Appetite gone, Claire tossed aside the rest of her muffin. "We fought the whole month he was home," she recalled. "The only reprieve we had was when you and Brianna came to stay for that weekend." She pulled a face, striving to make this light again. "And the two of you were so attentive to each other and so loving, while Steve and I snapped each other's heads off."

"We were clinging together as a survival mechanism," Nate retorted. He threw his own frozen muffin next to Claire's. "I was never so glad to leave in my life. I still remember Steve's puppy-dog eyes as we drove away."

His tone invited her to see the funny side. Claire managed a smile. "And then we had another fight when I shrilly demanded to know why he couldn't be as nice to me as he was to Bree and he said, 'because Bree isn't being a bitch.'" Actually, in hindsight, it was humorous. Smiling, she shook her head. "And off we went on another round."

"When he came back to base, we all took one look at him and steered clear," Nate commented. "He was one mean bastard, acing every training exercise. When we drilled unarmed combat, there wasn't one of us who wanted to step in that circle with him. He gave Dan a black eye."

"You should have seen what I did to Lewis's teddy bear," Claire deadpanned.

Nate laughed. "Our first night on leave, Steve drank himself shit-faced, then started crying into his beer and saying, 'I can unload and identify twenty-four different makes of gun, I can kick you guys into next week, but I can't get the temperature right in a baby's bottle or puree the frickin' lumps out of an organic carrot, according to my ever-loving wife.' We didn't have the first clue what to say. In the end, Lee suggested Steve write you a letter since you couldn't talk without arguing and we jotted notes on a cocktail napkin. But Steve was still way too fixated on the carrot thing, so the exercise never came to anything."

"Oh, my poor Steve." She chuckled, but there were tears in her eyes. Nate extended a comforting arm and it seemed natural to lay her head on his shoulder. "We were all so reckless with love," she said, watching the swallow break up the lump of muffin. "You guys played the field and Steve and I treated marriage like a soap opera. Like it was a renewable resource that didn't need nurturing and tending. And yet I miss those days of being young and heedless of consequences."

I miss the courage to love without regretting the cost. Wait, how had she ended up on the therapist's couch when this was about helping Nate?

"You and Steve grew smarter," Nate said. "I'm not so sure about the rest of us."

Claire straightened. "You haven't seen Dan with Jo, or Ross with Viv. Those two were such players, but they're changed men. Nate, are you sure—"

"Positive." He stood and stretched. "How about I start dismantling the electrics?"

Frustrated, she watched him pack up the basket, incurably neat, like all army guys. "Why won't you see them?"

"I can't be who they want right now.... It'll only end in more hurt."

"You're okay with me."

He was silent, replacing the lid on the muffin tin.

"I know the ambush was bad," she said. "You wouldn't have stayed away from us, from Dan and Ross, if it wasn't. But there must be a vanilla version you can give Lewis."

He went into the wheelhouse and started inspecting the circuit board.

"Or you could tell him some of the things you're telling me. The day-to-day stuff."

"Any chance you can pass me that toolbox?" he said.

After dumping it beside him, she settled to hand sanding the grooves in the handrail. So much for coaxing him into opening up. Mentally Claire regrouped. "The worst thing about deployment is that it puts your relationship on the back burner for months at a time," she commented as though Nate hadn't just shut her down. "Whatever you've got in the pot when you leave keeps on simmering. For both of us, it was resentment."

The sandpaper abraded her fingers and she paused to pull on gloves, not daring to look at him. "Steve thought I was unreasonable wanting him to quit when I'd married a career soldier, and so he stopped telling me anything that might fuel my argument. That just made me more paranoid we were drifting apart and that Lewis and I sat low on his list of priorities."

She concentrated on sanding. A couple of minutes passed.

"Steve could be a stubborn bastard," Nate said and she breathed a sigh of relief. "It was one of his best and worst qualities. I think he hated deployment through that period as much as you did."

"Really?" Claire glanced up. He was busy tracing the jumble of red, black and yellow wiring back to the control panel. At the time, her husband hadn't given an inch.

"He hated missing all Lewis's milestones. Crawling, his first steps, his first words... We watched Lewis's first birthday party on DVD a month late and Steve grew very quiet. He said, 'My baby doesn't remember me when I go home.'"

Her throat tightened, as it always did when she thought of father and son together. "When Lewis was little, we'd talk to Steve's picture every day. I spent ages teaching him to say *dada*, except he said it to Dan instead...so funny. You should have seen Steve's face."

Nate looked over his shoulder. "So that's why Steve taught Lewis to call Dan, Dumdum."

When he smiled like this, she realized how much she'd missed him. Claire nodded. "And then he taught Lewie to call Ross, Rose."

"Ross said if he was going to be called a damn rose he'd at least be an iceberg rose." Nate's grin broadened. "Over the years it was shortened to Ice."

Claire laughed. "I never connected those two nicknames. So much for the hard-man reputation. I'll have to tease Ice about that.... Did you know he's got this big campaign going to get Viv to marry him?"

"Yeah, I heard. And that he's finally given

up on reaching operational fitness." Returning to Afghanistan had been Ross's driving ambition since the ambush, but his leg injury had proved beyond rehabilitation. He'd returned to the SAS in a noncombat role. Grin gone, Nate returned to examining the wiring. "How's he handling that?"

Claire looked at the new tension across his shoulders. "Phone him," she suggested gently. "Find out."

But he didn't respond, and she got no conversation from Nate for the rest of the morning.

CHAPTER TEN

"RECEPTION'S FINE IN New Zealand," Zander complained the next day. "I call my family there. Don't pull that stunt again."

Nate shifted the cell to his left hand and removed the last screws from *Heaven Sent*'s control panel with a screwdriver. "Fair enough."

"We'll frickin' compromise—God, I hate that word—come home now and we'll forget about it."

That was a compromise? "I can't." Nate calmly attempted to explain it all again, but Zander cut him off.

"Okay, enough Mr. Nice Guy. If you're not home within twenty-four hours, I'm making the stand-in permanent." The rocker was renowned for threats and ultimatums, but this was the first time he'd tried them on Nate, who'd made it clear he'd walk if he did. Clearly the rocker had forgotten.

"You do what you have to do, Zee, and so will I."

"Don't go all war-hero noble on me, Nate. I hate that shit."

"If the new guy doesn't work out, let me know. I can recommend others." Unlike his employer, Nate followed through on his ultimatums.

"Screw you, then." Zander hung up on him.

"I guess that means no reference," Nate said to the dial tone. And sighed. The rocker would regret his action but Nate didn't have the patience—or the emotional reserves—to play games. He needed both for Claire.

"Everything okay?" Claire's head popped over the gunwale as she climbed the ladder to *Heaven Sent*'s deck.

"Peachy," he said. "Zander's missing me." Hell, some badgering from Claire for another story about Steve and his day would be complete.

Claire frowned as she donned gloves. "If you need to return to L.A.…"

"Nice try." She'd been in town all morning finalizing quotes. Not even pretending that he had a snowball's chance in hell of influencing her decision. He ripped the control box from the wheelhouse wall, and rusty paint flakes showered onto the chart table. "Got another sanding job for you," he invited.

"Nate, you're here of your own free will," she

pointed out. "If you'd signed the papers when I asked you to, you could be in Hollywood right now."

Yeah, pointing out the obvious really helped. Forgetting his vow of patience, Nate dumped the control box on the deck and returned to disconnecting the mess of wiring in the switchboard. "You gave me that message loud and clear two days ago—I'm here under sufferance."

"I love having you here," she said, surprising him. "You might not change my mind, but your advice is saving me money.... I've just confirmed that reconditioning the engine is a way better option than replacing it."

He wasn't in the mood to be placated. "So now you're patronizing me."

"Wow, you're determined to pick a fight, aren't you? Fine, put up your dukes...." She started dancing from one foot to the other, fists raised. "C'mon, I can take you."

Nate clamped his mouth against a smile. She'd pigtailed her hair and in those coveralls, dancing around, looked like a feisty kid.

"You've been sniffing paint, haven't you?" She'd started varnishing handrails before she left for town; the acrid smell still lingered.

"Yep, I'm all varnished up.... C'mon, Buff Man, show me what you've got."

His mouth twitched. "You calling me a poser now?"

"Yeah, whatcha gonna do about it?" She fist tapped him, once on the chest, once on the biceps. "After dealing with a sulky thirteen-year-old, a sulky thirty-four-year-old doesn't scare me."

"I'll wake you at six with a cheery song and a smile," he growled.

"That's fighting talk." She tapped him again, harder. Whaddya know, it actually had power.

Folding his arms, Nate affected a sneer. "Do you seriously think you'll be hauling in game fish with those puny muscles?"

"I'll buy an electric reel…or hire beefcake like you."

"Made of money, huh?"

"I will be when you sign the damn papers." Another hit, harder this time. His biceps started to smart. He gave her a head-to-toe inspection.

"Spend some on yourself and maybe I will."

Self-consciously, Claire raised a hand to her hair and in a trice he'd grabbed her hand and spun her into a choke hold, his forearm pressed lightly across her throat. "Hey!"

"Too easy," he teased, a pigtail tickling his nose.

In one smooth move, Claire leaned into his body, hooked a leg behind his and leveraged out of his hold, shoving a knee into the back of his legs and knocking him off balance. Nate found himself on his knees, one arm twisted behind his shoulder blades.

"Nice," he approved.

"I've got a great business plan and you've read enough these past two days to suss that out. Admit it." Claire twisted his arm harder. "You're trying to gauge whether I'm emotionally stable."

"And this is supposed to convince me?"

With a chuckle she released him. "Cards on the table, Nate."

"You seem sane enough." He circled his arm to return the blood flow as he got to his feet. "But I'm pretty good at fooling people myself, so maybe we should give this another couple of days."

It was the closest he'd come to admitting he was still hurting. Instinctively, Claire wanted to put her arms around him and tell him his friends accepted him as he came, but she knew it wouldn't be welcome. Nate would let her in so far, but no further. And crossing that protective space he kept around himself was too risky.

She didn't want to lose him again.

"Well, it's not like you haven't proved useful," she replied. "With your free labor, I'm ahead on the refit. And you can't leave until you confess the big secret."

For some reason, he froze. Claire studied his guilty look. "Nathan Wyatt, did you make that up to lure me in? Steve didn't nearly get you all killed?"

"He did," he insisted gruffly. But his attention had gone beyond her to the roller door, which they'd opened to take advantage of some spring sunshine. Following his gaze, Claire saw Ellie's Audi pull alongside the boat shed. She turned back to Nate, but he was already gone.

With an exasperated sigh, she went to meet her mother-in-law. "Hello, there," she said as Ellie opened the driver's window. "What brings you to my neck of the woods?"

"I've been visiting a new supplier, a farmer's wife who does exquisite satin robes, and thought I'd drop by with afternoon tea." She eyed Claire's varnish-crusted coveralls. "Can you stop?"

"Sure." She resisted the urge to look over her shoulder. "Let's go to the bach, it's more comfortable there."

Ellie undid her seat belt. "Give me a tour of the boat first."

"You're not dressed for it," Claire said easily. "And we can't risk wet varnish on that gorgeous coat." Ellie wore a trench coat that was the same forest-green color as her car. Checking the lacquer smears on her coveralls were dry, Claire climbed into the passenger seat. "You make me feel like a scruff by comparison."

Spend some on yourself and maybe I will.

He'd said it to distract her, but since Nate's arrival she'd become conscious of her appearance in a way she hadn't been for a while. Probably because he'd grown so stylish in Hollywood. Even in old work clothes, he looked put together somehow. Her thoughts touched briefly on the woman he'd brought home in L.A. before she gave herself a mental shake. Nate's love life was none of her business.

In the bach she washed her hands and made tea, encouraging Ellie to chat about her latest seamstress. "Her robes are lovely, let me show you a sample." She dropped a bakery bag on the counter and returned to her Audi.

Glancing after her, Claire noticed Nate's shoes inside the patio door. Oh, hell. As she hurried to pick them up, she heard the slam of a car door, then the click of Ellie's heels on the concrete path. No time. "I was thinking of painting the ceiling," she called. "What do you think?"

Ellie looked up as she stepped inside. "Not just the ceiling. Honey, the whole bach needs a fresh coat of paint."

"It's in my game plan." As Ellie rummaged in a carrier bag, Claire nudged Nate's shoes under the couch. Crisis averted. The robe proved a slither of sensual white satin. Conscious of her roughened hands, Claire handled it carefully.

"It's beautiful."

"And in your size…keep it."

"Even though I have no use for it?" But she stroked the satin again.

A pained expression crossed her mother-in-law's face. "I never thought you'd lie to me, Claire."

"What do you mean?" she said, startled. "I'm not seeing anyone."

"Then why are you hiding men's shoes?"

Her face heated.

Ellie folded her arms. "There's a man's jacket hanging on the dining chair, too."

Clearly the game was up. "It's Nate."

Her mother-in-law's jaw dropped. "Nathan Wyatt's your lover?"

It was Claire's turn to be shocked. "What? No, of course not! He's home to dissolve the trust."

"Nate's here? Oh, I can't wait to see him."

"He doesn't want to see anyone while he's home," Claire blurted.

Puzzlement wrinkled Ellie's brow. "But why?"

Claire scrambled for an acceptable reason.

"He doesn't want the publicity," she said hastily, refolding the robe. "Remember how much he hated the fuss when he was awarded the medal. The press was all over him. He's worried it might happen again."

The whole country had been captivated by his story, and couldn't understand why he wouldn't return for the medal presentation. The current-affairs show *Sixty Minutes* had even tracked him to L.A., wanting an interview with the man they called the reluctant hero. Nate had told them briefly and politely to go to hell. That only made people more fascinated by his story.

"I can keep a secret," said Ellie. Which meant she only told other people in confidence. "Of course Nate will want to see me.... Won't he?"

She couldn't hurt Ellie. She just couldn't. Steve's mother adored Nate, always had. "My second son," she'd called him. But Claire had no idea if Nate would cooperate. She hesitated.

NATE HEARD CLAIRE RETURN and called, "In here." He'd retreated to the cabin, and was fitting the sink.

Then he heard a second person climb the ladder and froze. Claire wouldn't do that to him. Steve's mother popped her head around the door. "Nathan Wyatt, I could smack you, I really could." Advancing into the cabin, she threw plump arms around him. "I can't believe you've been here a week and haven't called me."

"Ellie," he said flatly. Over her head, he glared at Claire.

"She saw your shoes," she said cheerfully. "I told her you didn't want to attract any publicity while you were here, which is why you didn't contact her." Her eyes pleaded with him.

Ellie pulled away and he thought she'd aged ten years.

"You look exactly the same," he lied, and she knew he lied because she smiled sadly as she patted his cheek.

"Who cares about me, let me look at you." Nate suffered her scrutiny, a smile fixed on his face. "My goodness, you've been having facials," she said. "I can tell by your pores." She picked up his hands, inspecting his nails like a mother. "Manicures, too. And your haircut." She ran a trembling hand through his hair, desperately trying not to cry. "Nathan, you've gone pretty on me."

Without a word he put his arms around her, and she sobbed into his chest. Claire hugged herself.

"I'm sorry," he said helplessly. "Ellie, I'm sorry." He didn't know what he apologized for, Steve's death, his remoteness of the past eighteen months, only that shame filled him.

Claire was strong, he'd known that when he'd left. Ellie, he realized now, wasn't—despite her bravura. She was a mother who'd lost her son and needed support. "I'm sorry," he said again.

"I know, Nathan, I know." She fumbled in her bag for a handkerchief, finding none. He found a clean rag and gave it to her and she mopped ineffectually at her cheeks. Her mascara had run into the laugh lines around her eyes.

"Let me." Gently, Nate cleaned her up.

"I had no idea that was going to happen," she said, embarrassed. "I did this constantly when Steve passed." She gave Claire a watery smile. "We both did, didn't we, honey, but not so much now. I guess it's the shock." She turned away to compose herself and Nate glanced at Claire.

"Thank you," she mouthed. Her eyes were wet, too. Or maybe it was his. He blinked hard.

"This is such an improvement." Inspecting the cabin, Ellie mustered her old enthusiasm. Nothing had changed since he'd worked on it close to two years ago—clearly, she hadn't been on *Heaven Sent* since Steve's death. "I only bought two cream buns." She added gaily, "So we'll have to share. Come back to the bach with us for afternoon tea. I want to hear everything you're doing in Hollywood."

He had no option but to go along. Ellie seemed to sense his reluctance because despite her demand for information, she carried the conversation with lots of anecdotes about her little dog—"You remember Collette, don't you?" And her shop. All the while watching him, her gaze soaking him up until Nate felt desiccated from her need. With Claire's help they managed an hour together and conversation got easier.

"So we're keeping my visit a secret," he stressed as he and Claire walked Ellie to her car. "Next time I'll see everyone else."

"But Lewis has to see you."

Claire threaded her arm through her mother-in-law's. "Nate can't catch up with everybody in such a short visit and he doesn't want to offend anyone," she said. "He'll be back soon, won't you, Nate?"

"Sure," he lied.

When Ellie drove away, he looked at Claire. Too raw for the gratitude he saw, he said bluntly, "How much time have we got?"

Wisely she gave him space. "If I prick her conscience with daily phone calls, maybe three days."

He frowned. "Couldn't you have passed my shoes off as Lewis's?"

"Too expensive and too big…. Nate, does it really matter?"

"Yeah, I'm not here for a reunion." He

thought fast. "You asked me to lay my cards on the table." He gestured to the outside table and they took a seat. "Assuming you're doing this for all the right reasons, my biggest concern is the meager amount of money left after you've set up the business. There's no buffer should things go pear shaped."

"I'm aware of that," she said. "But all start-ups have an element of risk."

Nate had a brain wave. "How would you feel about me retaining a half share in *Heaven Sent?* We split the costs of the upgrade, minus the specialist gear related to your sports-fishing venture. That would reduce your capital outlay and make it easier to break even."

Her blue eyes narrowed. "Sounds great for me, but what's in it for you?"

He couldn't let even a hint of charity into his offer. Nate kept his tone brisk. "I'll recoup any money I invest in the upgrade when we sell, whether that's to your business or an independent buyer."

Claire was already shaking her head. "Not good enough."

"Let me finish." He thought fast. "And you'd pay ongoing maintenance costs, insurance and mooring fees." He thought about adding, "or there's no deal," and decided that was laying it on too thick. She was still looking doubtful, so he added, "And when I visit, I can stay on the boat…plus get a free pass on fishing trips."

"But will you visit, Nate?"

"I can see myself coming home twice a year." He just didn't say which year. "And retaining my share in *Heaven Sent* would give a reason to."

Claire stared across the estuary considering, her hands jammed in the pockets of those tatty navy coveralls, chewing her lower lip in thought.

"I'll always have a soft spot for her," he said.

Her cheeks had lost their hollow look, and the fresh breeze flagged them pink and pulled golden strands loose from her ponytail. There was a dab of varnish on one eyebrow. It hit him that he was going to miss this woman. A lot.

"I accept," she said and held out her hand with its roughened skin and short nails.

Nate took it.

"If you promise to come home within the next six months for a visit," she added.

Hell, he could always cancel. "Sure."

"If you don't," Claire warned, her grip tightening, "I'll come get you again."

"Fine," Nate said easily. Anything could happen in six months. And he'd given her a fighting chance of making this business work. "Phone the real estate agent so he can contact the buyers. Notify the bank and Jules. I don't trust Ellie's secret-keeping, so let's supercharge this thing. If I can borrow your car I'll go into Whangarei and organize a new switchboard and control panel for the wheelhouse. I want to be gone within forty-eight hours."

He wanted to be gone, but he had nowhere to go. When Zander cooled down, Nate might be able to beg for his job back. Yeah, when hell froze over. At least the rocker's reputation as a prima donna meant Nate's reputation wouldn't suffer by a dismissal.

She dug her cell out of her coveralls and started making calls. Nate went to change clothes. Claire came inside as he shrugged on a leather jacket. "A minor setback," she said cheerfully. "Adam reminded me that the buyers won't be home from Fiji until Friday to sign papers." Nate scowled. He'd forgotten he'd bought them off.

"I'm delighted," she said. "I get an extra day of free labor. Besides, we can have everything else nailed down before then with the bank and the trust. Jules is coming to dinner tonight to talk over the process."

Nate didn't like it, but he didn't have a choice. He couldn't leave until the sales contract was signed. "I was thinking.... You can book the engine in for reconditioning now as well as give the canopy company the green light. I'll credit some money to your account tonight to cover costs and you can reimburse your half when the house money comes through." Claire was looking at him strangely. "What?"

"You're a good person," she said.

"No, I'm not." His recoil was instinctive. "I'm the guy who stonewalled you for months, who won't see his friends or your son, who used his heroism medal to score a job in Hollywood...."

"Who's making sure my venture will succeed, who hasn't made me feel guilty about Steve, who listens without judgment. Why are you so hard on yourself, Nate?" She hesitated. "Is it because you survived and Steve and Lee didn't? You saved Ross, kept him alive for twenty minutes under heavy fire. I don't understand—"

He cut her off. "We're not having this conversation. Where are your car keys?"

"So I have to revisit painful subjects but you don't?"

"Pretty much." Nate checked the table, the kitchen counter. "The difference is that what you and Steve had is worth saving. I—" He stopped. "Where are the damn keys?"

"You're not?"

He spotted them on a hook by the door and

grabbed them. "I'll make sure I'm here for dinner."

Claire blocked his path. "I'm tired of you closing me down. Tell me what's riding you."

"Confession being good for the soul?" He'd wrestled with this dilemma for eighteen months. But it would only be shifting the burden.

"Maybe." She squirmed at his sarcasm but didn't back down. "Or if you can't talk to me, talk to Ross or Dan. They understand what you're going through."

"The only thing riding me is you three," he snarled. "When are you all going to understand that wanting a clean break doesn't make me damaged? Hell, hasn't that been your argument these past few days? I'm happy earning the big bucks in Hollywood and delirious that lives don't depend on me anymore. It's freedom, Claire, in the same way *Heaven Sent* represents freedom to you."

"You're not free," she retorted. "Let alone happy. And there's a big difference between my fresh start and your clean break."

"I don't see it."

"For one, I'm not in denial about still having issues, for two I haven't ditched my old friends."

"You want more quality time with me?" Sidestepping her, Nate grabbed the keys. "Then try giving me some space."

CHAPTER ELEVEN

POWERED BY FRUSTRATION, Claire blasted through the rest of the afternoon's tasks, including hammering a hefty discount on a bait freezer out of a secondhand dealer.

Ellie's visit had spooked Nate, and then Claire had gone and spooked him more, fracturing the tentative trust she'd been so carefully fostering this week. Nate's happiness was important to her, re-establishing their friendship had brought deep joy. She wanted to help him. The way he was helping her. If only the bloody man would allow it.

Distracted by their fight, it was late afternoon before Claire remembered Jules was coming to dinner and she had nothing to feed her. And no car to go shopping with.

Taking a deep breath, she phoned Nate's cell and wasn't surprised when it went straight to message. Maybe he was busy, more likely he was avoiding her call. *Fine, I'll be the grown-up,* she thought, smiled at her sulky resentment and felt better.

"Nate, it's me.... Okay, I won't mention the war." She hoped he still appreciated black humor. "Dinner's at six. Bring absolution."

Unsure whether he'd clear his messages, she phoned Jules with a shopping list, then showered and changed into black leggings and an off-the-shoulder knit in a pearlescent gray over a pink tank. After blow-drying her hair into a tousled fall, she put on makeup, smoky shadow to give her light eyes drama and added a sheen of pink lip gloss.

She was honest enough to admit she was taking pains with her appearance because of Nate's smartass comment about spending some money on herself. He'd said it as a tactical ploy but had left Claire with a strong desire to show Mr. Hollywood she could knock his Ralph Lauren socks off.

When Jules arrived, she was glad she'd made the effort. With her dark hair styled in a French twist, her friend radiated urban professional in a navy wool tunic dress, black patent-leather pumps and patterned tights.

Jules pulled out a bottle of champagne from one of the grocery bags. "To celebrate your new partnership with Nate... Where is he?"

"I scared him off." Claire unpacked baguettes and green-lipped mussels in their shells, salad ingredients and a gateau from the Cheesecake

Factory. "Well, me and Ellie." As she poured the champagne, she told Jules about her mother-in-law's visit. "This incognito stuff is driving me crazy."

Jules settled onto a stool at the counter that divided the living room from the kitchen. "We all have secrets we don't share," she said, accepting a glass. "Maybe you should respect Nate's privacy."

Claire thought of the anger at Steve that she'd never shared with anyone but Nate. Didn't he understand that she wouldn't judge him, either? "It's been a year and a half since he walked away from everyone who loves him, Jules. If he could fix himself, wouldn't he have done that by now?"

"I don't know him as well as you do, but he strikes me as the 'horse you lead to water and can't make drink' type. Anyway, he has made progress. He's here for you."

"True." Claire opened a container of aubergine dip and a packet of baby carrots and passed both to Jules. What was this increasing tug she felt toward him? Concern, affection, both of those? "I just worry about him, that's all."

"Well, stop, he's a big boy." Jules dunked a carrot into the dip. "And tonight's about celebrating, girl. Thanks to Nate you've got a better business model. I, for one, will be sleeping more soundly at night." She lifted her flute in a toast. "To your successful sports-fishing enterprise."

"To *Heaven Sent.*" Claire felt a frisson of excitement as she chinked crystal and took a sip. The bubbles fizzed on her tongue. As careful as she'd been in formulating her business plan, there were contingencies she couldn't allow for. A poor season—for fish or tourists—weather conditions. If she didn't have to fork out thirty thousand for Nate's share of the boat and he split the cost of upgrades—yes, like Jules, she'd be able to sleep at night.

"Every ongoing cost is mine," she told Jules as she scrubbed the mussel shells clean under the running tap. "Make sure of it when you're drawing up an agreement. And I want Nate to get ten percent of net profits. He's got to get something more than free board and fishing." They talked through a revised agreement while she sautéed garlic, onion and celery in butter, prepared a side salad and set the table.

By the time Nate returned, the bach was steamy and fragrant with the white wine she'd used to steam the mussels open, and Claire was adding cream to the sauce. She was also a little tipsy, which made it easy to deliver a natural greeting as she busied herself dressing the salad. But she couldn't look at him.

"We've already opened the bubbles," Jules

confessed, pouring him a flute. We'll make another toast at the table. But can I just say that you'll be getting another birthday card next year."

"I'll make sure I check the post." He sounded normal. Claire chanced a quick glance. He and Jules were exchanging smiles. *Oh, they'd be perfect for each other,* she thought, and her stomach dropped. She must be hungrier than she thought.

"We have to eat now or the mussels will be chewy," she called. "Jules, take the salad to the table."

"Yes, ma'am."

Nate came into the kitchen as she wrestled with the big pot holding the mussels. "Let me." He tipped the steaming shells into three bowls. "I got your message," he said in a low voice. "Sorry for overreacting this afternoon."

"No, I'm sorry for being pushy. I didn't even thank you properly for your idea. It's genius and I'm so happy." For some reason her eyes prickled with tears. "I just want you to be happy, too."

He gave her a hug. "I'm happy if you're happy," he said gruffly.

"I'm happy."

"Then you and I are sweet. Incidentally, you

look beautiful." He released her, spotted the glint of tears. "Claire?"

"I'm a little emotional," she admitted. "It's been a long journey.… Here." she handed him the bread, spooned the creamy garlic and white-wine sauce over the seafood. "Let's eat, I'm starving."

He took the hint. "This smells incredible."

They all sat down. Jules poured more champagne. "Make the toast, Nate."

He lifted his glass. "To fish."

Claire laughed. "To fish."

Jules didn't refill her glass. "I'm driving. Anyway, I need my head clear for the business part of this evening."

As they savored the meal, Claire filled Nate in on their progress. "The engine's getting picked up tomorrow for reconditioning. And the canopy company is coming to recheck measurements."

"Are you returning for the launch next month?" Jules asked Nate.

"He'll be on tour," Claire reminded her.

"It's so great that Zander came around," Jules commented. Nate blinked and dropped his gaze to his plate.

"Oh," Jules said slowly.

Puzzled, Claire glanced between them. "Am I missing something?"

"Yes, the last roll." Jules reached for the final baguette. "So, Claire wants to give you a ten percent profit share."

Nate's head jerked up. "Wait, we didn't discuss that."

"I wasn't born yesterday." Claire paused to savor a spoonful of creamy sauce. "I'm well aware this deal favors me, for all the smoke and mirrors you've used around my paying insurance and ongoing costs."

"But—"

"It's my deal breaker, take it or leave it."

Jules laughed as she buttered her baguette. "Normally I'm trying to get negotiating parties to consider the other person's point of view." She glanced between them as if struck. "You two fight in each other's corner."

Nate was still glaring at her. Claire repeated, "Deal breaker."

"Accept it," Jules advised. "She'll call the whole thing off otherwise. Our Claire doesn't get a single bee in her bonnet, she gets a whole squadron."

"Tell me about it," Nate muttered.

Claire took that as consent and relaxed. "Let's not talk business until after dinner," she suggested.

"Good idea," Jules approved. "Nate can tell

me what Zander's looking for in a woman instead."

"Compliance," Nate said, still looking at Claire, and she laughed. The conversation moved on to some of Jules's conflict-resolution experiences, including a current one with an unnamed couple who'd separated over his ignoring their twentieth anniversary. His wife had given him an ultimatum when he'd missed the nineteenth.

"It's clear they love each other, but they both have blind spots. He simply can't understand why one day in the year outweighs three hundred and sixty-four others. And she can't understand why he ignored it when she'd told him how important it was to her for those three hundred and sixty-four others. And both are so hurt and bewildered that neither is giving an inch. I can see it escalating to a divorce."

Claire drained her champagne flute. "They could still work it out." It was suddenly important they did.

"Except they can't talk without fighting. I don't expect you to understand that kind of lunacy."

Picking up the champagne bottle, Claire paused. "Why wouldn't I?"

"You and Steve never argued."

Claire refilled her glass. "We teetered on the

brink of divorce ourselves when Lewis was small. Until Steve wrote me a letter." She waved the bottle. "Get your guy to write his wife." In her peripheral vision she saw Nate sit back. Withdrawing from the conversation or disapproving of her third—or was it fourth—glass of champagne? Defiantly, she poured bubbles to the brim.

"That's so hard to imagine." Jules accepted the empty bottle. "You got on so well."

"We'd learned to live together by the time you met us. When Lewis was little, it was touch-and-go for a while."

"And a letter saved your marriage?"

"We wanted it to be saved," Claire admitted, "but yes, it was a turning point for us."

"It must have been some letter."

"It was incredible." Claire sighed happily into her flute and bubbles tickled her nose. "I can quote it verbatim. 'You're everything to me, my soul…'" The words trailed off as a sudden suspicion struck her. She looked at Nate. "Wait a minute."

"I'll clear the table."

She stopped him. "You said you all offered to help Steve write a letter once."

"It didn't come to anything," he reminded her.

"It was lyrical, it was romantic, it was perfect," she said to Jules. Too perfect. "Come to think of it, Steve would never use the word *soul mate*. Nathan Wyatt, was my love letter written by committee?"

"He asked for feedback only because it was so damn important," he hedged.

"Wait here." Pushing back her chair, Claire marched into her bedroom.

Nate looked at Jules. "Am I in trouble?"

"I don't know," she admitted. "Sounds like she really loves that letter."

Claire returned, carrying a sheet of handwritten paper in a plastic sleeve. "I cried over this so much I had to protect it." Narrowing her eyes, she thrust it across the table at Nate. "Give me an example."

Nervously Nate glanced again at Jules and then down at the page, cursing that he'd ever raised the subject. Would this make things better or worse? He was a guy, how the hell would he know? He cleared his throat. "Okay, Steve would start with something like, 'Without you, my life would be crap.' We'd workshop that into…" Nate found the quote with his finger "'—you make my life worth living.' Trying to put a positive spin on a negative statement," he added, risking a glance at Claire.

Her expression, as she eyeballed him over the edge of the champagne flute, gave nothing away. "Lee, being our romantic, suggested some of the poetic stuff…changing 'wife' to 'soul mate,' for example."

Claire exchanged glances with Jules but made no comment.

Nate stared at the letter, fighting that male sense of helplessness that told him nothing he did now would be right. "Okay, this line, 'We have so much fun, in bed and out of it.' That's all Steve's…except for the 'out of it' part. That change was group consensus—we thought it might look like Steve was being shallow." Nate told himself to shut up now, but the continuing stony silence only increased his verbal diarrhea. "The marriage vow thing, for better or worse. I think Steve wanted to write about things having to get *much* worse before he gave up.…" Desperately he scanned the page. "That sorta morphed into, 'No matter what, I'm committed to you for the rest of our lives.'"

Nate could see them all now, four bearded, dust-covered young men agonizing over this damn thing while Steve paced camp, occasionally bursting out with, "It's not frickin' right yet.… It's got to be right."

A lump in his throat stopped him. He looked up. Claire had her head bowed, so did Jules. Oh, shit. Claire's shoulders were shaking. "You're upset," he said helplessly.

A hoot escaped her...a hoot? She lifted her face and there were tears in her eyes. "Th-th-that's hilarious!" The two women collapsed in paroxysms of laughter.

Nate stared at them in amazement.

"Can't you see them?" Claire hiccuped. "Oh, Jules, can't you just see them?"

"Right down to licking the pencil," Jules managed to say, sending Claire into whoops again.

"It was a pen," Nate said stonily. "And I don't see what the hell is so funny."

"You're right, it's beautiful." With a last giggle, Claire wiped her eyes dry with a napkin. "Steve was so hopeless at this kind of stuff, and for him to do this, to lay it on the line in front of you guys...and for you all to agonize over it..." She leaned over and hugged him. "Nate, it's sweet and funny and, well, thank you."

He was placated. "Well, that's okay then."

"'In bed and out of it,'" Jules murmured, sending them both into more peals of laughter.

"And you call guys shallow," Nate complained. "Steve made us bleed out for you... and this is the thanks we get."

But he could feel something expand in his chest, a quiet pride, a connection with his dead buddy, with his mates that he hadn't felt in so long. They'd had some good times.

"I'd rather smile over this letter than cry over it," Claire said when she'd recovered her composure. "And now I can."

Nate noticed Jules had sat back and was eyeing them both with an appraising smile. For a moment he'd forgotten she was there. "What?"

"Nothing, excuse me... I need the bathroom." She disappeared toward the outside loo. Nate picked up the letter.

"You're really okay with this?"

"I'm really okay."

He wanted to leave it at that, but felt the need to explain further. "We couldn't let you guys separate. Not when it was so obvious that you two had something worth saving."

CLAIRE STRUGGLED not to smile. He was so transparent in his desire to reconcile her to Steve. And so damn sweet. Tipsy with champagne, relaxed with laughter, she could reassure him.

"Well, it worked," she said. "We recommitted to our marriage vows when he came home and lived happily..." She put down her drink, said brightly, "I'll clear the plates."

"I'll help."

She and Steve had also agreed how long he'd serve in a combat role that first leave after they'd reconciled. Which raised another question. After every tour the unit always took a couple of days' leave to decompress before shipping home. Claire glanced outside, no sign of Jules yet. "Nate, I need to know something." The champagne gave her courage. "I asked Steve this question after we'd reconciled and he hesitated before he said no."

Dumping the empty mussel shells in the trash bag, she faced him. "Did he cheat on me during that period?"

He stopped midstride between the table and the kitchen, salad bowl in one hand, breadbasket in the other. "No," he said.

"Then why the hell did he hesitate?"

It was his turn to glance at the door. "Jules will be—"

"I won't have the courage to ask again."

He dumped the plates on the kitchen counter. "We were at an expat bar in Dubai and Steve got drunk.… I mean, fall-down drunk. You'd fought on the phone."

"Yes." Her voice was steady.

"He started flirting with a woman at the next table, nothing in it," Nate reassured her, and she managed a jerky nod. Inside she felt sick.

"She dragged him onto the dance floor. At that stage, he pretty much needed to hold on to her to stand up. Next thing, she's got him lip-locked."

Claire moaned and covered her face. He pulled her hands away, held them tight. "Look at me," he ordered. She raised stricken eyes. "Steve yanked away and bellowed, 'Goddamn it, you guys are s'posed to be looking out for me.' He was totally indignant about the incident."

She let out a breath.

Nate released her hands. "Back at our hotel Steve used up half a bottle of mouthwash—to purify his mouth, he said, and then passed out. He was riddled with guilt when he sobered up."

"Good," Claire croaked, a weight lifting from her mind. She'd trusted Steve when he'd told her he'd been faithful, but the shock of his death had made her question everything. "And where were you while this was happening?"

"Organizing a cab to return his sorry ass to the hotel."

"Just as well!" She managed a shaky smile. Nate's gaze softened as he reached out a hand.

The patio door slid open and a cool gust blew in with Jules. "Brrr, it's cold out there," she commented. "What's for dessert?"

CHAPTER TWELVE

"I'VE GOT SOME NEWS," Jules said as Claire walked her out to her Volkswagen Beetle an hour later. "I've started dating again."

Claire stopped in her tracks. "That is news." She noticed Jules's hand was fisted around her car keys. "Are you expecting me to give you a hard time about it?"

"You're the first of Lee's circle I've told," Jules admitted. She glanced over her shoulder at the bach. Through the lit window they could see Nate moving through the room. "I'm testing the waters."

Impulsively, Claire hugged her. "You're only thirty-two, Jules. Of course you'll meet and fall in love with another guy."

"Whoa, slow down there, I said I'm dating, not looking for Mr. Right. I'm not a masochist."

The wind gusted and both women shivered. Claire said, "Let's get in the car for a minute."

Once they'd settled in the front seats, she turned to Jules. "Don't close yourself down to another love."

Her friend looked at her ring, absently twisted it straight. Why had she never had it fitted properly? It was almost as if she was reluctant to claim it. "And you're not an impostor," Claire added.

Jules raised startled eyes. "What?"

"You've always been uncomfortable wearing that ring. You pull away from family gatherings and commemorative get-togethers as though Lee's going to ghost up and say, 'I meant that ring for someone else.' Even when he was alive you doubted his love, when we could all see it as plain as day. I don't know why you think you don't deserve to be happy or loved or treasured, Jules, but don't use Lee's death as an excuse to pull back from letting a good man love you. More than any person I know, Lee lived life to the full and he'd want that for you."

"Claire," her friend said shakily, "you have no idea what you're talking about."

"Don't I?" Claire sat back. "Okay, my mistake."

"And anyway, what about you?"

"What about me?" Jules was deflecting, but Claire got defensive anyway. "Hey, I had a fourteen-year marriage, I have a teenager. I've already had a wonderful family life."

"See, you're not a masochist either."

"You lawyers twist everything," Claire complained, but feebly.

"Uh-huh." Jules sighed. "I'm lonely, Claire. Until Lee, I was perfectly happy being celibate."

"You were a workaholic nerd."

"Semantics." Jules waved a dismissive hand and her ring flashed by the subdued green light of the dash. "Sex was something I could take or leave." A faint smile curved her lips. "Lee ruined that for me. Now, as hard as I try, I can't put my libido back to sleep again. I need touch, sexual companionship."

"Remarket that as meaningless sex and you won't have any trouble finding takers." Jules was a good-looking woman with an intelligent "dare you" quality. She and Lee had been perfect for each other. He wasn't used to hearing no, and she wasn't used to saying yes.

"I've had one date with a guy I met through an online-dating website, but it's harder than you think to jump into bed with a virtual stranger."

"You slept with Lee on your blind date," Claire pointed out.

"I told you that in confidence," Jules scolded. "Anyway, I'm hitting the dating circuit and I wanted you to know. One, because I'm the type of person who always gets caught, and two, I need your blessing."

"Go forth and fornicate."

"I'm serious, Claire. I want you—everyone—to understand this doesn't diminish what I felt for Lee—"

"Jules, this is me." Claire covered her friend's hand. "I'm in the same lifeboat, remember? We've finally hit land and now the fearless one—that's you—goes ahead to check if the natives are friendly before the cowardly one leaves the boat."

Jules relaxed in the leather seat. "So, you miss sex, too."

"Marriage to a soldier gets you used to a life-style of feast or famine, but yes, it's been a long time between meals." She thought of the sexy lingerie in Ellie's shop, of the pang it had given her. "After fifteen years with one guy, I don't have a clue how to go about dating. And then there's Lewis to consider. He's at an age where the very idea of his mother wanting romance is disgusting. I have a new business to get up and running." She noticed Jules had raised a brow. "Does it sound like I'm making excuses? I am."

"What about Nate?"

Claire looked at her uncomprehendingly.

"You two have such a bond."

The penny dropped, and she was offended. "I've never considered Nate as more than a friend."

"Of course not, you loved Steve.... But I doubt you thought of Nate as a brother, either," Jules added astutely.

She took a moment to respond. "Being happily married gives you a free pass to appreciate a sexy guy.... It's not personal."

"You think Nate's sexy?" Jules widened her brown eyes. "I would only describe him as good-looking myself."

Claire got out of the car with as much dignity as she could muster. "Go home, you bad girl," she said. "You are not making me self-conscious around an old friend."

A wink was her only response. Claire slammed the door, watched the Volkswagen disappear into the dark with a twinkle of taillights. Shaking her head, she returned to the bach. Nate wasn't anywhere in sight. Faintly, she heard the shower running.

Don't go there, she told herself before she put a picture to that. Damn Jules and her warped humor. Rolling up the sleeves of her knit top, she plugged the sink and turned on the taps. Heard a muffled "Hey!" through the wall.

"Sorry!"

Shutting off the hot tap, Claire filled up the sink with cold water and started washing the dishes. Now he probably had a scalded ass.

Her brain threw up an image. She smacked her forehead. "Stop it!"

"Stop what?"

Nate stepped through the patio doors, bare-chested, with a towel slung around his neck and jeans low on his hips. "You've got soap bubbles between your eyebrows."

Claire grabbed a tea towel and patted her forehead dry. "Don't walk outside like that, you'll catch cold," she scolded, getting all mumsy in her embarrassment.

He shrugged. "I forgot to take a shirt. Maybe that's something you can spend your first year's profits on—interior access to the bathroom."

"Yes, let's talk plumbing," she said, relieved, then heard the double entendre and blushed.

"You okay?" Nate paused at the entrance to his room, a foot away from the sink. Amidst the sudsy detergent she could smell sandalwood aftershave. "You've gone red."

Experiencing an urge to close her eyes and follow her nose, Claire turned her burning face to the dishes. "Steam from the sink," she lied.

"Really?" With a doubtful expression he came closer and dipped his finger in. "It's cold." He dried his finger on the towel around his neck. "Maybe I should take another look at your thermostat."

Claire had to get out of this kitchen, but he

blocked her way, solid, half-naked, radiating heat. "Can you just…"

He stepped aside to let her pass and she found some extra space in the living room, found her breath.

"The thermostat's fine," she said. "I didn't want to affect the shower, so I used cold."

"Thanks." Absently, Nate lifted part of the towel and rubbed his hair dry, affording her tantalizing glimpses of his chest, abs and biceps. Claire's mouth went dry. Then she saw he was watching her under the toweling, his expression puzzled.

"You look fit," she said inanely. "You work out much?"

Nate draped the towel over one shoulder. "Zander likes a gym buddy."

"So you said earlier. I'm going to have to join a gym myself," she babbled. "If I'm helping clients haul in a ten kilogram snapper."

He assessed her body dispassionately. "I was only teasing in the boat shed. You're holding up okay." She felt the disinterest like a bucket of cold water. Idiot.

"You and Jules were deep in conversation when I went to the shower," he said.

"She's dating again," Claire replied, still caught in her mixed feelings. Then remembered

Jules didn't want that broadcast. "Keep that to yourself," she added.

"Okaaay," he said.

Claire stiffened. "What's that supposed to mean?"

"Nothing. It's a shock, that's all. The end of an era."

"The end of a very bad time and the start of the rest of her life," she said sharply. "You think she should take the veil or swear a vow of celibacy?"

"No, all I—"

"It's not like she'll forget Lee because she gets on with her life and takes a lover. Don't you dare go making her feel all guilty about getting her needs met!"

"That wasn't—"

"Hopefully one day she'll meet someone she can marry…and you'd better be bloody nice to that guy, Nate, when she does. You hear me?"

"I hear you," he said carefully. "So…are we still talking about Jules?"

She got flustered. "Of course we're talking about Jules."

"I thought maybe you were working up to telling me you were seeing someone."

"Well, I'm not." Claire folded her arms, realized that was defensive and unfolded them again. "But if I were, I'd expect the same support! You guys can't expect us to turn into sexless beings...." Oh, dear God, there was no retrieving this. "I'm off to bed. Good night!"

Without waiting for a response, she swept into her bedroom and jerked the curtain closed, cursing the smallness of the bach, Jules and her own confusion.

She hadn't cleaned her teeth or washed her face.... Well, she'd wait until he went to bed. In the meantime, Claire sat on hers, dropped her head in her hands and reminded herself that her future was all about control and self-determination. She couldn't possibly have sexual feelings for Steve's best friend.

A man subject to mood swings she couldn't fathom, who didn't want his buddies or her son to hear he was home. Sure, he'd been sweet to Ellie, but—

Imagine Steve's mum's reaction if they—

Exasperated, Claire flung backward onto the bed. Too much champagne had made her a suggestible fool. Well, that was stopping right now.

NATE FROWNED at Claire's departing back and wondered what had just happened here. One "Okaaay" and all hell had broken loose.

He took a tentative step in the direction of her bedroom and stopped. Anything he said now would sound patronizing.

"Of course I can understand Jules wanting to date.… She's young, she's attractive, she can't mourn Lee the rest of her life. He would hate that."

He felt a deep sadness for his friend's sake, but it was right and natural that Jules move on, and he honestly wished her all the best in her pursuit of happiness. Then he imagined Claire meeting someone else and experienced such an immediate and visceral rejection he was shocked.

Still frowning, he went into his room and hauled on a sweater. He'd only ever known Claire as his best friend's wife, and it was hard to accept her as single. Relieved, he raked a hand through his damp hair. Yeah, that was it. In the kitchen, he drained the sink and refilled it with hot water.

Her outburst had surprised her as much as him. Of course she'd be missing sex. "Ouch!" Nate jerked his fingers from the tap, turned it off and added more cold. She was a hot-blooded woman in her prime. He felt the pangs himself, though for Nate, celibacy was a personal choice. Relationships were rife with expectations and he didn't feel capable of meeting them anymore. His thwarted one-night stand with Mia had been exactly what Claire suspected— a way of holding her at arm's length.

Forearms deep in soapy dishwater, Nate smiled. *So much for that.*

He picked up the dish brush and washed the glasses. No question that when Claire was ready to date, there'd be men lined up. His smile faded.

She had that rare quality of being one of the guys while remaining unquestionably feminine. It must be innate, because he'd seen pampered beauties in Hollywood who couldn't emulate the gracefulness Claire managed in coveralls. Women might miss it, but men saw it. And when she applied makeup and matched a sexy off-the-shoulder sweater with tights that accentuated her shapely legs... Oh, yeah, when she was ready they'd be lining up.

A champagne flute clunked against the sink and broke in half. Carefully, Nate removed the pieces from the suds. Okay, he didn't like the idea, but his feelings were irrelevant. If Claire saw herself as single again, he'd just have to deal with it.

He had the opportunity to practice the next day.

The morning started well. After breakfast they walked to the boat shed, same as usual. Claire seemed bent on keeping the conversation strictly business, but Nate figured they needed to clear the air. "About last night," he said as they walked along the estuary. "I have no objection to Jules dating."

"I'll be sure to pass that on."

"C'mon, Claire, give me a break. It's natural to feel regret for Lee. That doesn't mean I don't want Jules to be happy." *Or you.*

She sighed. "I appreciate that."

Nate gave her a sidelong glance. "She and Lee weren't together very long. That must make it easier for her to move on."

"It's been over eighteen months, Nate." Uh-oh, snippy again.

"And she's an attractive woman," he soothed. "I'm sure she's had lots of offers." He waited. One beat, two. "I imagine a couple come your way too."

"Amazing, I know."

"Not at all." So, did the sarcasm mean Claire wasn't ready? His spirits lifted. She'd only talked about dating in principle; it might be months before she met someone. When the time came, he'd be happy for her, he really would. "Beautiful day," he added cheerfully.

The estuary on full tide was a gleaming mirror under a sky of translucent blue, its surface only broken by the occasional small fishing launch puttering out to sea and the shadows of swooping seagulls.

As Claire unlocked the padlock on the boat

shed, a white ute pulled up and a middle-aged
man climbed out of the cab with a cheery greeting. "Made better time than I thought," he said
as Claire introduced him as John, the canopy
guy. Shaking his hand, Nate noted that John
was freshly shaven, with recently combed hair
and a powerful aura of Old Spice.

"Nate's an old friend visiting from the States,"
Claire said, and the slight crease between John's
eyebrows relaxed.

The handshake became more enthusiastic.
"Good to meet you."

Releasing Nate's hand, he turned to Claire. "I
know how important this is to you, so I thought
I'd come out first thing and get things moving."

"That's so kind," Claire said. "I was under
the impression you'd got all the measurements
last visit."

Nate hid a smile.

"Always good to recheck them." John's neck
reddened slightly and he avoided Nate's gaze.
"Wooden boats aren't symmetrical, maybe
there's been some movement."

Nate put him out of his misery. "Sounds sensible to me," he said. "I'll leave you to it."

He took his time selecting tools, chuckling
silently as John set about trying to impress an
oblivious Claire. Doubtless some parts of his
job required skill, but his implication that tak-

ing simple measurements demanded surgical precision and crack-shot reflexes cracked Nate up. If this guy was an example of available men, poor Claire would find slim pickings. Taking the cover off the engine bay, Nate climbed into the cavity and started whistling as he disconnected the fuel line.

Claire appeared after John left, carrying a notebook and pen. "I hope you haven't got too far. I wanted to watch how you did it."

He was disconnecting the engine's fuel, cooling and electrical systems for pick-up later that morning. "I'm just about to do the transmission." He moved over to give her room in the confined space. "You've got quite the admirer in John."

She smiled. "He's so awkwardly sweet, it's very endearing."

The wrench slipped. Nate cursed and then apologized as he picked it up. "He's not someone you'd consider going out with, though.... Is he?"

"Poor John lost his wife eighteen months ago.... It took a lot of courage to ask me for coffee." Her shoulder bumped his as she moved closer for a better view. Unlike John's cologne, her perfume was a mere hint of the sensual Orient, an unsettling base note amongst the paint fumes and engine grease. "I made it clear it's a support-group kind of thing, not a date."

Nate turned his head, found her face very close and sat back on his haunches. "Claire, some guys will play on sympathy to get what they want. Sure, John seems harmless, but you're isolated out here. Be careful."

She laughed, and in that confined space her breath was minty-sweet. "I'm thirty-four, Nate, not sixteen. Steve was away half our married life and I've been widowed for over a year and a half. I don't need advice on looking out for myself."

"Of course not," he agreed, making a mental note to check the bach's security and do a security check on John.

He bent to his task. They'd been working closely for days, but suddenly she was in his space. Her hair fell across his forearm as he disconnected the electrical system, a tickling touch of silk. "Put your hair up," he said brusquely. "It'll get caught in the electrics."

She gave him a puzzled look. "You've disconnected everything."

"Safe practice."

"Fine." She reached across him to the toolbox where a pink scrunchie sat amongst the spanners, screwdrivers and pliers, and the side of her breast pressed briefly against his arm.

Nate gritted his teeth. It was that stupid conversation last night that was making him self-conscious. It forced him to see her not as Steve's widow, but as a woman. He didn't like it.

He suffered her proximity another five minutes before he sat back. "You're kinda blocking the light."

"I'm in your way, aren't I?"

"A little."

"Then I'll go start on the hull's second coat."

"Great idea."

He could breathe again when she'd gone. Except he still found himself watching her over the course of the morning—the way she lifted her arms to tighten her ponytail, the sweet roundness of her bottom as she bent to dip her brush in the paint can, how the coveralls tightened over her curves as she stretched to apply paint to the upper hull.

She caught him staring and raised a brow. "What?"

"Nothing."

It was a relief when the marine mechanics arrived to pull the engine and take it away for reconditioning. They were young guys in their twenties with cheeky grins and eyes for a pretty woman. Their appreciative gazes followed Claire, and when they used a portable gantry to lift the engine from its bay into the back of their specialized ute, they flexed their biceps in their muscle shirts, showing off for her.

Their flirting was harmless and in good fun and his irritation at their macho posturing made Nate feel like a grumpy old man. What the hell was wrong with him this morning? On the other hand, Claire wore a wedding ring. They should show some respect for the institution. Some guys might read too much into her open, friendly smile. And that habit she had of twirling a loose strand of hair around her finger could easily be interpreted as a come-on.

Nate stood back as she signed all the paperwork, arms folded and a frown on his face. Hell, for all she knew, these idiots could be gang members. But then, she'd always been too trusting, picking up strays throughout her married life, himself being a case in point.

"So, any chance of some work now," he said when they'd left.

Claire raised a brow. "Excuse me?"

"I'm trying to do as much as I can before I leave," he said impatiently.

Narrowed blue eyes assessed his mood. "Oh, don't you worry about that," Claire said sweetly. "I can easily organize a replacement."

CHAPTER THIRTEEN

EVERY TIME CLAIRE TURNED AROUND, Nate seemed to be scowling at her.

Dipping her brush into the can of paint sitting on the stepladder beside her, she applied it to the hull. By unspoken agreement they'd moved to opposite ends to paint, but eventually they'd have to meet in the middle. Hopefully, by then he'd have found some perspective.

She'd woken this morning determined to think of him as a friend only, and his disapproval had made it easy. It didn't take a rocket scientist to figure out he was uncomfortable with the idea of her dating. And that annoyed the hell out of her.

She'd had to rebuild her life one day at a time. And she'd done it. Stepping out alone had been terrifying; at times it was still terrifying.

The acrid paint fumes collected in her throat. Briefly she left her station to open the second roller door.

When she'd noticed his smirk at John's clumsy attempts to impress her, she'd been an-

noyed enough to say yes to the tradesman's invitation. John was a nice man, trying his best to
move forward after his wife's death. He needed
encouragement, though she'd emphasized that
having coffee was a friendly gesture only.

Obviously, Nate required a reminder that it
was her decision when she resumed a love life.
And that was a lesson Claire was more than
happy to deliver.

The breeze created by the through draft lifted
the corner of a drop sheet.

"Careful," Nate warned, but it had already
flapped across the hull, leaving a streak in
Claire's new paintwork.

"Damn it!" She pinned the sheet with a paint
can and glared at Nate, who had the sense to
keep his mouth shut.

When the young mechanics had started flirting with her, she'd flirted back, assuaging the
small core of hurt left by Nate's dispassionate
scan last night. His disapproving face had only
made it more fun. Recalling it cheered her up.
As she feathered out the streak, she picked up
the tune Nate had been whistling earlier.

On the last chorus he joined in. "I've been a
jerk," he said.

"Yes, you have." Claire swept the brush
across a new section, leaving a bright swath

of cobalt on the gray undercoat. "It felt like I was ripped in half when Steve died," she said. "If it wasn't for Lewis and Ellie needing me, I would have lain down on my bed and never got up. It's taken a long time to get to the point where my life feels like it's mine again. Where I'm excited about the future."

She bent to refill her brush then covered the patches the first stroke had missed. "Maybe I'm not quite at the point of dating again, but I want to approach the process with an open mind." She glanced sideways at Nate. "I don't need you making it harder."

"Fair comment," he said in a low voice. "Just...be careful."

"I will."

They resumed painting, but Nate was still restless. She lowered her brush. "What!" Swear to God, one more crack—

"I'm sorry I couldn't be here for you after Steve died."

It was the last thing she'd expected. Claire took a few seconds to reply. "That's okay," she said. "It wasn't something you could make better."

Shaken, she wiped a spot of paint off her forearm with a solvent-soaked rag. Grief was a personal journey and everyone's road to recovery was different. She was further along that road than Nate—and she was starting to understand why.

He was a protector. Even in his new persona he hadn't given up looking after people, albeit a spoiled rock star. He did volunteer security for a women's shelter. Safeguarding people was a primal need for him. That's why he took Steve's and Lee's deaths so personally.

Realizing she was staring at him, she scrubbed at another paint splatter on her wrist.

Nate was punishing himself with exile because he hadn't saved Lee in the ambush. But the odds of Nate's finding him while an attack raged—and with a critically wounded Ross to save—were tiny. No one knew whether Lee survived the initial blast that threw him clear of the vehicle. Claire prayed not. Believing he'd been conscious, dying when the rebels strapped him with explosives was too terrible to contemplate.

She dropped the rag and moved her stepladder along to the next section of unpainted hull. Did Nate feel guilty because he'd survived and Steve—the family man—had died? It would explain why he didn't want to see Lewis. In hindsight, telling Nate about her son's troubles hadn't helped. But not all Lewis's delinquency could be attributed to being fatherless. Some of it came down to being a stroppy teenager.

Nate needed to see that.

And Ross was no longer the bitter disabled soldier Nate still believed him to be. He needed to see that, too. It wasn't enough to tell him.

"I need some fresh air," Claire said abruptly, putting down her brush.

His gaze searched her face. "You okay?"

"I will be."

As always her mind settled as she took in the sweep of water narrowing as it wended its way out of sight into the bush-clad hills. Nate hadn't found it easy seeing Ellie again, but it had been good for him, good for Steve's mother. An old man fishing from the footbridge lifted his hand in a wave. Claire waved back. In this peaceful place, bound by tides, she could always see the big picture.

It was the big picture that helped her reach for her cell.

By LATE AFTERNOON the following day they'd coated one side of the hull with the glossy blue paint and were nearly finished the second. It was a late-spring scorcher, heralding a hot summer. The iron roof creaked and groaned as it expanded in the sun, the corrugated sides absorbing the heat and releasing it inside.

The sinking sun streamed through the open

roller doors and made the space even hotter. But the doors had to stay open to vent the fumes.

Claire peeled down her coveralls and tied the sleeves around her waist, working in a baby tee. She worked distracted, trying to remain positive by not dwelling on what she'd done yesterday. Her nervousness had grown as the day progressed and the moment of reckoning approached. She was standing at the roller doors, restirring the paint drum prior to refilling her can, when Nate put down his brush and removed his shirt. Rolling it into a ball, he tossed it out of splatter range and raised his arms in a spine stretch.

She blinked. A couple of nights ago there'd been tantalizing glimpses of his torso through the towel, but this…

With an effort, she resumed mixing. Unlike the young marine mechanics who'd flexed for her, Nate's body reflected long years of Special Forces conditioning, with each muscle clearly defined under skin tanned honey by a Californian sun. He bent to pick up the brush and his torn jeans tightened over a muscular ass and solid thighs.

His brain calculating completion time, Nate stepped back to assess the finish of his section and decided he was pleased with it. The surface reflected like a mirror. He could even see Claire behind him, slowly stirring paint with a stick.

Her gaze drifted down his bare back, and up again, lingering on his shoulders, and he froze. Her teeth caught her lower lip and she seemed to shake herself, refocus on the mixing, before her eyes lifted, almost guiltily, for another scan. Nate's breath caught, his groin tightened at the very feminine assessment. He didn't know what to do, what to think. How to think.

If the surface hadn't been wet, he'd steady himself against the hull. Instead, he concentrated on replenishing his brush. Okay, he'd imagined it. Some trick of the light. Or the fumes getting to him. As he lifted the brush, his gaze returned inexorably to her reflection. He clenched his teeth. Hell, Claire, you can't go around looking at men like that. You'll end up... Nate had a sudden vivid mental image of where she'd end up and stared at the paint dripping down the hull because he'd forgotten to stroke the excess out of the bristles.

Inwardly cursing, he feathered it out. Okay, Claire checking him out had nothing to do with him and everything to do with being celibate for nearly two years. That didn't explain the sudden hopeful leap of his pulse.

He had to put a stop to this.

Nate turned, deliberately catching her in the

act, his gaze challenging. Hers dropped, hot color flooded her cheeks. Yeah, that was better. Control. This wasn't personal. It was just the male-female dynamic, his response a reflex.

Her lashes lifted, she met his eyes with a "got me" smile that held another element that years of friendship made easy to interpret.

Shy invitation. It punched Nate in the gut because her response was so intrinsically Claire. She'd always been courageous in her willingness to be vulnerable.

For a timeless moment he saw possibilities so bright that they blinded him. Saw everything he'd ever wanted, everything he'd believed beyond his reach. "When do you know you've found the right woman?" he'd once asked Steve. It had been after his breakup with Bree and he'd been dating women who ticked all the boxes but one. He couldn't love them.

And his friend had answered, "When even the tough times with her are better than good times with any other woman." The truth of that struck Nate now with blinding clarity.

His fingers tightened on the handle. Where was Claire's judgment? He was the last man she should be attracted to. He'd run away when she'd needed him, been derelict in his trustee duties, in their friendship. She knew he was relationship trouble. He'd dumped one of her friends, for God's sake.

And he'd left her husband to die alone.

He remembered Steve the last time he saw him, the anguish in his eyes—"Tell Claire I'm sorry." Guilt jerked him back to reality. "Let me tell you another story about your husband." It was Steve she had to love, Steve she had to forgive, and Steve who would always stand between them. They both needed a reminder of that.

There was a pregnant silence. "I'll just refill my pot."

When she returned to her end of the boat, he saw the flush of humiliation fading on her cheeks. Ruthlessly Nate closed his mind to her hurt.

He could live with her thinking him a cold bastard; he couldn't live with her seeing him as worthy.

CLAIRE RESUMED PAINTING in an agony of embarrassment. She thought she'd seen a bounce-back of attraction when Nate caught her looking. Her encouragement had been instinctive, without considering consequences. Turned out she'd horribly misread the situation.

What must he think of her? Maybe she was overreacting, maybe Nate hadn't understood her smile.… No, that was a faint hope. He'd understood and he'd shut her down. Now she experienced shame in front of him, as though she'd denigrated Steve's memory. Except she hadn't been thinking of Steve. Oh, God, she was so confused.

She wanted to talk about this, but what if that only made things worse? No, all she could do was minimize the humiliation. Gaze glued to the hull, she picked up her brush and cleared her throat. "What story do you have for me?" she managed to say casually. *Now* he wanted to talk about Steve. Another blush heated her cheeks.

"The one about how he nearly got us killed," Nate said, and reflexively she glanced over. He was grimly intent on his painting. "It was the tour before last and we'd been driving thirty-six hours to a rendezvous point for pick-up. Steve drove into a ditch. Our vehicle ended up on its side, wheels spinning."

Embarrassment turned to shock. "Was anyone hurt?"

"Scrapes and bruises, Steve had a mild concussion…nothing requiring an air-vac. One of the other vehicles winched us out." He glanced over, but she wasn't ready to meet his eyes yet.

"He'd lost concentration worrying about you dealing with the miscarriage alone. More bad news was the last thing you needed, so we all agreed you'd never find out."

Nate paused, clearly waiting for a response, but her throat had tightened.

"Steve became like a machine after the accident," he continued. "Didn't matter what reassurances we gave, he couldn't get past the fear of endangering our lives. I wonder—" Nate stopped.

Slowly she turned her head. "You wonder?"

"If he took the next deployment because he felt he still had restitution to make."

Defending Steve. She loved and hated him for that. "I don't believe he had any intention of quitting," she said. "You know why? Because he didn't tell you about our deal at the beginning of the tour. I even know why he didn't tell you."

His turn to avoid her eyes. Oh, yes, Nate knew, too. Claire said it anyway.

"Because he didn't want you badgering him to do the right thing." Blindly she set down the brush.

"Hell, Claire, don't torture yourself."

She found herself caught to a broad, bare chest and kept her arms rigidly by her sides, overwhelmed by an avalanche of conflicting emotions—sadness, anger, a resurgence of grief for Steve, along with a dawning suspicion that her life was sweeping in a direction she hadn't anticipated.

"I only told you about the accident to show how often you were in Steve's thoughts." Nate's chest lay warm and smooth against her cheek, his rapid heartbeat at odds with the gentle stroke of fingers on her hair. Claire closed her eyes on a horrified revelation. Lust was bad enough, but this…not this.

She pushed free, shielding her face so he wouldn't see her confusion. "I'm okay."

His hand landed on her shoulder, tightened. "I figured if you knew how much Steve loved you…"

She'd forgive him. "I don't doubt that Steve loved me," she said, because one of them could be comforted. That didn't fix everything, but Claire wasn't going to go into it with the guy threatening to tilt her world on its axis.

If she ever fell in love again it would be with a man wholly unconnected to her past, to Steve, to the SAS. Not her husband's best friend, not the guy still mourning him. The hand on her shoulder suddenly felt like a weight, a burden. She didn't need these feelings, didn't want them.

Suddenly his earlier rejection felt like a lucky escape.

CHAPTER FOURTEEN

"THAT'S SORTED THEN." Giving him an impersonal smile, Claire moved away, all bustle and purpose, and Nate dropped his hand. "We need to clean up if we're going to catch low tide. I'll rinse out an empty paint pail.... It's perfect for collecting shellfish. You wash the brushes."

What could he say, "don't shut me out"? He'd rejected her shy overture to achieve precisely this outcome. "That's right, I can't leave without a feed of pipi fritters," he said. Steamed, then chopped and mixed in a beer batter, the small, sweet shellfish were a must-eat culinary experience during a Stingray Bay stay.

As he soaked the brushes in turpentine, Nate told himself he'd won. He'd done his job as trustee, redeemed Steve in Claire's eyes and resisted the temptation to risk their friendship by taking it to the next level. Watching the paint dissolve in the solvent, he strove for a sense of victory, but all he felt was hollow, scraped out inside.

But he did his best to match Claire's light

chatter as they walked across the mudflats to where the estuary twisted in a thin ribbon out to sea.

He'd get past this. Once he was back in L.A., thousands of miles from this woman, he'd be okay again. Nate crouched to dig in the wet sand, his fingers scrabbling for the shellfish. The water was chill, out of the hothouse that was the boat shed, and the sun had lost its power to a gusty wind channeled along the exposed sand.

Claire wiped her hands clean on her pants, then untied the coveralls' sleeves around her waist and covered up, loosening her hair in the process. It streamed out behind her, accentuating the fine bones of her face. Something clenched inside him, Nate fixed the image in his memory. He wasn't going to torture himself by coming home again.

She turned to him, her hair whipping across her cheeks and he battled an impulse to smooth it away. Then Nate saw the apprehension in her blue eyes. "What is it?"

"We have visitors."

He followed her gaze to the bach. Three figures stood on the deck. A waving tow-haired youth, flanked by two men, who stood with arms folded and legs planted. Nate swore. "Ellie broke her word."

"No," said Claire. "I did."

His attention swung back to her. "Goddamn it, we had an agreement!"

She took a deep breath. "You need to see them, Nate, as much for your sake as theirs. I think it will help you."

"I don't need help. I need to be left alone."

"I wish there was time for me to be subtle about this, but there's not. You've been left alone for eighteen months and you're still screwed up about the ambush. And this isn't just about you." She returned her son's wave. "It's about Lewis who lost his dad and shouldn't have to lose his uncle Nate, too. It's about giving Dan one less person to worry about as his wife approaches her two-year checkup after a mastectomy." She read his shock. "That's right, Nate. Jo had cancer. He didn't tell you because he didn't want to worry you."

He would not be manipulated like this. "Coming out swinging doesn't further your cause."

"It's still better than being terrified by how much you'll hurt my son if you walk now."

Shit. She had him. Reluctantly, he raised his hand and returned Lewis's greeting.

Apparently satisfied, the three watchers disappeared into the bach. "Thank you," Claire said unsteadily and bent to rinse her sandy hands at the water's edge. Nate picked up the bucket of pipis. In a low voice, she added, "Right now, I'm as eager to have you gone as you are to go. But this is about doing what's best for everybody, not just me."

He was too angry to pretend not to understand her. "How can you be attracted to a man like me anyway? You said yourself, I'm screwed up. I'm transient and I dumped one of your friends. And that's only scratching the surface of why we shouldn't do anything about this."

Damn. He'd acknowledged he felt something in return. And by the flare of cognizance in her eyes, she'd picked it up, too. Things had just got harder.

She wiped her hands dry on her coveralls. "I don't want our relationship to change. My life's finally getting simple."

"So we're agreed," he said. "We forget it."

"Yes, let's forget it." She didn't hide her relief.

"Good," he said gruffly.

They headed back and the water-laden sand sucked at his bare feet with every step.

"Dan and Ross are only here overnight," she said. "All I ask is that you keep an open mind."

"You're expecting a Hallmark moment." Nate gave a mirthless laugh. "Those guys are going to crucify me."

"WOMEN AND CHILDREN FIRST," Nate said when they reached the bach. He so wasn't ready for this.

"It'll be fine," she reassured him, and entered with a smile. "Where's my sheep-dagging expert?"

Nate stopped at the threshold, watching riveted as Claire threw her arms around the lanky teenager. Lewis rolled his eyes but returned her hug with a quick convulsive squeeze that suggested he'd missed her.

God, he'd grown. Taller than Claire, blond fringe falling over his eyes, this wasn't the eleven-year-old who'd clung to her hand through the funeral service.

Claire went to kiss his cheek and Lewis warned in a deep voice, "Mum, be cool. I've only been gone a week."

"Hey, I'm allowed to miss you, aren't I?" But laughing, she let him go, crossing to hug Ross and Dan who stood up from the couch. But Nate couldn't tear his attention from Lewis.

Achingly familiar hazel eyes met his, Lewis said with awkward casualness, "Hey." Then blushed because his voice had hit a high note.

Nate just stared at him.

Lewis's blush deepened. Clearly embarrassed, he gestured to the bucket Nate carried. "Mum makes everyone who comes to stay collect pipis. She thinks of it as a must-do Stingray Bay treat." He ducked his head. "Sorry, I forgot. You've been collecting pipis here forever."

Nate realized he should say something. "You look a lot like your dad."

"Yeah, everyone says that." The teenager shuffled his feet and Nate inwardly swore. He'd said the wrong thing. Defining the kid first by his loss.

Nate set the bucket down. "Bad luck, mate, when you might have inherited your mum's good looks."

Lewis's head jerked up, he gave a snort of laughter. Hand outstretched, Nate moved forward, though it felt like walking on broken glass. "It's good to see you."

Swallowing convulsively, Lewis's hand grabbed his and Nate couldn't stop himself hauling the teenager into a bear hug as emotion swamped him. He'd been an honorary uncle to this kid.

"You too," Lewis said, and the break in his voice had nothing to do with puberty. "I missed you."

When they broke apart, Nate looked over at Ross and Dan. "Guys," he said.

Neither of them responded, except by a tightening of jaw, an accusing stare. The silence grew awkward, heat rushed to Nate's face. He set his own jaw.

Claire moved first, hooking her arm through a puzzled Lewis's. "Let's go outside and soak the pipis in fresh water to make them spit out any sand," she suggested. "There's nothing worse in fritters. And I want to hear all about your holiday."

She cast Nate an anxious glance as she and Lewis left, and he returned a grim smile. Not so confident now she'd done the right thing.

By unspoken consensus, they waited for the sound of voices to fade away. It gave Nate an opportunity to study the two stony-faced men opposite.

Despite the season, Dan was tanned from his new life as a farmer. Like Nate, he'd grown out his military haircut, and his brown-gold hair flopped untidily over his forehead. Shep. The good shepherd. Flying home, Claire had told him that Dan had weathered survivor's guilt. Now he'd learned his friend's bride, Jo, had battled cancer.

A blowfly swept in the open door then buzzed, distressed, around the window. Ross let it out. As he crossed the room his limp was pronounced and Nate averted his gaze. It had been torture listening to the increasing desperation in his voice when Ross phoned to talk up his rehab progress. He lived for deployment. His mate had recently conceded defeat and accepted a teaching position within the SAS.

When he'd passed through L.A. last month en route to New York with Viv, Dan's sister, Nate had made excuses not to see them. He couldn't face the Iceman in his final disillusionment. As for finding true love, Ross was clearly scrabbling for some kind of substitute. All Nate foresaw was an emotional pileup further down the track when Ice realized it and broke Viv's heart.

The fly was released and Ross turned from the window, his gray gaze hard. "You better have a good explanation for this, Nate. What the hell are you playing at, coming home and not telling us?"

"I didn't expect to be here more than a couple days. I figured there wasn't time to catch up properly."

"Don't treat us like fools," said Dan. "You've cut us loose."

Fine, if they wanted it blunt. "If I can't be the person I was, then it's better this way."

"You dumb asshole," said Ross. "You could be a freakin' amoeba and you'd still be a brother. And the only reason I'm not throwing a punch right now is because you had such a dipshit upbringing you don't get that."

"We should never have pandered to his wanting to be left alone." Dan turned to Nate. "The only reason we left this intervention so long was because we were both in the same crazy headspace."

Nate felt the pressure build. He couldn't let these men bulldoze themselves back into his life. He wasn't one of them anymore.

Ross's voice softened to a growl. "You seriously think I'm going to abandon the guy who saved my life?"

Something inside Nate snapped. And for what? Permanent disability, for a slow painful disillusionment, for a half life. "And are you glad, Ross? You can't be a real soldier anymore, do the thing you loved most. And don't bullshit me that teaching is doing it for you, I won't believe it."

He waited for Ross's blow, but it was Dan who hit him. Nate glimpsed the fist in his peripheral vision, and was too surprised to duck. Dan pulled the punch at the last second, but it was enough to send Nate flying across the living room and crashing into the dining table, toppling two chairs in the process. He landed on his ass, half jammed under the table, the chairs across his legs. His jaw ached and he touched it gingerly, still astonished.

Shep had hit him. Shep, who'd led the retrieval team, who'd argued with the surgeon who wanted to cut off Ross's leg and who'd supported Claire through the funeral because Nate couldn't.

"Well," Nate said, cradling his jaw. "This is one fun reunion."

Dan looked dazed. "I didn't know I was going to do that. I'm sorry."

"Make your goddamn apologies to me," Ross snapped. "I don't know who I'm more pissed with. You, Dan, for thinking I can't defend myself, or Nate for believing I'm still a monodimensional prick. FYI, Nate, the only thing my disability does is level the playing field for you. Even now I can whip your ass in close-quarter combat."

There was the sound of running footsteps and they all froze. None of them had thought of Claire and Lewis in this. Dan righted the chairs; Ross hauled Nate upright by his T-shirt.

Lewis burst into the bach, Claire on his heels. "We heard a crash," said the boy.

Ross massaged his leg. "My fault, still a little clumsy. I knocked over a chair."

Claire's gaze settled on Nate's jaw and her eyes widened.

"I dived for the chair," he preempted the question. "Went for a skate."

"Is that why the side of your face is all red?" said Lewis.

"He clipped it on the table when he fell," Dan supplied.

Nate saw the instant Claire realized what had happened. Her eyes narrowed, her mouth tightened. Walking over, she laid her open palm against his aching jaw. Her hand was icy cold from the outside tap and the chill immediately soothed the pain.

"Better?" she said softly.

The ache moved to his heart. "Sure."

Hand cupping his face, she said over her shoulder, "Lewis, there are frozen peas in the shed freezer. Go get them for me, will you, hon?"

When he'd left, Claire lifted her palm, then hit Nate's cheek in a short, sharp slap that made his eyes water. Stepping back, she glared at each of them in turn. "If you guys need to do this, fine, but next time make sure it's nowhere near my son. And this better have a happy ending because I sure as hell can't take another tragic one. Am I clear?"

"Next time I'll take him into the dunes," Dan promised.

"We can go now if you want," Nate retorted. "If it helps, I'll even let you win."

"In your dreams, Hollywood. You're in the real world here."

"I'll take on the winner," Ross said. "Show you both how it's done."

"Cool," Lewis returned, tossing and catching the packet of frozen peas like a football. "Can I watch?"

Claire closed her eyes. "I'm making you all chamomile tea."

"Mummmm," said Lewis in an agonized tone, but Nate smiled. It hurt.

CHAPTER FIFTEEN

CRADLING A CUP OF COCOA, Claire watched her son with Nate across the flames. Nate was tuning Lewis's acoustic guitar while the teenager stifled yawns. It was after ten-thirty and he should really be in bed, but she couldn't bring herself to send him. His time with Nate was too short, too precious.

After dinner, they'd built a bonfire on the beach like the old days and all sat around it on deck chairs carted down from the bach. Beside her, Dan and Ross talked rugby with the endless enthusiasm that Kiwi men had for their national sport. They'd behaved themselves since this afternoon's incident, but she had a sense they were biding their time.

Nate finished tuning the guitar and gave it back. Lewis launched into a version of "Hotel California." Showing off with more enthusiasm than skill. Across the blaze Nate met her eyes, his own dancing with amusement and firelight. The red patch on his jaw had shrunk to a small bruise.

She'd forgotten it had been his skill that had sparked her son's interest in playing, forgotten how he'd patiently taught eight-year-old Lewie his first chords. Claire could hold a tune, but Steve had been tone-deaf, though that never stopped him singing along.

Claire experienced a pang for her late husband, embraced it like the old friend it was, then looked at the man she was trying not to fall in love with. She'd been glad Nate had admitted to feeling the same attraction. Glad because it got rid of the shame, made the bond more than the pathetic imaginings of a lonely widow.

Of course, they wouldn't do anything about it. She was completely in agreement with him on that. Neither of them needed this complication in their lives, the timing was all wrong, and it was highly possible that for both of them, this attraction was linked to grieving for Steve.

Except she'd never developed feelings for Ross or Dan in the eighteen months since Steve's death. Unwittingly, Claire sighed. No, it was Nate who quickened her pulse, Nate who roused a dangerous tenderness, a reluctant longing.

She and Steve had once talked about finding someone else if one of them died, and she'd said jokingly, "Another woman? Over my dead body." More serious, he'd replied, "If you find a guy who can give you what we have… Honey, I want you to be happy." At the time she'd admired his unselfishness, now she wondered if his magnanimity was because he understood divided loyalties, already knew the SAS held a prior claim to his heart. She couldn't think like this, didn't want to. The same old endless circuit, she was tired of it.

"Claire," said Dan. "Settle an argument. Best kicker in the All Blacks, Carter or Weepu."

"Oh, Carter certainly," she said without a clue, and Ross hooted.

"Told you, Shep."

The men resumed their argument, leaving her free to watch the interaction across the fire. After an awkward start, Lewis and Nate now seemed relaxed in each other's company. She'd made a tough call, but the right call.

Lewis yawned again, his gaping mouth all but obscuring his face. Claire smiled and made another one. "Time for bed, son."

He started to protest.

"Or you can skip the early bridge jump and stay up," said Dan.

It was a long-standing tradition that visitors to Stingray Bay jump off the footbridge on an outgoing tide then float the half mile to the bach.

"Fine, I'll hit the sack," Lewis said grudgingly.

"Are you joining us, Claire?" Ross said, and she encountered four male grins.

She played the game. "Try and stop me."

"Mum, you know you'll chicken out. You do it every time."

"Well, if she does, she can paddle home in the kayak with me," Ross said. Claire saw Nate glance at his friend's damaged leg, then away. *He's made his peace with it,* she wanted to say, but this was for them to resolve privately.

"I think I'll turn in, too," she said.

Collecting the empty mugs, she bent to hug Ross, realizing only when she was hugging Dan that it would seem odd if she left Nate out.

Self-consciousness hit her as she turned and saw the tension in Nate's shoulders. He'd realized the same thing. "Sleep well," he said, his gaze just left of her ear.

Steadying herself on his shoulders, Claire leaned forward to give him a light kiss on the cheek. Misreading her intention as drawing in for a hug, Nate turned his head. Mouths brushed, noses bumped. Instinctively, each recoiled. Claire stepped back and tripped over Ross's bad leg. His arm shot out to catch her.

"I'm so sorry."

"No harm done." Ross's gaze flickered between her and Nate. In her peripheral vision, she noted a sudden stillness in Dan's posture.

Casually Nate gave his empty mug to Lewis. "Take this up for me, will you, buddy.... Got the flashlight?"

"Yep." Lewis switched it on, the glare full in Nate's face. It was as red as Claire's felt. "Oops, sorry." Lewis angled the beam downward.

"Lead the way, honey." Claire escaped the circle of firelight. "Good night, everyone!"

Cheeks flaming, she followed the dancing beam up the path cut into the bank that connected the estuary to the bach, feeling the foliage of the agapanthus shrubs brush against her jeans. They might as well have put a sign up. Awkward attraction here. Lewis strode ahead oblivious, pointing the flashlight at the bank in a hunt for rabbits. "Did I tell you we went possum hunting one night, Mum?"

"No, I hope you didn't catch any."

"They're pests. They strip the bark off trees."

"Sounds like you had a great stay at the farm."

"Yeah, I really liked it. It'll be good to get gaming again, though. Some guys at my new school said as long as you've got a microphone you can set up your computer so you can all talk to each other during the game. If I had headphones we wouldn't disturb you."

Claire smiled. "That's so thoughtful."

"You wanted me to interact with the kids at my new school," he reminded her.

She laughed. "I was talking about in person."

"That reminds me. Remember Callum in my new soccer team has a pool party in Whangarei for his birthday. Now I'm home early, I can go, right?" Without giving her a chance to reply, he added, "You liked his mom, remember? And Callum's a nerd, your favorite kind of friend for me."

Claire ignored the sarcasm because she didn't want to fight on his first night home. "Still an exaggerator," she said lightly. "Yes, you can go."

"They live around the corner from Nana's. I could stay with her afterward to save you driving to pick me up."

Claire was touched. "That's very thoughtful, Lewis."

He shrugged. "I have to stay with her one night through the holidays. Might as well get it over with."

Shaking her head, she made up the other bed in Nate's room while he was in the bathroom brushing his teeth. The other guys had pitched a tent in the yard.

Lewis came back in his pajamas and dumped his clothes at the end of the bed. "You think Nate will stay longer if I ask him?"

"Zander Freedman's going on tour. Nate needs to get back to his job."

"I wonder if they ever play guitar together."

"You can ask him tomorrow."

"I can ask him when he comes to bed."

"I doubt you'll be awake, the guys have some catching up to do."

Lewis climbed under the covers. "Yeah, well, so do I.... Is my wet suit here? The water's too cold to do the bridge jump without."

"Yep, I brought both of ours."

He laughed. "Mum, you are so not going to jump tomorrow. Just admit it."

"One day I'm going to surprise you."

"Sure you are," he said in that patronizing tone teenagers reserved for parental delusions. God help her, she'd even missed it.

Claire turned off the light. "Love you, Lewie."

She waited, hopeful. Maybe being away—

"I know," he said.

With a silent sigh, she went to bed.

THERE WAS A LONG SILENCE after Claire and Lewis left. Nate bought himself time by dropping more driftwood on the bonfire and sparks rose like fireflies, winking out as they cooled.

He didn't even try to turn the subject. In special ops, you evolved the capacity to read each other's gestures, even minds sometimes. Survival depended on it.

"I suppose it makes sense," Dan said at last. "You and Claire were always close."

Nate stiffened. "If you're suggesting I've spent years lusting after my best friend's wife—"

"Don't insult my integrity by suggesting I'd question yours," Dan rebuked sharply. "Or Claire's. We know each other better than that."

"Nothing's going on," Nate clarified. "Nothing will. Claire and I are agreed on that." Willpower had triumphed over emotion, but it didn't feel like victory.

Ross snorted; Dan shook his head.

Nate glanced suspiciously from one to the other. "What?"

"The desperation," Ross answered. "We recognize it, that's all."

"I don't get it."

"The point is, you don't owe us an explanation," Dan said. "It's none of our business."

Incredulous, Nate stared at him. "You should bloody care. This is Steve's widow. You're supposed to be protecting her from guys like me."

"Women who choose military men are strong women," Dan said. "They have to be. Claire doesn't need our interference, only our support."

He gave a wry smile. "There's a difference, apparently, one my wife is still teaching me."

"But if this attraction goes anywhere," Ross added, "then yeah, you'll have to get your shit together and stop pretending you're happy in Hollywood."

"What time did you say you were leaving tomorrow?" Nate said bitterly.

Ross looked at him. "You think you're not hurting us? You're hurting us, Nate. We've been family to each other for ten years, and you're breaking our frickin' hearts."

Nate was shaken.

Ross eased his leg out to the fire. "And to answer your earlier question, yeah, there were times I wish I hadn't survived. But having to come to terms with this injury has made me a better man."

"I miss Steve and Lee so bad sometimes," Dan said. "Eighteen months and sometimes it's as raw as when it happened. Survivor's guilt is difficult to come to terms with."

Nate's throat tightened. "I can't talk about this stuff."

"Look around this fire," Ross said. "There are two men missing. We have no choice about that, but we do have a choice about losing you."

"If what Steve would think is the only thing

holding you back from Claire, then don't let it," said Dan. "He only cared that she was happy."

"But you'd have to make her happy," said Ross, and Nate felt as if he was under attack by the tag team from hell. "That's a big commitment. It can't be tied up with grieving for Steve—for either of you."

"Look, we don't need to talk about it because it's not going to happen," he tried to end the conversation. "I'm leaving as soon as the papers are signed. Day after tomorrow."

Dan stretched his hands to the fire. "If there had never been an ambush we'd all be sitting here now," he commented as though Nate hadn't spoken. "Lee would have been housebroken and making us laugh with some outrageous story. Steve would be lounging back, sipping a beer and radiating the smug contentment of a happily married man. I have that smugness now," he added. "I recommend it."

"I will have it once Viv commits to a wedding date," said Ross. "Can you believe it, she even called the engagement ring a friendship ring to wind me up. I can't believe I'm actually begging a woman to marry me. It's a crime."

"It's frontier justice," Dan retorted. "And remember, you have to be on your best behavior for a year before I'm letting you hitch your star to my little sister's."

"This visit—" ignoring Dan, Ross addressed Nate "—I'm pinning her down to a date."

Despite himself, Nate smiled at his earnestness. Unfortunately, Ice took that as encouragement. A glint entered his eye. "Viv's flying in from New York Sunday night and she'd love to see you. And Dan and Jo will be in Auckland on Monday for Jo's two-year checkup. Stay another few days," he suggested.

"Yeah, mate," Dan added quietly. "Stay and see that it's still possible to be happy."

Their affection settled over him, as warm and familiar as a child's comforter. Nate pushed it away. "I can't. Zander's heading on tour, I've got to return for work." He looked at Dan. "Why didn't you tell me about Jo's cancer?"

"Would you have come home?"

He remained silent.

"Something happened during that ambush that you're not telling us," Dan said. "Don't shake your head.… I had to peel your fingers off the gun barrel. You're trying to protect us— because that's what you do. Protect Claire if you must, but not us. Whatever went down, we can handle it."

Nate disagreed.

Dan read his face and sighed. "We're here for you, mate. Anytime, anywhere."

"I appreciate that," he replied politely.

Ross said nothing. He had his Iceman's face on, unreadable. But his fingers beat a frustrated tattoo against his good leg. Never a good sign.

"Get the cripple another beer?" he said to Dan.

"You're perfectly capable of getting your own beer, Ice."

"Humor me."

A look passed between them. "You want a can, Nate?" Dan asked.

"Thanks—" he stood and stretched "—but I'm heading to bed."

"Ten more minutes," said Ross, and it wasn't a request. Nate raised his brows. "Please," Ross growled.

Reluctantly he sat down again.

"The problem with grieving," Ross said when Dan was gone, "is that it makes you selfish. You forget your responsibilities to the living. That's a lesson I just learned, one I'm passing on. Shep needs his friends around if things don't go well with Jo's checkup. That's all I have to say."

Nate stared into the fire. This was why he'd made a life among strangers. His friends still had expectations of the man he used to be. Claire had taken a big risk bringing Lewis home and he'd sensed her tension as Nate responded to Lewis's eager questions about life in Hollywood and suffered the boy's hero worship. While his guilt returned, heavier than lead.

Dan returned, tossed Ross a beer. The conversation returned to sports. Nate made his token contribution. Inside he was in turmoil. *Don't need me. I'm unreliable, I'll let you down.*

"I'm turning in," he said abruptly.

"Yeah, it's time we all did."

They doused the fire, kicking sand over the traces, and then carried the empty cans and deck chairs up to the bach. "Night, guys."

Dan grabbed him in a hug. He wasn't expecting it and had no defense for the emotions that swamped him.

After the ambush, Dan had shadowed Nate through his darkest days. When he'd said, "I can't get over this," Dan had grabbed him by the shoulders and shaken him.

"You don't disrespect their memory by holding your own life cheap, you hear me. I can't lose you too." He'd wept as he'd said it and Nate had thought dully, *He's right, death is too easy. It's much harder to live.*

So he'd said yes to the antidepressants, he'd bared his soul to a military psych who'd told him it wasn't his fault and he'd left the friends he no longer deserved and made a life among people who didn't give a damn about him.

Over Dan's shoulder he met Ross's eyes. Saw a plea where there hadn't been one before.

"Call me as soon as you get results from Jo's specialist," he heard himself say to Dan. "If you need me around, I'll stay."

CHAPTER SIXTEEN

NATE ONLY REALIZED he was sharing with Lewis when he pushed back the curtain and saw the boy asleep in the spare bed, mouth slightly open in a light snore. As the light shafted across his face, he shifted restlessly. Nate dropped the curtain and swore softly under his breath. It was clear Lewis wanted to talk about the ambush and Nate wasn't ready.... Never would be.

"Is there a problem?"

Closing the patio doors en route to the tent, Ross paused. Talk about the devil and the deep blue sea.

"No." Steeling himself, Nate yanked the curtain open, flicking off the kitchen light at the same time. In the small bedroom he stood quietly waiting for his eyes to adjust to the darkness. Then, slipping off his boots and jacket, he crawled over the baseboard and lay down fully clothed. Lewis had stopped snoring.

"Nate?"

He deepened his breathing, mimicking sleep. The springs creaked on the other bed, and he sensed Lewis standing over him. Wanting to wake him, wanting to ask. A tentative hand touched his shoulder. "Nate?" the teenager whispered.

Turning as if in sleep, Nate rolled away. More seconds passed, ten...twenty. At last he heard the soft squeak of springs as Lewis returned to his bed. Within minutes the boy's breathing had deepened into sleep.

Nate lay awake, staring into space.

Around 2:00 a.m. he saw Claire's silhouette through the open curtain, moving silently around the kitchen as she found a glass and got herself some water. She paused at the doorway. Through half-closed lids, Nate watched her as she checked Lewis, and then glanced in the direction of Nate's bed. Her face was in darkness, but he heard a soft sigh before she disappeared from sight.

Nate buried his face in the pillow to smother a groan. The next few days were going to be torture.

CLAIRE WOKE TO THE SOUND of her son's excited voice, followed by a grown male's. "Keep it down, you'll wake your mother." She rolled over and peered at the clock: 5:55.

"I'm awake," she grumbled. "And waiting

for tea. And it better have two sugars if it's not six yet."

Silence.

"Still a morning person, huh," Ross muttered.

"I heard that!"

Five minutes later, Lewis came through the curtain, grinning ear to ear, carrying a mug of tea and fluttering a white hankie. "They said I'm expendable," he said cheerfully.

"Ugh." Claire accepted the tea. "You're taking after your dad, aren't you? Why can't I have a teenager who stays in bed until noon?"

"We have to do the bridge jump before breakfast," he reminded her. "Dan and Ross have to leave straight after. You can stay in bed if you want."

Taking a gulp of tea, she set the mug on the bedside table and flung aside the covers. "Give me ten minutes."

Claire wrestled into her full-body wet suit, wondering if Catwoman had this much trouble as she dragged the resistant rubber over her feet and hands.

The guys were already on the beach when she walked out onto the deck, Lewis and Nate hauling the kayak down to the estuary while Ross limped behind with the paddle. The sky was overcast and a breeze ruffled the gray water and chilled the early-morning air.

Nate looked as if he hadn't slept and Claire tried not to be glad about that. His impending departure would be painful; she wanted him to feel it, too. He, Dan and Lewis were in wet suits—Nate must have borrowed one from Ross, who wore board shorts and a wet shirt. They were fine-looking male specimens, supremely fit, and Claire paused to admire the view, trying not to discriminate by lingering too long on Nate's powerful build.

"Yeah, we're hot," Dan boasted, and they all struck a pose for her, like the old days. She looked at her son's scrawny frame as he strained his biceps and laughed, alive to the joy of the moment, as well as its poignancy.

There would be other bumps in the road to adulthood, but she experienced a sudden conviction that she and Lewie were over the worst.

In her wet suit, she walked down the track, intensely conscious of Nate's glance at her body, no longer cursory, no longer dismissive, before he said gruffly to Ross, "So, are you getting in the boat or what, princess? You'll need a big head start if you're paddling against the tide."

"Sure, let's make this a competition," Ross retorted. "See who gets there first."

"Running on these sharp shells with bare feet," Claire protested.

"Lewis, your mother's gone soft, mate," Dan

said. "We're relying on you to toughen her up now you're home." Then yelped as Claire kicked a splash of water over him. "I was caught by surprise," he protested when everyone laughed.

In the kayak, Ross used his paddle to push off, sticking close to shore where the tidal pull was less intense.

"C'mon." Lewis beckoned the runners. "We can't let him get away."

Nate and Dan jogged the roadside verge, a longer distance but easier underfoot. Claire and Lewis stuck to the beach, but the shells definitely slowed their progress. Claire braved the icy water to run in the shallows—the shells weren't as close to the surface in the estuary—and picked up speed, though she had to work harder as her feet sank deeper in the sand.

Ross heard her coming and arrowed farther out into the estuary, a more direct route, but one that forced him to paddle harder to counter the current. Lungs burning with the unaccustomed effort, Claire ran out of steam. "Lewie," she hollered between gasps. "Tag."

Teen coolness forgotten, her son detoured toward her, arms pumping, a grin splitting his face. She high-fived and he sprinted ahead, splashing through the shallows like an exuberant dog.

Nate and Dan eased into a jog. "Win this for us, mate!"

Lewis drew level with the kayak and droplets streamed off the paddle blade as Ross dug furrows through the choppy surface. Lewis inched ahead. Her son's hand slapped the wooden pillar seconds before the kayak shot underneath the bridge. Claire dropped to a walk, pressing a knuckle into the stitch in her side and laughing. "We rule!"

There'd been a time when these old games would have been too painful; now they seemed a celebration of everything that had been good about her life with Steve.

"Nice strategy, Langfords," Dan approved as he and Nate reached the bridge. "Local knowledge and teamwork wins." He walked ahead with Lewis, leaving Nate to wait for her, a deliberate move, she realized.

Claire wasn't sure how she felt about that tacit permission.

"Oh, my gosh, do I need fitness," she huffed as Nate reached out a hand to pull her up the bank. And it was there again, that electric awareness.

He released her hand. "Okay if I stay another couple of days?" he asked, and she felt a leap in her pulse. "Depending on Jo's test results. If they're clear, I'll leave tomorrow night as planned. If she needs treatment…" His voice trailed off.

Claire bought a minute by wiping her sandy feet on the grass. Great that he was prepared to support their friends. She and Nate had agreed not to follow up their attraction and if there was one quality they shared, it was willpower. But that didn't mean her feelings for him wouldn't get stronger. The pulse leaps weren't something she had control over. She liked having him around, but she didn't want to need him around.

Except Dan might need him and Lewis could spend more time with his favorite. No contest.

"Of course you can stay," she said casually.

"Come on, you guys," Lewis bellowed. "We want to jump."

"Coming," she called. They started walking along the bridge.

"I thought I'd sleep on *Heaven Sent* now the cabin's cleaned up. Give Lewis his space."

"It'll be good for security, too," she said, relieved. "With all the deliveries we've had recently, I'm concerned about break-ins. I'll pick up a padlock when I'm in town later."

"That's settled then."

Yes, they understood each other perfectly. And if he stayed longer, they had a chaperone. Lewis wouldn't let Nate out of his sight.

"Mum, you can go first," her son said when they reached the launch spot. "That way you're less likely to chicken out."

"As if," she scoffed. Claire leaned out and waved to Ross, who'd beached the kayak at the shoreline. Then clutching the railing, she climbed over and took her first look at the fast-flowing water below. Closed her eyes under the familiar surge of fear.

As a kid she'd been teased about her inability to jump, but neither taunts nor bribes, not even her own stubborn determination, had ever counted against the stark terror she always experienced at this point. She ended up clinging limpet-like to the railing and scrambling back over. "Next time," she'd promise—to herself as much as everyone else. Defeat was not in her nature.

She hadn't attempted the bridge leap since Steve's death and having gone through so much, she'd sincerely believed today would be different.

So why the heck were her fingers grabbing the handrail in a death grip?

"C'mon, Mum," Lewis said impatiently.

Claire swallowed again. "Give me a minute." She took another look at the estuary. It wasn't even that far, only twelve feet. Her toes gripped the edge of the boards like another pair of hands.

"Mum!"

"Lewis," Dan said quietly, "Just *wait!*"

Claire barely registered the comment. "One more minute," she sang out in a nervous falsetto, conscious of growing frustration. She'd come through a black cloud of grief, found a new passion in her business, rescued her son from bad company. Surely she could jump off this damn footbridge!

"Count of three," she croaked. "One…two…" Her knees threatened to buckle. "Two point one." She crawled back over the railing. "Next time," she promised. "Today I'll go in from the shore."

The guys didn't tease her. These tough guys, to whom this kind of thing wasn't even a blip on their adventure radar. She loved them for it.

Her son had no such compunction. "Told ya." Shaking his head, Lewis sprang onto the railing and balanced there with athletic ease.

"Show-off," Claire grumbled. "Be careful around Nate. He'll push you."

Nate grinned. Ross's laugh echoed from below. "Tell Lewis that story," she encouraged. After a slight hesitation, he did, and her son listened closely to every word.

"I want to learn to parachute," he said when

Nate finished. "And I'm not scared of heights. Maybe I'll join the SAS."

Claire bit back her instinctive "no" as Dan threw a casual arm around her shoulder. "What happened to game designing?" he asked.

"Well, there's heaps of competition," Lewis said, blithely dismissing SAS selection as easy. "I don't know if I'm good enough." A wind gust made him sway and he flung out his arms to regain balance.

"Design a battle game," Ross called from the water. "Make some money. You don't want soldier pay."

"Or become a farmer," Dan replied. "You've got the right attitude."

"Being a bodyguard pays well," offered Nate, Claire suspected to evoke a disgusted snort from Ross.

"How about working in the family business with me?" she suggested, and evoked the same response from Lewis.

"You just want slave labor, Mum."

"Enough talk, hotshot," she said to her son. "Show me how this should be done."

He leaped with a whoop and a boy's fluidity. Climbing onto the railing, Nate and Dan opted for bombs. All three came up openmouthed and gasping.

"Sh...ooot, that's cold," Nate said, swimming

against the current to stay under the bridge. "I'm glad I'm in a wet suit."

Lewis flipped onto his back, as graceful as a seal. "It's too cold to hang around. Let's go."

"That settles it," Claire said. "I'm not even getting wet. Ross, I'll hitch a ride with you." She scrambled down the bank under the bridge to join him. "Huh, I see you threw in an extra paddle."

"Oh, I know you'll jump," he assured her, watching the swimmers. "It's only a matter of when."

Claire told herself it was only coincidence he was looking at Nate. Until he turned to grin at her.

LEWIS DIDN'T HIDE his disappointment. "You don't have to sleep in the boat," he told Nate. "I don't mind sharing my room."

"It's your snoring." Nate baited the teen's fishing rod. "It kept me awake all last night."

Lewis scrutinized him. "You do look tired."

It was late morning; the guys had left three hours earlier and Claire was in town bulk-buying fishing supplies. "Forget working on the boat," she'd said. "Go fish off the bridge with Lewis."

Nate was still nursing a sense of grievance over that. How could he say no when the kid was right there? Handing Lewis his baited rod,

Nate picked up his own. "I thought you hated fishing."

"I do." Gingerly, Lewis swung the baited end away from his body and flung it haphazardly into the estuary below. "But this might be my only chance to talk in private about the ambush."

Shit. Crouching, Nate cut another strip of soft bait and threaded it over his hook. "Your mum said she told you what happened."

"I know Dad died instantly and everything.…" Lewis made a few nervous turns of the reel, backward and forward. Nate realized he was waiting for reassurance and lifted his gaze.

"Your dad didn't suffer."

The boy's shoulders relaxed. For a few minutes the only sound was the soft whir of the reel as he spun the handle. "The thing is," Lewis ventured, "I want to know what Dad did on his last day, what he said and what he was thinking. I mean, it just seems so weird—" the words tumbled faster, one after another "—that someone can get up and eat breakfast and do the same patrol as always and end up dead at the end of it." The line was a hopeless tangle of nylon around the reel. "I know this makes me sound weird, too," he finished miserably.

"Give me that thing before you break it." Rescuing Lewis's rod, Nate swapped with his own. "Try again."

Red-faced, Lewis recast his line.

"We'd had a good day," Nate said, and felt the kid's attention latch onto him like a leech. He concentrated on untangling the snarled nylon. "Between patrols we were stationed in this little village, it was one of those enclaves you see on TV, stone and mud, high fortress walls—hell, mate, how did you make such a mess of this in such a short time?"

"Dunno." Clutching the rod, Lewis stood rooted, his gaze as hopeful as a spaniel's.

Untwisting the last knot, Nate reset and recast the line. The sinker landed in the estuary with a solid splash and the current drifted it closer. "Breakfast was army rations, but a villager had baked naan," Nate continued in the same curt tone. "That's flat bread, cooked the way your dad liked it, spicy and oiled. As a last meal…" His throat closed, Nate concentrated on his line. "Getting any bites?"

"Um—" Lewis refocused on the fishing "—not anymore."

"Check the bait."

Lewis did as he was told. The hook broke the surface, trailing raggedy white shreds.

"Rebait it," Nate barked.

The boy hesitated. "Can't you do it?"

"No."

The teenager finished reeling in. "You're mad," he commented nervously. "Dan said to be really careful how I asked because you had such a bad time." He caught the swinging hook. Nate frowned at the implication he was somehow fragile.

"I'm not mad," he said. "I'm—" Guilt-stricken, gutted, devastated. "It's…fine you asking," he lied. "It was dawn when we drove out." Nate tried to take the gravel out of his tone. "The sky is an incredible blue that early. In the desert it seems to whiten out by noon. As we left, the dogs started barking—I swear those bloody Afghan mutts make better sentries than we do."

Lewis stood riveted, the hook dangling from the rod, glinting in the sun. "Bait," Nate prompted, and the boy crouched by the pail, wrinkling his nose as he dipped into the bucket for the slab of defrosted soft bait.

"Cut a centimeter cube," Nate advised, and then winced as Lewis slashed at the bait with the razor-sharp knife. "Here, let me show you before you slice a tendon." Wedging his rod in the railing, he knelt to demonstrate technique. "Either Claire's a poor teacher," he commented, "which I doubt, or you have trouble listening to your mother."

Lewis scowled. "You know I do," he said ingenuously. "Mum must have told you why we moved here."

"I didn't get details. Share a few." However much he might have improved, Lewis could benefit by an attitude adjustment around his mother. Sunny enough when things were going his way, the teenager quickly turned sullen if Claire requested help with small chores—the same tasks he happily knuckled down to when asked by Nate, Ross or Dan.

"No, I don't want to go into it." Lewis finished baiting his hook and wiped his hands clean with a rag.

Nate didn't press him. They resumed fishing and Lewis glanced over expectantly. "Well?" he said after a couple of minutes.

"Well, what?"

"You're telling me about Dad."

"No, I don't want to go into it."

Lewis only took a second to get with the play. "That's blackmail," he protested.

"Yep." The line pulled as a fish nibbled the bait; Nate jerked the rod.

"I shoplifted," Lewis said grudgingly.

"What did you take?"

"I took iPod earplugs at an electronics store.… They had surveillance cameras."

"So you weren't a very good shoplifter?"

Nate glanced at Lewis as he spoke and saw a flash of annoyance before the teen shrugged and let out more line. "Guess not."

"So how many times did you get away with it before you were caught?"

Lewis glanced up, shocked. "What? N-n-never."

"You know another animal you see everywhere in Afghanistan? Goats… I've hooked something." Nate started winding his reel. "That morning Lee discovered one had somehow climbed high enough to steal two pairs of his underpants from the clothesline."

Lewis laughed.

"Yeah, we all thought it was pretty funny. Not Lee though, but he'd been grumpy all tour. Your dad said—" Nate stopped. A small kahawai broke the water, its sides flashing silver as it wriggled on the hook.

"Dad said…?" Lewis prompted.

"We'll let this baby grow a bit more, shall we?"

"Sure."

Seizing the struggling fish, Nate freed it with one deft twist.

"So Dad said…?"

"How many times did you shoplift before you were caught?" Nate released the gasping kahawai into the water, watched it surge out of sight.

Silence. Nate rebaited his hook. Cruel to use a dead father as a negotiating tool, but he had no doubt of Steve's blessing.

"Three," Lewis admitted in a small voice. "A bar of chocolate from the supermarket and then a T-shirt. I bought one and wore another under my own. And a prepaid phone card. My friend distracted the teller."

The hint of pride in his voice faded as he met Nate's hard gaze. "I am sorry now," he assured him hastily. "I won't ever do it again. Don't tell Mum."

"I won't." Claire had enough on her plate. "Were you prosecuted?" Nate threaded more soft bait onto the hook.

"No. Nana knows the store owner really well. I just had to apologize and clean up around the store's trash bins every Sunday for six weeks."

"You're bloody lucky Ellie had contacts."

"That's what she says."

"So why'd you do it?"

"It sounds lame now."

That's encouraging. "Tell me anyway."

"The first time to prove I wasn't a wimp." Lewis shrugged. "A mummy's boy. It was scary, but it was also kinda exciting after I'd got away with it and it snowballed, I guess. School and stuff seemed a bit pointless and the kids I skipped classes with were fun to hang out with. They didn't give a sh—damn about all the school rules. But they're not my friends now. Even if Mum let me, I don't want to see them anymore."

Nate recast his line. The lure of cool kids, those sullen little badasses—as he'd once been—who strutted around acting as if they had all the answers. He knew well their attraction to a boy who'd lost his way. He glanced at Lewis. Or a boy whose whole world had been turned upside down.

"You think I'm an epic fail, don't you?" Lewis said.

"We all make mistakes. I got into worse trouble when I was your age."

"Yeah?" The teen pricked up his ears. "What did you do?"

"Similar stuff," Nate hedged. Fortunately, he'd never been caught, at least not doing anything serious enough to affect his army application later. But he'd been a lot street smarter than this kid.

"Tell me!"

"So your dad said to Lee—" Nate took up his story again "'—Lighten up, General Lee, it's another be-u-ti-ful day.' He was buzzed from getting a letter from you a few days earlier."

Fortunately, Lewis was diverted. "Yeah?"

"Steve still had it in his pocket. God help us, he kept reading out the knock-knock jokes."

"Oh, man," Lewis groaned. "I forgot I was into those."

"Your dad's favorite was, knock knock, who's there?"

Lewis covered his face with one hand. Nate grinned.

"Eve," he answered himself.

Lewis squirmed. "Don't—"

"Eve who?" said Nate, and waited.

"Nate!"

"Eve who me hearties!"

Lewis groaned again, trying not to laugh. "Really, his favorite?"

"Cross my heart… What's happened to all the fish?" Nate checked the bait. Still there.

Lewis gave his line a cursory tug. "That joke scared them off.… So, will you talk to Mum for me? Ever since the shoplifting and stuff, she doesn't trust me." He hit Nate with "help the puppy" eyes. "And I've been perfect at least two months."

Nate laughed. "Kid, you've made so many withdrawals from the trust account you'll be paying interest for the next six months at least. But if you want to bank brownie points, then be nicer to your mum." He held the boy's gaze. "Treat her with the same respect your dad did."

The teen broke eye contact first. "I'll try.… So, what else do you remember…about Dad's last day."

But Nate had reached his limit. "That's it."

"Ross said the road had only been checked for IEDs hours before."

Unable to help himself, Nate put his hand on the boy's thin shoulders. "We never knew what hit us," he said honestly. "But up to that point, I promise your dad had a really good day."

Lewis nodded. "Cool." Then without warning his face crumbled. Dropping his rod, he buried his face in Nate's side.

Nate wrapped a comforting arm around him, instinctively grabbing the dangling rod with the free hand holding his own. "It's okay, mate," he managed to say, though they both knew it wasn't.

"I feel bad that I'm forgetting him—" Lewis's voice was muffled against Nate's shoulder "—but I was only eleven."

And you're still only thirteen. "Doesn't matter," Nate insisted stoutly. "Steve was your dad—he's in your DNA. Nothing will ever change that." One of the rods jerked in his hand. He ignored it.

Stepping back, Lewis wiped his eyes dry with a sleeve. "Did you stay away because we remind you of the bad times?"

"No." Nate swallowed. "Because you remind me of the good times."

"That doesn't make sense." The rod jerked again, attracting Lewis's attention. "Have I got a fish?"

"I think so…here." Nate untangled the two rods, doing the handover just as the line bowed.

"Whoa!" Lewis grabbed the pole with both hands. "I think it's a big one."

His grief forgotten, he started reeling in and a fish jumped out of the water, a fair-size kahawai, ready for a fight. Nate seized the distraction.

"Drop the line, then reel in a little bit," he advised. "Yeah, that's it. She's a beauty."

They lost it, but it didn't matter because somehow they'd started enjoying themselves. When Claire's car pulled over beside the bridge to give them a lift home, Nate even checked his watch, astonished by how quickly the afternoon had passed.

"Catch anything?" she said when they'd walked to the car with their fishing gear. She wore a black, slim-fitting skirt that accentuated her small waist and the curve of her hips.

Another one that got away. Nate rattled the empty bucket. "We won't be filling up your bait freezer."

"Now, that's a shame. I—"

"Mum," Lewis interrupted. "Remember all those knock-knock jokes I used to send Dad? Nate said he read out bits of one of my letters the morning he...of his last tour."

"Really, that's so great." Her eyes met Nate's, glowing with a gratitude he didn't deserve. He busied himself loading the fishing gear in the trunk.

"It's Mum's fault I got hooked on knock-knock jokes," Lewis said. "She tells the lamest jokes."

"Hey," Claire protested. "I tell great jokes. What fish do road-menders use? ...Pneumatic krill."

"See." Lewis rolled his eyes at Nate. "She doesn't even wait for you to answer before giving away the punch line."

CHAPTER SEVENTEEN

IN SOME WAYS, signing the sales agreement on her house felt like Claire's wedding day. An exuberant celebrant— Adam, the estate agent, could barely contain his excitement over the sales commission. Her dress was a little tight.... She'd put on five pounds over the past ten days. And it was a moment of change that would close a chapter and catapult her life in a new direction.

Claire watched as Nate leaned forward to sign the document. The pen hovered over the blank space as he sent an unspoken query.

"Don't even go there," she warned and, smiling, he signed. Claire added her own signature with a flourish.

"Congratulations, everyone!" Adam retrieved a bottle of champagne from behind his desk. "I know it's only noon. But I think we've all earned it." Popping the cork, he poured the fizzing liquid into paper cups. Claire turned to the couple who'd been so patient.

Peter and Felicity Durell had the relaxed

happy demeanor of two people who'd spent a week reigniting their marriage through a combination of sand, tropical sun and sex. Claire raised her glass in a toast. "I hope you'll be as happy in the house as we were," she toasted.

"Thank you." Felicity was three months pregnant. After toasting, she put the cup down as gingerly as if it was a detonator and smiled at Nate, who looked particularly handsome in dark jeans and a moss-green cashmere sweater that clung to every defined muscle. Remembering her reaction to Nate last time she'd drunk champagne, Claire set down her own cup, untasted. It didn't help the lust. A light had been switched on inside her and she couldn't switch it off.

"This time next week, honey, we'll be home owners." Peter leaned over and kissed his wife. They'd gone for a quick settlement. Claire needed cash to finish the boat and she wanted to reimburse Nate quickly. She'd already transferred some things to the bach—kitchen appliances, newer beds and linen. All that remained was to box up what she intended keeping and send it with the furniture to storage.

She glanced at her watch and stood. "I hate to sign and run but Nate and I are due at my lawyer's."

As long as Jo's medical checkup went well—please, God—he'd leave tonight, taking a feeder flight from Whangarei to Auckland to catch a connection to L.A.

And keeping busy was the way Claire avoided dwelling on that.

The first thing Jules did when they reached her office was try to talk Nate out of resigning from the trust.

"I've changed my mind. I think you've got a lot to offer." She glanced at Claire. They'd discussed this briefly on the phone, but Claire had left Jules to raise the idea with Nate. His choice, she'd stressed. Maintaining the trust would safeguard the bach against the possibility of claims against Claire's new business venture.

Nate shook his head. "It's too complicated with me living in another country."

"Not if we modify the trust so that Claire and I sign for cash withdrawals up to a pre-agreed amount and organize an electronic signature for you." Jules had agreed to replace Steve as third trustee. She sat back in her office chair and crossed her legs. "Really, you're only looking at an annual general meeting and that can be done over Skype."

"Leave it now, Jules," Claire said after a glance at Nate. "Excusing Nate from the trust was part of our deal when he agreed to come home. I'll ask Ellie to step in for him." She'd hoped Nate might have changed his mind, because Jules was right, his advice had proven invaluable, but she completely related to his need for a safe distance.

"Okay… But it'll take me another few days to sort out the paperwork."

Nate straightened in his chair. "I thought we were signing everything off today."

"I figured you'd agree, so I didn't prepare alternative documents."

Claire frowned. "But I told you that Nate's leaving tonight if Jo gets the all-clear." Nervously she checked her watch. Nate should be getting a call from Dan anytime now.

"Tonight?" said Jules. "I thought you said Tuesday." Five days away? She thought no such thing, Claire decided. Their friend was trying to play matchmaker.

"Well, where the hell does that leave us?" Nate demanded.

"It leaves us with Jules putting a rush on documents, doesn't it, Ms. Browne?"

Jules returned a limpet gaze. "It would, except I've got back-to-back appointments today and tomorrow. Then it's the weekend. What say we meet again Monday?"

"No," Claire and Nate said together.

"In that case—" Nate's cell rang, interrupting her, and they all tensed.

Nate checked the number and swallowed.

"It's Dan…. Hey, mate. How'd the specialist's appointment go?"

"She's clear." Dan's voice was jubilant. "Jo's been given the all-clear. We've passed another hurdle."

Relief swept over him like a wave so powerful that Nate forgot his annoyance at Jules. "That's great." He gave the two women a thumbs-up and they shrieked and jumped up and down, hugging each other. "Dan, that's great news."

"You're telling me…. Hell, my hands are shaking."

"It's reaction," Nate said. He was feeling a little shaken himself. "Can you hear Claire and Jules?" He held out the phone, they yahooed louder, then returned the cell to his ear.

Dan laughed. "We have to celebrate this," he said. "By hell crikey, do we have to celebrate this." He whooped suddenly, a sound of joy and release. "We're coming up Saturday night— me, Jo, Ross and Viv. And don't give me any bullshit about leaving tonight. I need you to celebrate with us, plus you owe Jo big-time for not showing up to our wedding. Tell Claire to book a restaurant in Whangarei. We'll stay in a hotel. No way is our first baby being conceived in a tent…. Hang on… Yeah, honey, we're making babies…. Nate, I'll confirm details later. I have to go kiss my wife."

Nate rang off and gave the others an update, too elated to immediately consider the ramifications of staying. "That's fantastic," Jules said. "And it takes the pressure off the paperwork."

Nate turned to Claire. "Looks like you're stuck with me until Monday." Her eyes revealed her thoughts when she forgot to guard them and he saw the same mix of dismay and reprieve he felt himself.

He wanted to go only slightly more desperately than he wanted to stay.

DURING LUNCH WITH ELLIE, Nate and Lewis at the waterfront restaurant, Claire made two trips to the bathroom, solely to panic. Her second visit she sat on the closed seat in a toilet stall and obsessively shredded toilet tissue into tiny squares, trying to regain perspective. What was another few days really? They'd handled it so far, hadn't they?

Except she felt like a marathoner within sight of the finish line who'd just been told the race had been extended another fifteen kilometers. Frankly, Claire didn't think she had the reserves. Nate had to leave for her to regain her emotional equilibrium.

Sitting jammed next to him in one of the restaurant's small booths didn't help. Every time he moved, a warm shoulder or thigh brushed against hers. She knew Nate was as self-conscious as she was because he kept asking the waiter if one of the bigger tables had come free. Even when perfectly innocuous conversation flowed between and around them, their sexual awareness only got stronger for being repressed.

She couldn't sit here forever; they'd wonder where she was. Standing, Claire lifted the toilet seat, let the myriad scraps of toilet tissue flutter to a watery grave and flushed. Hopefully, Lewis and Ellie would have finished dessert by now; she'd ask for the check on the way back to the table.

She exited the cubicle, washed her hands and grabbed a paper towel, resisting the urge to shred it. She could have kissed Nate this morning, seeing Lewis so happily recalling his dad. Claire imagined that chaste peck of gratitude turning into a carnal, tongue-thrusting, body-grinding… Oh, my God. Returning to the basin, she turned on the tap and splashed cold water on her face, then stared at herself through dripping lashes.

Four more days. She dried her face on a paper towel, practiced her yoga breath and straightened her shoulders. "I can do that."

She returned to the booth as Nate was saying, "So while we were trying to talk to him—" He saw Claire and stopped.

"Mum, have you heard this story?" Lewis demanded, his eyes shining. "About how Dad and Lee saved a baby's life?"

"No." Somehow her son could draw Nate out where Claire had failed—and she rejoiced in it for both their sakes. She slid into the booth, bracing herself against the inevitable touch of Nate's warm thigh.

"Keep going," Ellie urged. "You'd been patrolling for weeks, collecting intel." The slang sounded strange on her tongue.

Glancing at Claire, Nate pushed aside his empty plate. His reluctance to tell stories was to do with her, she realized, and tried not to be hurt by that.

His leg accidentally touched hers. "Where was I?" he said distractedly. At least he was finding their physical proximity as hard as she was.

"You weren't making any progress with this village headman," Lewis said. "That's like the boss, Mum," he clarified importantly.

"Even though his village was being raided by the insurgents," Nate added. He picked up his water glass and took a sip. "One visit we were trying to find common ground with him, when this young woman approached Lee. We'd been in the area long enough for him to have treated a few locals—she must have known he was our medic. She carried a little girl, who was fever-ish, semiconscious. The second he spotted her, the headman started screaming and shooing her away. Sobbing, she argued with him, but he didn't budge. Other villagers pulled her into a building."

Claire leaned forward. "Did you follow her?"

"We're trained to respect local customs," he said. "If they want help, great. If not, we accept the headman's authority."

"But her baby needed medical treatment," Ellie protested.

"Their country, their rules," Nate said, and there was a soldier's inflection in his voice. "It's tough, but it's necessary to gain their trust. Except then Lee muttered to Steve, 'Symptoms match that baby I treated last week.' Unfortunately, that village sought our help too late, the baby died."

Claire shivered, her gaze going protectively to Lewis, but though his eyes widened, he said, "What happened next?"

"Through an interpreter, Steve started reasoning with the headman," Nate said. "The elder kept shaking his head. It was the same week you'd taken a tumble," he said to Lewis, "and been in the hospital overnight with suspected concussion. Suddenly your dad lost it. He started yelling at the old man, said he deserved to have rebels wipe out his goddamn village if he couldn't put a child's life before his pride."

"How did he take that?" Ellie said, aghast.

"Glared back, not saying a word," Nate replied. "When Steve ran out of steam, we shoved him in the truck because it was clear he'd blown whatever chance we had of getting onside with this guy.

"Next thing, the headman is standing in front of the bull bar beckoning Lee. We got out. The elder shook his head and pointed. Only Lee." Nate took another sip of his water. Clearly, he found this difficult.

Lewis propped his chin in his hand. "And then?" he prompted.

"Your dad said no, and the headman walked away. Lee insisted he'd take his chances. He disappeared with the elder, leaving the rest of us to sweat it out, rifles cocked. Thirty minutes later Lee reappeared. Another hour, he said, and the little girl would have been past saving. The interpreter said the old man relented because Steve had lost it. 'Then,' said the interpreter, 'he know you geev a sheet.'"

"What does a sheet have to do with it," said Ellie, confused.

"A shit, Nana," Lewis clarified.

Ellie frowned. "Language." She dabbed her

eyes with a napkin. "But what a wonderful story."

"It is," Claire said softly.

Nate looked at her. "Later, Steve said that if he couldn't be there for his own child, he could at least be there for someone else's."

Her anger sprang out of nowhere. One second Claire was trying not to cry, the next struggling to swallow bitter words.

"That's so like Steve," said Ellie. "Always putting other people first. Just like his father."

Claire stood abruptly. "I need some fresh air." Ignoring their astonished faces, she escaped the restaurant and stalked across the waterfront piazza. She stopped at the edge of the quay where she struggled to bring her temper under control by counting the spars and masts of the small yachts bobbing in the marina.

"Honey, what's wrong?" Oh, no, Ellie had followed.

She'd never told Steve's mother about her son's decision to accept one more tour. It would be too cruel to add another "if only" to the ones already haunting Ellie. But today the urge to scream, "Your bloody son broke his word, that's what's wrong!" was so strong that sweat broke out on Claire's forehead. "I'm not feeling well," she managed to say.

"You don't have to pretend to me." Her bangles jangled as Ellie hugged her. "Nate's story upset you, didn't it?" Claire tried to return her mother-in-law's affectionate embrace.

"Yes," she said tightly. "It upset me."

"How about I take Lewis shopping for a couple of hours, give you space to have a good cry? You let Nate drive you home and I'll drop Lewis off later."

"Bless you, Ellie." There was no reserve now in her hug.

Nate exited the restaurant, pocketing his wallet, Lewis behind him. Claire avoided Nate's gaze. Only he had the information to join the dots, understand that this was anger, not grief.

"You okay?" he said quietly.

Ellie took charge. "She's not feeling well. Nathan, take her home so she can have a little lie-down. Lewis, I'm taking you shopping for those Converse skaters you wanted."

Her son's worried frown lightened. "Cool, thanks... But are you really okay, Mum?"

He glanced at Nate then added valiantly, "I can look after you if you want."

Despite her distress, Claire was moved. "It's only a headache." She touched his cheek. "Nothing a nap won't cure. You go with Nana."

She dreaded Nate raising the subject when they were alone, but he didn't say a word until they were thirty minutes into the drive. "The stories about Steve haven't helped, have they?" he said. "To forgive him."

Claire stared out the passenger window. Green fields rolled by, pastoral and peaceful, grating on her nerves. "Don't take this on yourself. It's not your war!"

He didn't respond. A woman, she thought sourly, would have tried to make her feel better, told her it was okay to feel snarly and mean. Nate's silence felt like disappointment. Claire glared at his profile.

"What do you want from me, Nate?" she demanded. "Reassurance that I'll always love Steve? Of course I will. You want me to focus on the good times instead of the bad? Okay, let me tell you my favorite memory. After every deployment, Steve would walk in the door, drop his bag, open his arms and holler, 'Daddy's home.' And our little boy would hurl himself at his father."

Even distressed, she felt the buoyancy, the sheer joy of that moment. "As Lewie grew older he got self-conscious and would hesitate. And Steve would boom, 'Get over here, son, and give your old man a hug.'" Her voice cracked. "'Don't you know, Daddy's home?'"

She returned to staring out the window. They were traversing the mangroves, nearly in Stingray Bay. Close to full tide, some of the smaller trees looked to be on tiptoe trying to keep their leafy heads above water. Claire knew how they felt. "Steve had a big heart and there was always plenty to go around," she said bitterly. "But in the end he put the SAS first."

Nate's free hand closed over hers, clenched in her lap. "Even if I can forgive him for leaving me," she said, "I can't forgive him for leaving Lewis. He needs his dad more than ever and Steve's not here because he wanted one more tour. When Lewis acts out because he's lost, because he's hurting…that's when I want to rage at Steve. If he couldn't put me first, he should have put our son first. I should have *made* him!"

His grip tightened. "Blaming yourself won't help anybody."

"Coming from you…" she said with a weary laugh, opened the window, let the wind dry her wet cheeks. "You know the last thing Steve said to me before he left for tour? 'I swear, honey, I'll make it up to you when I come home.' And I said—" Her voice broke, tears streamed down her face. "'The only promise I need from you is that you'll stay safe.'"

Loosening her hand from Nate's, she opened the glove box and fumbled for the box of tissues. "So that's two promises he reneged on." She dried her eyes, blew her nose and hardened her resolve. "You ever wonder why I don't ask for more details of his death, Nate?" The car bumped gently over the uneven ground of the shared yard. "Because I'm so terribly afraid his last thoughts weren't of us."

"Of course they were." He sounded appalled that she'd think any different.

"You don't know that," she said, beyond weary. "Nobody knows that."

The car stopped beside the bach. Nate jerked on the hand brake. "You were," he repeated fiercely.

Shaking her head, Claire got out of the car. "Believe that if you need to," she said. "I can't."

NATE STARED AFTER Claire as she disappeared into the bach.

Steve's last words rang in his ears, resonating on a whole new level. "Tell Claire I'm sorry."

Sorry that he was leaving her? Or sorry he was breaking his promise? It dawned on Nate with blinding force that he held the missing puzzle piece that might help Claire forgive Steve.

He'd wrestled with telling her many times after the ambush, desperate to be punished when self-hatred wasn't enough. But he could never justify the pain that would cause her.

Instead, she doubted Steve's love, doubted his love for their son. Which pain was worse? The scales that had always been weighted against telling her the truth were now finely balanced. For some ten minutes he sat in the car agonizing.

Which was the lesser evil, which the greater good?

She had to know. For the sake of her relationship with Steve. For the sake of Steve's relationship with Lewis, because Claire might not always be able to contain her anger. This then was his ultimate penance—telling the woman he loved that he'd left her husband to die.

He glanced at the dashboard clock. They had a couple of hours before Lewis arrived home. Nate could pack and leave before then, because once he told Claire, she'd want him gone. Sick to his stomach, he followed her.

He'd never allowed himself to consider a future with her. This shouldn't hurt as much as it did.

She was emptying her bag on the dining room table when he walked in. "I don't want to talk about this anymore," she said, picking out a Tylenol bottle from the debris.

Nate forced himself to say the words. Forced himself because it was the right thing to do. "Steve didn't die instantly."

Claire turned. "What?"

"The explosion twisted the front of the Humvee and trapped his lower leg."

"Oh, my God." She fumbled to pull out a chair and sat down hard, her expression stricken.

Nate looked at the floor because it was the only way he could finish telling this. "I tried to free him after we'd stabilized Ross." Involuntarily his fingers flexed. He could still feel the weight of the crowbar, slippery with blood and sweat, still recall his increasing desperation as he strained every muscle to bend the twisted bull bar.

His body might be standing in a living room in Stingray Bay, but he was back in Afghanistan, struggling to free Steve. "We were under heavy fire," he said. "They had an RPG launcher. With every shot, their aim improved." There was a tremor in his voice, a tremor in every limb. "Steve told me to go," he rasped. "I did."

He heard Claire suck in a breath. No sugarcoating this.

"I told him I'd come back for him, but we both knew there wouldn't be time for that. As I hauled Ross over my shoulder, Steve said…" Nate lifted his gaze, met Claire's shell-shocked eyes. "'Tell my family I love them. Tell Claire I'm sorry.'" He returned his gaze to the floor. "I should have stayed. I used Ross's life as an excuse to save my own. In battle, a soldier has only one certainty. That his brothers will never leave him…" The trembling in his limbs reached his voice. "That he'll never be abandoned." His eyes burned, but he would not cry. He had no right.

Instead, he waited, arms held rigidly by his sides, for whatever punishment Claire wanted to mete out. If she told him to crawl out of here like the yellow-bellied coward he was, Nate would do it. For the first time he registered that his shoes were flecked with grass—the mowing contractor had been in their absence.

He could hear Claire's breathing, halfway between a sob and a gasp, but made no move to touch her. That would only be adding insult to injury. Her chair scraped across the floor as she stood up.

Claire stumbled into him, her arms encircling his waist. She rested her cheek against his chest. For a moment he stood frozen in bewilderment. "What are you doing?"

Her arms tightened—such a powerful clasp for a small woman. "It's not your fault." Then she began to cry, great wrenching sobs that forestalled further argument. Gently, Nate freed his arms, shepherded Claire to the couch and held her while she wept.

CHAPTER EIGHTEEN

CLAIRE FELT THE SAME horror, the same shocked disbelief as in those early days following Steve's death. Nate left her briefly to find a box of tissues and a blanket, which he laid over her shoulders. "Just tell me he didn't suffer," she sobbed as he gathered her close again.

"He didn't suffer." The conviction in his voice comforted her.

"It's so hard to bear, Nate," she wept. "So hard."

He rocked her in his arms. "He died loving you and Lewis so much," he said brokenly. "Maybe his last words were an apology? Forgive him, Claire, please. Don't abandon him like I did."

She struggled to a sitting position and fumbled for the tissues. "I'll forgive him," she said when she'd blown her nose, "when you forgive yourself."

Nate's mouth tightened.

"Steve would never think three men dying instead of one was justified. If the situation had been reversed, you would have done exactly the same thing."

"You don't know that." Bleakly he repeated her earlier words. "I don't know that."

"Yes, I do." Integrity was in every fiber of this man's being. "You had no choice but to leave Steve and carry Ross to safety and he had no choice but to make you," she argued passionately. "Because you're both good men." She wept again for all of them. "Can't you see it took as much courage to leave as it did to send you away?"

"I was running for cover when the Humvee got hit, and the blast threw me into a ditch. I came to with Ross sprawled unconscious on top of me, looking at a patch of blue sky through the black smoke. And my first feeling was relief that I was still alive. Not concern, not grief but gladness, Claire. That's what I can't live with."

"Oh, Nate." Her heart broke for him. "Our primary instinct is survival, don't blame yourself for that."

He shook his head and she felt helpless against his guilt. He would never have left Steve if he didn't have Ross's life to save. He always put others before himself. And Steve had used that to make Nate go. Suddenly she saw her way forward.

"Steve saved your life," she said. "Don't you dare dishonor his sacrifice by wasting it in misplaced guilt." Claire gathered all the sternness she could muster. "Don't be selfish."

Nate winced. "Have I been selfish?" he said, and she had to frown to hold back tears.

"Yes." Steve had made the wrong decision in going on tour and she and Lewis would forever pay the price of that. But he'd made right choices, too. Unable to save himself, he'd saved Nate, and by saving Nate, he'd saved Ross. For the first time since his death, Claire understood him, and in understanding him she let go of the anger. It had always been a defense mechanism. Her heart overflowed with love—for Steve, for Nate, for herself and Lewis. There was enough to go around again, for everyone.

She cupped Nate's jaw in her hands, looked deep into his eyes; let him see the truth in hers. "I forgive Steve," she said. "And I forgive you, Nate. Do you hear me? And if I can forgive you, then it's only arrogance that stops you forgiving yourself."

Tears filled his eyes. She couldn't ever remember him crying, not ever, even when Steve and Lee died. He bent over his legs and wept and she wrapped her arms around his broad back, holding him while he did, her own grief spent.

"It's going to be okay," she told him. And believed it.

By the time Ellie dropped Lewis home, it was dark. They arrived with a newspaper parcel of fish and chips, which the four of them ate with squeezes of lemon juice, to cut through the delicious grease of the battered schnapper. Claire licked her fingers when she finished and said it was one of the best meals she'd ever eaten.

She could feel more tears building for another cry later, but she couldn't regret Nate's confession.

Showers hadn't done much to repair the effects of this afternoon's catharsis; both of them looked like wrecks, pale with red-rimmed eyes.

Claire told Ellie she thought she had a cold coming, which had triggered her headache. Ellie looked at Nate and suggested he might be catching it, too, which enabled him to plead an early night and leave for the boat shed immediately after dinner.

Claire waited until he'd left, then said, "Oh, I forgot to mention something about tomorrow." Running after him, she hugged him briefly and hard. "Sleep well, Nate."

He returned the pressure, dropping a light kiss on her hair. "Good night, Claire."

They both needed to be alone now, but as he walked into the darkness, the flashlight beam dancing ahead, she felt easy about him. He was going to be okay. She was going to be okay. She had to believe that.

On her return a few minutes later, Ellie and Lewis were watching TV. "Stay the night," she said to Steve's mother. "Drive home in daylight. You take my bed and I'll sleep in Lewis's room. I'll lend you nightwear."

"You know I will," Ellie said. "It's been a busy day."

"Let me make you a hot chocolate."

"Should you be in bed, honey?"

"Soon."

After she'd delivered the drinks, Claire nudged in between them on the couch, suddenly loving them so much that she could have cried again, simply for the gift of them in her life.

Ellie glimpsed her watery eyes as she passed her the hot chocolate. "Don't you give me your cold," she warned. "It's full on in the shop this week."

Claire laughed. There went her precious moment. "I'm thinking it's more a spring hay fever thing. Really, I'm feeling a lot better. What's on the box?"

"Top Gear," Lewis said, his gaze glued to the television. His favorite British motoring show. He crossed his feet at the ankle, showing off his new Converse shoes—bright red suede.

"Cool shoes," said Claire, and he gave her a swift grin.

"I know."

"Thank you, Nana," she prompted.

"I already said it."

She jabbed him in the ribs.

"Thank you, Nana."

"You're welcome, sweetie.... I wouldn't be surprised if you're getting a cold, Claire. This bach needs more insulation."

"Are you chilly?"

"A little."

"Here." She reached for the blanket folded over the back of the couch and covered everyone. Lewis frowned but didn't protest when Claire snuggled closer. They watched television and sipped their hot chocolate.

Nate had said Steve didn't suffer. She had to keep reminding herself of that. Tears threatened, and she blinked them away. Shortly after his death she'd worked out what she'd been doing at the time of the ambush. Rushing through the supermarket, hurrying to make sure she was home for Lewis when school finished. And now she knew that across the world her husband had been sending his last goodbyes.

"You know, I will turn in," she said.

"Want anything, sweetie?"

"No, I'll leave a nightgown for you on my bed. Good night." She bent to hug her son, distracting him from the television with her intensity.

"What?" said Lewis.

"I love you."

Lewis hesitated. "Me, too." He was already returning his attention to the screen. Claire laughed and embraced Ellie.

"Love you, too," she told her mother-in-law.

"You're very affectionate this evening." But Ellie held on equally tight. "I think your color's returning," she added when they separated.

"I think so, too."

Claire collected nightwear for Ellie, a new toothbrush and clean towel and laid them on her bed. In Lewis's room, she folded back his covers and laid out his pajamas, feeling Steve's presence as she went through the domestic rituals. What mattered was that she'd been keeping the home fires burning when he'd said his goodbyes.

Lewis had taken a framed picture of his dad to Dan's. She noticed he'd finally unpacked and replaced it on the nightstand. Picking it up, Claire looked at the man who'd shaped her adult life, then hugged it to her breast. "Goodbye, my darling," she whispered. "Rest in peace."

THE BOAT SHED WAS COLD when Nate unlocked the side door. Pointing the flashlight at the barometer in the wheelhouse, he saw the temperature was actually warmer tonight than it'd been the last couple. Odd. The smell of varnish and new paint mixed with packed dirt permeated the air and the handrail slid smoothly against his palm as he descended the narrow stairs into the cabin and found the switch.

He stood for a moment after turning it on, looking around the cabin's womblike interior, conscious of the jewel colors of the soft furnishings, the golden glow of the kauri table and galley counter. Kicking off his shoes, he lay on top of the bedcovers and stared at the pearlescent white of the low ceiling overhead, its smoothness a testament to Claire's careful painting.

His mind was an exhausted blank, but his senses were alive to his surroundings, sensitive in a way they hadn't been for a long time. To shapes and colors, to temperature, to smells. He fancied he could even distinguish the lingering aroma of coffee left in the plunger on the counter from this morning.

On impulse, Nate got up and warmed some in the microwave, adding two sugars and milk. He cupped it in his hands, and the warmth permeated to the bone, then lifted the mug to his nose and inhaled deeply. The first taste was sweet. Two and he'd had enough of the richness.

Satisfied, he put it down and returned to bed,

stripping to his underwear before sliding between the sheets. The cool linen softness bringing unexpected tears to his eyes. He wiped them away with his forearm, felt the skin prickle as they dried.

He closed his eyes without turning off the light. Only then did Nate register the silence. The boat shed was exposed to the elements and any breeze rattled the loose roofing iron. It was eerie somehow. Even unnerving.

And then faintly, high in the eaves, he caught the faint chirrup of baby birds through the open cabin door. He'd forgotten to shut it and the light was disturbing them. Reluctantly he flicked the switch and prepared for another insomniac's night.

But tonight the darkness was friendly. *Tomorrow,* he thought, his body growing heavy as he relaxed into sleep. *Tomorrow I'll tell her the rest.*

But it would be okay because there was nothing left to be ashamed of.

CHAPTER NINETEEN

TWO DAYS LATER Nate stuck his head around the door of the Whangarei house. "That's the tools sorted," he said to Claire. "A sweep-out and the garage is done." She was sitting on the wooden floor in the living room, taping up the last of the boxes destined for the bach. Only the furniture going into storage remained and the movers would pick it up this afternoon.

She started almost guiltily and picked up the tape. "Oops," she said. "You caught me slacking off."

"It's been a long morning." He hesitated. From the kitchen came the bang of a cupboard door where Ellie was scrubbing out shelves. Even from here, he could smell the cleaning products. "You okay?"

"Fine," she reassured him, pulling tape along the box. "I've been moving on for a while."

There were dents in the carpet from the coffee table, pinholes in the wall left by the picture hooks and a couple of scuff marks on the skirting board from a ball or skateboard. A good house, a family house.

"Still, it can't be easy leaving a place you and Steve lavished so much DIY on," Nate said. It had become a standing joke in the unit, the Langfords spent years renovating.

As he'd hoped, Claire laughed. "And it only took fifteen years to knock into shape."

"Lewis, take that dratted ball outside!" Ellie's raised voice wafted from the kitchen. "I've just washed that cupboard door."

"It was an accident!"

Claire pushed to her feet and picked up the taped box. "Time for an intervention."

"Let's take a break," Nate suggested. "We've been working all morning."

"Good idea, there's a picnic hamper in the car."

"I'll get it. Here, give me that." He took the box from her. "Get some fresh air."

Smiling, she touched his arm. "Thanks."

There was an understanding between them now, a quiet and considerate tenderness. Physical awareness was still there, but it was muted, patient, waiting for the right time. This period was a deep breath between the past and the future. Steve was forefront on both their minds, but gently.

Nate felt like a man woken from a coma—

tentative, stretching limbs, unable to believe his luck. He was waiting for a relapse into guilt. It didn't come. Quietly, he accustomed himself to peace while Claire mourned Steve again. For now, being near was enough.

While Claire unpacked lunch on a blanket under the apple tree, Nate competed with Lewis to see who could bounce a soccer ball on their knee the longest. Lewis was winning hands down.

"Twenty-seven, twenty-eight..." The ball angled off the grinning teenager's knee and landed in a rosebush. "Don't destroy the garden," Ellie scolded from the rug. "They're not your plants anymore." She was fragile this morning.

"Man," Lewis muttered, "I can't do anything right today."

Nate rescued the ball from the rosebush. "Let's shoot basketball hoops instead."

"What, so I can whip your ass in something else?"

"Lewie, watch your language," called his grandmother.

Scowling, Lewis opened his mouth for a retort, but Nate forestalled him. "Ellie, you were a good netballer, weren't you?" Steve had once told him his mother had played competitively. "What was your position again?"

She looked over from the picnic rug, shading her face with one hand. "Goal shoot."

"Come help me teach your grandson a lesson."

"Heavens, Nathan, I can't leap around a basketball hoop now. Not with my knees."

"You can't move with the ball in netball, is that correct?"

She nodded. "Once you're in possession you have to ground one foot."

"So we'll set a mark and shoot from a stationary position."

"I don't think so," she said doubtfully. But she was tempted, he could tell.

"Go ahead, Ellie," Claire encouraged. "I'll finish getting lunch ready."

She glanced at her grandson who was trying not to laugh and a glint came into her eyes. "What do you think, sweetie, can an old lady play?"

"If she wants to." Lewis shrugged, obviously humoring her.

Nate shared a conspirator's grin with Claire. Steve's competitive gene hadn't come from his dad.

"Set the distance, Ellie," he said, and threw her the ball.

She took her time to settle on a distance some

four feet away from the goal then marked it with a branch snapped from a hydrangea.

Nate resisted the temptation to tease her about that. Ellie bounced the ball a few times, assessing its weight.

Then she raised her arms, stretching one leg behind for balance, as gracefully as a dancer, her gaze intent as she gauged the distance to the hoop.

Curiosity raised Lewis's brows.

Ellie launched the ball—it fell short by a foot. "Damn it!"

"Language, Nana!"

"I'm out of practice."

They gave her five shots to warm up and then she took them both to the cleaners, winning with a score of eleven from twelve hoops. By the end of the competition, everyone was having fun. A light mood that lasted through lunch.

Nate was in the hall, returning from dumping a load of boxes in the car when Claire called his name.

He turned. In three quick steps she walked over to him. Before he could register her intent, she stood on tiptoe and brushed a kiss against his mouth. "Thanks," she said, and walked on to the kitchen with the picnic remnants.

Nate stood rooted, his mouth still processing the sensation of their first kiss, warm and fervent. Promising so much more. Then he caught sight of Ellie standing in the living room doorway with a box, her eyes full of dismay.

Nate held his composure. "You want me to stow that in the car?" he said.

She looked down at the box as if she'd forgotten she was carrying it.

"It's not heavy," she said, "but there're another two in the living room. If you could carry those?"

"Sure." He moved past her, unable to talk about this. It was too uncertain, too new. She waited for him and they walked to the car together.

"When are you heading back to L.A.?" she blurted as he stacked the boxes in the station wagon's trunk.

Nate met her gaze calmly. It was natural for her to feel this way. "I haven't confirmed a flight yet," he said. "I figured I'd reassess after the weekend." Lewis was staying with Ellie tonight while Nate and Claire attended Jo's celebratory dinner. It would be the first occasion since Lewis had come home that they'd be alone together.

The same thought must have occurred to Ellie because she frowned. "I'm very fond of you, Nathan."

He braced himself.

"My daughter-in-law has experienced a lot of change over recent months—working to launch a new business, giving up her job, moving to the bach. And that's on the back of the very hard time Lewis gave us, all on top of Steve's death."

Her gaze returned to his. "All that has taken a toll on her, though she'd deny it. I don't think Claire realizes how vulnerable she still is." Ellie paused, as if searching for the right words. "She's severing another major tie today. Sometimes you jump into things to distract yourself from the gap. It's so difficult, you see, after losing the love of your life as we've done." Her expression softened as she laid a hand on his forearm. "You've been a good friend to Claire, Nathan. I hope you'll accept my advice in the intended spirit."

"You two are close," he said. "You're looking out for her."

"Steve would want me to."

He nodded. "He would."

She searched his face, and then, satisfied, returned to the packing. Nate stood by the car another minute. The house was in a well-established suburb and the street was overhung with flowering cherries. In mid-October their frilly pink blossoms shed like confetti on footpaths and verges, extraordinarily pretty.

Absently, he caught a petal as it fell, then

dropped it and pulled his cell out of his jeans pocket. "Jules, I need the trust stuff ready for signing first thing Monday morning. And no excuses this time. Incidentally, don't tell Claire I lost my job. I'm cool with it and you know she'll only feel guilty." Which hopefully would guilt Jules into keeping his secret. She was as protective of Claire as he was. Nate's second call was to Air New Zealand. "I'd like to book a flight for Monday night."

"Zander rang," he told Claire later. "If I'm not airborne within forty-eight hours I'll lose my job." He was old friends with guilt and told the white lie easily. Even when it broke his newly healed heart all over again.

You RUSHED THINGS with that kiss. Clearly Nate isn't ready. Give him some space.

Claire repeated that mantra constantly the rest of the day, but common sense did nothing to dispel the sense of hurt, even betrayal, she felt. Fair enough if Nate had to return to L.A., but did he have to be so anxious to leave?

As she showered for the celebration dinner that evening, she reminded herself that Nate didn't owe her anything. He'd made no move toward a romantic relationship. This new closeness was all to do with bonding over Steve and anything else was in her head.

Some stubborn inner voice insisted it wasn't, but Claire shut that down with logic and the blow-dryer. From the moment she'd kissed him, Nate had become aloof and uncommunicative. On the two occasions they'd been left alone, he found some pretext to leave.

It hurt.

Wrapped in a towel, she left the bathroom, crossed the deck and went inside the bach. Nate had been nowhere in sight when she returned from dropping Lewis at his grandmother's—hiding out on *Heaven Sent* probably—though their ride was due in thirty minutes and the boat had no shower connected.

In her bedroom, she opened the dresser drawer, grimaced at the sexy robe Ellie had given her and pushed it aside to find underwear.

Boohooing and feeling rejected wouldn't change the fact that Nate wasn't ready. Neither would a confrontation. The very worst thing she could do was to start coming across as needy.

From her closet, she pulled a red dress, the one she'd bought for her leaving function at work, the one that heralded the advent of Captain Claire, bold, bright and fearless.

It was better this way.

Briskly, Claire zipped up the dress and started applying makeup, using the mirror above the dresser. She could concentrate on establishing her business and Nate would have time to settle his thinking—miss her, hopefully. And after a couple of months she'd go get him.

Maybe.

If she had the courage.

If he sent the right signals.

If he didn't take a lover in the meantime.

Claire realized her shoulders had slumped and straightened them, picking up the eyelash curler Ellie had foisted on her. "Stop panicking," she admonished her reflection. "You haven't given up on him. You're just giving him space." Ugh, that tweeniespeak. Claire screwed up her nose. She was thirty-four, for heaven's sake. She shouldn't have to deal with this crap.

Scowling, she darkened her lashes with mascara, made her eyes mysterious and smoky, and chose her most luscious lipstick. That would show him.

Lack of recent practice meant she smudged it. With an expletive, Claire scrubbed off the excess and reapplied it. Who was she kidding? She'd never been good at flirty games. So she'd quietly assess the situation over the next couple of months, and decide her move from there. Carefully, she blotted the excess lipstick with a tissue. She didn't have to be Braveheart tonight.

Only Monday, when she said goodbye.

NATE LEFT IT AS LATE as possible to arrive at the bach to shower and change, tapping on the patio door as he passed to let Claire know he'd arrived. The bathroom was still steamy from her shower, the mirror fogged and the air fragrant with feminine potions.

He showered quickly, and then dressed in dark pants and an open-necked white shirt, topped with a dark gray jacket. Styling himself came automatically now, but as he shaved using the small bathroom mirror, slightly mottled with age, he wondered what Zander would make of him.

It occurred to him he'd miss the bastard— despite Zee's faults, they'd been mates. Zander would miss Nate more because the rocker had so few real friends. But he also knew that asking for his job back would be tantamount to posting a Kick Me sign on his butt. Anyway it didn't matter. Nate's professional reputation was sound; he'd have no difficulty picking up another A-lister. The thought depressed him.

Mentally bracing himself, he entered the bach. Claire was standing in the middle of the living room inserting gold hoop earrings. She blinked when she saw him. "Wow," she said lightly. "It's not hard to get the Hollywood back. You look gor…very smart."

Nate remembered to close the slider. "So do you."

Understatement. Her scoop-necked dress was an overlay of chiffon tiers over a silk sheath, sleeveless and very sexy in traffic-light red.

Red for stop, Nate reminded himself, but he couldn't tear his eyes off her. One shoulder of the dress had a tie feature and as he stared, she twisted it into a chiffony bow. Like a present just waiting to be unwrapped.

Setting his jaw, Nate checked his watch and then walked to the window looking for head-lights. "You'll get cold without a coat."

"I have a pashmina shawl."

It was winter-white silk and cashmere, noth-ing provocative about it. His brain threw up an image of it wrapped around her naked body. Nate stared out the window, desperate for head-lights. "So we're meeting Jules at the restau-rant?"

"Uh-huh." Behind him, Claire squirted on perfume, an Oriental fragrance, sensual and spicy, entirely in keeping with the red dress.

Briefly he closed his eyes and when he opened them a double-cab behemoth of an ute was bumping over the grass. His white char-ger tooted.

"They're here, let's go." He turned around.

"Are we okay, Nate?" There was something

in her quiet directness that made him realize he'd hurt her.

"Sure we are." He smiled reassuringly. Of course this was tough—the right path always was. "If I've been distracted, it's because I'm thinking of all that needs doing when I get home." He used the word deliberately, though L.A. had never felt like home to him.

It worked. Claire stopped searching his eyes and dropped her own. "It'll be fun going on tour," she said lightly. "Berlin first, isn't it?" She picked up her bag, a glittering beaded thing that matched her strappy stilettos. "How exciting."

"Yes." His spirits heavy, Nate opened the ranchslider and stood aside to let her pass. "I'm looking forward to it."

If the conversation got any more stilted they could build a pole house on it. As she walked by, another scented tendril tangled around his senses. Grimly, Nate followed her to the ute.

The powerful engine was idling and as they approached, the front passenger door opened and Jo climbed out, dressed in an emerald-green dress that suited her red hair. The two women met in an emotional embrace. "I'm so happy for you," Claire said.

Over her shoulder, Dan's bride smiled at him. "Hi, Nate." He hadn't attended her wedding, but there was nothing but warm affection in her hazel eyes.

"Hey," he said awkwardly, and hugged her, lifting her off the ground a few inches. "Great news, Jo."

"It hasn't sunk in yet," she confessed as he put her down. "But I'm sure champagne will help. I should warn you, we've already started drinking—" she lowered her voice "—to calm our nerves."

Puzzled, Nate looked toward the ute. Dan's little sister waved through the driver's window. "Our hugs will have to wait," Viv called, pushing a strand of shoulder-length brown hair out of her eyes. "I can't get out or Dan will hijack the driving. You two are in the back with Ross." Nate hadn't seen Viv since her twin's wedding years ago, but Dan had regaled the unit with terrible-twin stories for years, so he knew her as living, breathing dynamite.

"Dan and I are riding shotgun," Jo said, and giggled.

"You *have* been drinking," Claire commented. "You're not a giggler."

"It's nervous hysteria." Jo giggled again.

"Jocelyn Swann Jansen!" Viv warned. "Sisterly solidarity, remember?"

"Yes, ma'am." Winking at Nate, Jo climbed

into the front next to her husband. Dan winced as his sister shoved the gear stick into his thigh.

"Why you have to drive a manual is beyond me," she said, graunching the gears. Her brother groaned.

Ross slung an arm across the back of the seat, behind Claire. "You're doing great, honey," he reassured his fiancée. "These overpriced imports are always tough drives."

Across Claire, Nate stared at him. Ross was anal about driving.

"You're as rusty as hell, sis," Dan complained in the front.

"All the more reason to get practice in while I'm home," she answered cheerfully. "Just remind me to stay on the right side of the road."

"You mean left," everyone chorused in unison.

"She meant the correct side of the road," Ross clarified. "Sheesh, will you all relax! You might want to take your foot off the accelerator a tad here, babe. We're coming up to a T-intersection."

"It's so hard to see without streetlights," Viv commented. "Oh, wait, I've got my lights on low beam." She flicked a switch on the dash. "That's better."

"Okay, that does it," Dan said. "Pull over, I'm driving. Do your refresher in daylight."

"Stay where you are, honey," advised Ross. "Jo gave me shit for years about being a sexist pig when it came to women drivers. I want to make Bridezilla happy."

"You're all heart, Ice-cream." Jo glanced over to the backseat, her dark red curls bouncing with every bump in the road. She grinned at Ross. "Hey, Viv, *Vanity Fair* had an article about the benefits of a long engagement. Remind me to show it to you."

"On the other hand, Viv," Ross said to his love, "we don't want you overtiring yourself trying to keep left and right straight. I've got big plans for our first-night reunion."

"We've talked about this, Ice." Dan twisted his head to complain. "No sexy talk with my sister while I'm within hearing."

"Okay, Shep."

Dan faced forward again and Ross leaned forward to caress Viv's neck. Ice was a guy who needed to be behind the wheel in every endeavor, yet here he was completely relaxed, trusting this madcap woman to carry them safely through a pitch-black night. Nate shook his head in disbelief and beside him, Claire laughed softly.

"Told you things had changed," she murmured.

He found himself laughing, too.

He loved these people. Dan glanced behind to grin at him, then tightened his arm around his wife's shoulders. Jo leaned into him. These two had been friends all their lives, a shift in perception and now they were married.

Nate was conscious of the sweet curves of Claire's body pressed against his side. If he slung his arm across the back of the seat there'd be more room, but that was an intimacy he couldn't indulge.

Ellie was right. This woman was still vulnerable. Just because confession had cleansed his soul didn't mean he'd earned a green light to pursue his buddy's widow. She needed more time to get over the emotional aftermath.

"Are cows an issue on country roads?" Viv said. "I see a shape looming ahead.… Oh, it's okay, it's a tree." She negotiated another sharp bend, sending Claire sliding into him, all soft femininity and seductive fragrance. Inwardly, Nate groaned as he double-checked their seat belts. Monday couldn't come soon enough.

CHAPTER TWENTY

"When did you know," Claire said to Jo, "that your feelings for Dan had changed?" When did your friend become your love?

Claire put down her glass, damning the alcohol that had loosened her tongue.

"When he told me he loved me," Jo said. She looked toward the dance floor of the bar they'd ended up at where her husband boogied with Jules, Viv and Ross. Nate was at the bar replenishing drinks.

"Actually it was a terrible moment," Jo continued. "My health was uncertain, so was my fertility and I'd already decided I couldn't marry him." Struggling with survivor's guilt, Dan had organized their wedding without Jo's consent.

"But he talked you into it?"

"He wore me down. I realized he wasn't going to go away, but more important, I realized he needed me as much as I needed him.... Sometimes you're destined to save each other."

She smiled at Claire with way more comprehension than she could handle. Nervously, Claire sipped her champagne.

Jo took pity on her. "'Course, it was one-sided for Viv and Ross," she said loudly as the couple returned to the table. "She did all the saving. I like to think of my sister-in-law as a little yellow bulldozer reducing the iceberg to rubble."

Claire laughed. Ross and Jo liked nothing better than winding each other up.

"Very droll," he said, pulling out Viv's chair.

"Little pieces of rubble," Viv agreed, planting a kiss on his lips before sitting down.

"Brave words from someone too chicken to set a wedding date."

"I'll marry you next time Nate comes home," said Viv.

Returning from the bar with a tray of drinks, Nate nearly dropped it.

Ross looked at him with spaniel eyes. Hell, Dan was right. His bubbly little sister was diabolical. And not just Viv. Dan, Ross and Jo had spent the whole evening trying to pin him down to a return date.

"Nice try," he said in a tone even Ross knew not to argue with.

"C'mon, babe." Ice pulled his fiancée out of her chair again. "They're playing our song." And dragged her, protesting, onto the dance floor.

Nate took his seat at the other end of the table from Claire and Jo and brooded over a scotch. Dan sat down next to him five minutes later.

"Why don't you ask Claire to dance?"

He wasn't in the mood. "Leave it, Shep."

"Then take your turn dancing with Jules. She's finding tonight hard."

Nate looked across the table at Jules, recognized a kindred spirit and stood. Turned to Dan. "Yeah," his buddy said. "I'll dance with Claire."

"I've only just sat down," Jules protested when he asked her.

"Please don't turn me down," said Nate. "Everyone's watching."

She laughed. "Fine, I'll take pity on you."

He spun her around the floor and discovered she had some skill. Lee had liked to dance; those two would have been something to see.

The music changed to a slow tempo. To Nate's surprise Jules pulled him close, glancing over her shoulder to check Ross and Viv's proximity. Locked in each other's arms, four feet away, they were completely oblivious.

"What the hell are you doing walking away from Claire when you're in love with her?"

Nate was so startled he stopped dancing. Another couple swung into them. "Sorry." He began moving again. "I don't..." He couldn't lie about loving Claire. "Look, this isn't something I'm comfortable discussing with you."

"It's obvious she returns your feelings and yet you're burning her off."

He remained silent. This was none of her business.

Jules gave him an impatient shake. "I'm not backing down, Nate," she said in a loud voice.

Frowning, he steered them to the far corner of the dance floor. "She's making a new life," he said. "I come with baggage from her past that maybe she needs to leave behind." He wasn't articulating this very well. "Right now she's vulnerable and I'm another complication."

"Ellie's been giving her two cents' worth," she said astutely. "Steve's mother is a wonderful woman, but she has a problem with transference. It's Ellie who's feeling vulnerable, not Claire."

"Six months to a year for things to settle," Nate said, guiding her off the dance floor before she could talk him into doing something he shouldn't. "Then I'll come back."

She stopped him as he turned toward their party. "Because there's always tomorrow?" she challenged. "We both know that's not always true. There's only today to tell someone you love them, to put aside your fears and prejudices and neuroses and defense mechanisms, Nate."

Her grip had tightened on his forearm. He removed her hand and cupped it between his own. "I'm so damn sorry you won't get a life with Lee. He was…" Words failed him. How did you encapsulate a man who'd always been larger than life?

"A one-off," she finished for him. "Don't set yourself up for regrets, Nate. Don't ever miss an opportunity through—" She stopped. Forced a smile. "Now I'm doing the transference thing. I'll shut up."

He hugged her. It was easier than words. But she hadn't changed his mind. What Ellie said had struck a chord because they echoed his own doubts.

"I'll keep in touch this time," he said. "I promise."

"NATE'S GOT SOME MISTAKEN idea that you're this fragile flower he has to protect. Damn it, Claire, take the initiative!"

Dragged to the ladies' room on the pretext she had panda eyes, Claire studied Jules's outraged expression in the mirror, then reapplied lipstick in the same siren red as her dress. *False advertising,* she thought. "Jules, I'm not chasing a reluctant man."

"But Ellie—"

"Is right," she interrupted. "I *am* vulnerable." She stuck the lipstick in her clutch bag and closed it with a snap. "So is Nate. No more browbeating. He's not ready to have a relationship and his second thoughts have given me second thoughts."

"Have you kissed?"

Claire blushed. "Not the way you're thinking."

"Then kiss him, Claire, make the first move."

Claire replaced the lipstick in her bag. "I've never kissed an unwilling man and I'm not starting now."

"He's not unwilling, he's scared and noble and... God, this is all bullshit!"

"Why is this so important to you?" she asked gently.

"Because I can't stand for you both to screw this up for lack of courage."

There was something more going on here, but a ladies' room in a busy restaurant wasn't the place to dig deeper.

"So I kiss him," Claire said to placate her. "Let's say the incredible happens and we end up in bed. He still has to fly back to L.A. Monday to go on tour for six months with Zander Freedman."

Jules waved an impatient hand. "Zander fired him days ago," she said.

"What?"

"When Nate decided to stay and make sure you were doing the right thing by throwing all your money into the business."

"Zander fired him?" Claire repeated stupidly.

Jules seized her hands. "And you don't let a guy that decent walk away without putting up some kind of fight."

"WE'RE ALL AT YOUR PLACE FOR breakfast first thing tomorrow," Ross told Claire when she and Jules returned from the bathroom. "Nate suggested making it early to coincide with Ellie and Lewis being there."

"Great idea," Claire said. So Nate was banking on safety in numbers, was he?

"Don't worry about supplies," Jo said. "We'll stop at the supermarket in the morning."

"I'm thinking lots of red meat to replenish energy," Ross said wickedly and pulled a laughing Viv onto his lap.

"With plenty of iron for the mother to be," agreed Dan.

Jo said, "Lover, it could take time to get pregnant, you are aware of that, aren't you?"

"Not the way we do it," Dan promised.

"This sexy-talk embargo works both ways," complained Ross. "But I expect to be the godfather."

"You would," said Jo. "I think we'll go the

celebrity route and have multiple godparents to counter your influence. Heavens, I'm talking like I'm pregnant already." She smiled at her husband. "Your confidence is contagious. I need to touch wood or something to avoid jinxing this.... Ross, bend your head."

"I won't be able to make it," Jules said. "Sunday's the only time I can catch up on billing. Which is why I should go." Despite protests, she hugged everybody and picked up her bag, sending Claire a private wink.

Smiling weakly, Claire lifted her empty glass. "Is there any champagne left in the bottle?"

After Jules disappeared from sight, Jo commented to Claire, "She was sad tonight. Were we too much for her with all the loving-couple stuff?"

"No," Claire said empathically. "It's good to be around happy." She'd hated how Dan and Ross had tiptoed around her after Steve died. It only reminded her of the crippled part of herself, not the survivor's part. "Jules is at a crossroads, that's all."

"Lee would hate that she's lonely," Ross said. "He'd want us to find her another guy."

Claire kept her mouth shut and with a glance reminded Nate to do the same.

"Wow," said Jo. "I hate to say this, Ice-cream, but that's actually a brilliant idea."

"But is she ready?" Viv asked Claire.

"I think so." She spoke cautiously, trying not to telegraph insider information.

"It's a tall order," said Dan. "Who the hell could match Lee?"

"There are a couple of nice guys at base," said Ross.

Claire forgot to be Switzerland. "Are you insane? Jules doesn't want another soldier." She realized as soon as the words left her mouth that Nate would read that the wrong way and a quick glance confirmed it.

"Okay, a desk jockey," Ross said reluctantly. "I guess between the three guys we could rustle one up?"

Nate held up his hands. "Hey, I'm not getting involved. It's a crazy idea."

"It's not something we can leave to these women," Ross explained patiently. "They'll give too much credence to charm, money and good looks. We'll end up with someone we can't respect. I can't do that to Lee."

Only his fiancée attempted to hide her smile. "Now, everyone," Viv cautioned, "you need to encourage Ross's new nurturing side, not mock it."

"Damn right," he said, rewarding her with a smacking kiss. "Keep protecting these quivering, vulnerable feelings and name a wedding date. I'm not pinning my hopes to Nate's schedule once Zander Freedman gets hold of him again."

Claire glanced at Nate, but he was looking into his whiskey.

Viv shook her head, but her tone was admiring. "You never give up, do you, babe?"

"Giving up is for wimps," Ross declared. He grinned at Jo. "Right, Bridezilla?"

The redhead grinned back. "Right, Icecream."

Nervously, Claire picked up her glass and sculled the last of her champagne. And so say all of us.

CHAPTER TWENTY-ONE

THE FOOTBRIDGE ARCHED in a shadowy span above the dark estuary, but a full moon lit their way. Claire waited while Nate paid the cabdriver. The taxi had dropped them off in Stingray Bay South, which shortened the journey from Whangarei by twenty minutes.

They walked to the bridge in silence, her stilettos resonating once they reached the wooden boards. The tide had turned toward the sea and it gurgled past the concrete piles. A fish jumped, landing with a startled splash. *Moonstruck,* thought Claire.

She stopped to lean over the railing and gazed across the black water, sparkling with the reflected gleam and glitter of the night sky.

"Amazing, isn't it," she said, "how much brighter the stars are out of cities."

Nate had walked on ahead. He turned reluctantly and she thought, *What am I doing? He doesn't want this.* "The height doesn't look so daunting at night. Maybe I should get you to push me."

He smiled at that. "Somehow I don't think I'd get the grateful thanks Steve gave me."

"No." Did he know how badly she wanted to touch him? "This is something I have to do for myself."

Returning to her side, Nate leaned his elbows against the railing and looked down. "What stops you? Do you worry you'll hit the surface too hard? Sink too deep?"

"No, it's the gap between bridge and water. The sensation of freefall." Her pashmina slipped from one shoulder. Claire adjusted it. "Do you really have a job to go back to?"

He hesitated. "No."

"You're really keen to get away from me, aren't you," she joked because it hurt too much to do otherwise.

"I'm looking out for you."

"Because I can't do it myself?" Oh, yeah, sarcasm was a wonderful seduction tool.

Eyes wary, Nate faced her. "What do you want from me, Claire?"

Everything. The knowledge bubbled to consciousness like a spring of clear water. She swallowed, trying to find the courage to say it. Silent seconds passed. Nate gestured toward home. "We should walk."

"I can feel you looking at me when you think

I don't notice," she blurted. "It makes my skin tingle."

"That's the cold," he said. Shrugging off his jacket, he held it out at arm's length. "Here."

Claire shook her head. "I don't feel it."

"Only because you've been drinking," he said roughly. Stepping forward, he draped his jacket across her shoulders, the silk lining still warm.

"Three glasses over six hours," she clarified. He stood close, fastening a button to keep the oversized jacket on her smaller shoulders. "Funny, isn't it?" Claire stared at his shirt. "I drank to do something about us and you drank not to." His hands stilled on the button. He must hear her heartbeat. "Unfortunately, like jumping off this bridge," she managed to say, "I find when it comes to the leap I can't quite make my move."

Silence. Claire dared to look up.

Moonlight illuminated a clenched jaw. His expression was impassive, but the yearning deep in his eyes made her suck in a hopeful breath.

"Are you going to kiss me or not?"

He released the jacket. "Not," he rasped.

"Then I'll kiss you." Cupping his nape, she drew his head down, but Nate laid his fingertips over her mouth.

"Some things you can't take back."

Claire lifted his hand. "Some things you don't want to."

Closing the gap, she pressed her mouth tentatively against his. Nate pulled away, catching her fingers in a painful grip. "You're beautiful," he said. "You're the most incredible woman I've ever known. Brave, smart, strong." He dropped her hand. "Emotions have been intense since I told you what happened. Let's not rush into anything."

And suddenly she understood. "You think this might be motivated by pity?"

"I think," Nate said carefully, "that we're both susceptible right now and I'd be taking advantage if I took this further tonight."

Really, perfectly reasonable, yet part of her raged against it.

He must have sensed her frustration. "I will come back," he added quietly.

Claire resisted the urge to tell him she'd heard that before. From Steve. "Fine." She shrugged. "Let's do the sensible thing."

"Claire…"

"You go ahead. I'll catch you up."

Ignoring him, she leaned over the railing and fixed a fierce gaze on the moon reflected below. It reminded her of a shivering white bather treading water. Pathetic.

"I'll wait at the end of the bridge."

"You do that." She was over waiting for a man she loved. As soon as Nate began walking, she shrugged off his jacket, dropped her shawl and stepped determinedly out of her heels. By the time he'd reached the end of the bridge and turned, she was already on the other side of the railing.

"What the hell!"

"One way or another," she called, "I'm moving on tonight."

"Claire, no!" He ran toward her. Closing her eyes, she jumped.

Her body hit the water with a resounding splash and as it closed over her head, cold squeezed the last of the champagne bubbles out of her bloodstream and constricted her lungs. Claire broke the surface on a giant gasp. "It's freeeeeezing," she yelled, every molecule burning.

Above, Nate was hastily stripping off his clothes.

"No, I'm fine!" she hollered. "Bring my stuff." The current drifted her shivering body downstream, her dress, lightly billowing in chiffon petals.

Expression anxious, Nate hesitated and Claire waved reassuringly and kicked into a fast crawl while she still had blood flow. The silk sheath of the underdress wrapped her body like a second skin, fortunately short enough not to impede her kicks.

And that was luck—she hadn't given safety a second thought. Maybe she was tipsier than she realized. The icy water made its languid way into her bones and Claire kicked faster. This is insane. But she felt more alive than she'd felt for months. *We did it,* she told the little girl she'd once been. *We climbed our Everest. We can do anything now.*

She lifted her head to check distance and spotted Nate jogging alongside, her stilettos and pashmina clutched in one hand. "Swim to shore," he bellowed.

"No," she yelled defiantly. "I'm nearly there." Teeth chattering, she resumed her swim, determined to go the distance, though her arms got heavier and heavier. At last the bach was alongside. Claire angled into the shore and stumbled through the shallows, feet numb, muscles convulsing and grinning ear to ear.

NATE WAS SO FURIOUS he had to consciously unlock his jaw. "You didn't even bloody jump at the right place!"

Claire's dress clung to her body like tattered flags. Her nylons were torn and covered to the ankles in sticky mud. "Th-that…wa-was… f-f-f-fun," she said.

Roughly he wrapped her in the shawl, jerked his jacket across her shoulders and frog-marched her up the path. "Do you know how cold that water is right now?"

"P-p-pooh! Y-y-you d-d-did it."

"We were in wet suits!"

Claire stumbled and impatiently he picked her up and carried her across the grass, over the deck and into the bach, where he tugged off the jacket and pashmina. He yanked the bedraggled chiffon bow loose then spun her around to undo the zip on the back of her dress, ignoring her blue-lipped protest.

"Hey, you wanted me to do this half an hour ago." Unceremoniously he stripped Claire to her underwear, then grabbed a couple of towels from the bathroom and briskly rubbed her dry.

"W-w-want sss-sssssshower."

"Not for hypothermia." At least she was shivering; that meant it was mild. He steered Claire into her bedroom and bundled her under the covers. "Take off your bra and pants while I find something warm for you to wear." He rummaged through the dresser drawers and settled on a fleecy nightdress.

Claire was still fumbling with her bra clasp when he turned.

"Here." Thrusting the nightdress into her arms to protect her modesty, he undid the hooks. She disappeared under the covers and two scraps of sodden underwear dropped onto the floor.

Grimly Nate picked them up and dumped them into the laundry hamper, then began another search for additional layers of warmth, finding a beanie and a woolen scarf. Claire emerged from the blankets dressed in flannelette, hair plastered to her head and looking like a half-drowned rat. Dropping the woolens beside her, Nate sat on the bed and roughly towel-dried her hair, then pulled the beanie from the heap and covered the damp tangles. Claire began to laugh. "Th-th-this is ssssssilllllly."

"Hypothermia is no joke," he scolded. Now she was okay, he allowed his fright and frustration free rein. "You could have hit your head in the dark. You could have got cramp. As for jumping in a goddamn dress—what the hell were you thinking?"

"Ssssssorry," she said cheerfully. Nate narrowed his eyes. Winding the scarf around her neck, he gave the ends a light tug, warning her not to push him too far, and then tucked the blankets in until she was swaddled like a baby.

"Stay covered," he ordered. "I'll make a warm drink."

"Yyyyesssss, ssssir."

Ignoring that, Nate went to the kitchen,

boiled the kettle for cocoa, adding plenty of sugar. Claire was curled up when he returned. With relief he noticed her shivering had abated.

"Sit up," he said brusquely. When she held out a trembling hand for the cup, he stopped her. "You'll spill it, let me hold it."

Obediently she took a sip, her teeth knocking against the rim of the mug. Then grimaced. "Sweet."

"Drink it." Her icy hands covered his on the mug. She took a couple more sips. Putting the mug on the nightstand, Nate picked up her hands and rubbed them between his own chilled fingers. For the first time he registered his own dishevelment. His shirt untucked, the buttons half undone. So was his belt buckle, because his first thought had been to follow her into the water, until she'd convinced him she was okay. Claire shivered again, a violent paroxysm.

"Hell." Kicking off his shoes, Nate joined her under the covers. Body heat was the quickest way to warm her and no point pretending otherwise. "Put your arms around my waist and snuggle in."

She did so without hesitation, one knee instinctively going between his for maximum contact. Her feet were two blocks of ice against his calves, which helped keep his focus on the task, instead of the woman in his arms. Her woolen beanie prickled the underside of his chin and the hands splayed against his back were as icy as her toes, but gradually the shivering stopped until only Claire's nose, burrowed into his chest, retained a vestige of cold.

Something in him began to unravel. Her breathing slowed to match his, their ribs rose and fell in instinctive synchronicity. Nate became aware of her breasts under the flannelette pressing against his chest, the warmth of her breath feathering his collarbone and—he closed his eyes—the tension in her body that told him Claire was as acutely conscious of the seductive possibilities of this moment as he was.

He wanted her so badly.

One last inhale of wool, salty skin and woman-heated flannelette, then Nate rolled away from the warm clasp of her arms to the edge of the bed, and to his feet. "I'll sleep in Lewis's room tonight in case you need anything."

She looked up at him with those blue eyes, and touched a self-conscious hand to the beanie. "Good night, Nate."

Resolutely he left the room, headed straight to his monastic bed and told himself he was doing the right thing, though every part of him trembled as he fought an internal battle to do nothing.

Minutes later the living room light switched on. "You need something?" he called.

"No, I'm having a shower. Is that okay, Doc?"

"Yeah."

The water went on forty seconds later. The shower cubicle lay on the other side of the bedroom wall, which meant Claire was only a couple of feet away while she soaped the salt off and shampooed her hair. Nate groaned and turned over, putting a pillow over his head to drown out the sound of water splashing over her naked body.

Which is how he missed her return until something bumped against the foot of his bed.

Nate took the pillow off his head.

"Ouch," said Claire. "It's dark in here."

"What's wrong?"

"Wait." She bumped his mattress again, then the curtains swept back and moonlight cast pale beams into the room, enough to see she wore a white satin robe belted at her waist. And it was clear from the way it clung to every swell and indent that it was all she wore.

"There's sand in my sheets," she said.

CHAPTER TWENTY-TWO

NATE CLOSED HIS EYES because it was the only way he could think, but the image of her nipples under the robe had already burned his retinas.

Claire said, "Nate," and he opened them as she sat on his bed, her scent as fresh as a summer shower. "First, let's get something straight. I'll always love Steve. I don't want you having any doubts about that."

Relief was bittersweet. "I'm glad."

"And I've fallen in love with you." She opened her robe and moonlight fell on the slope of her shoulders, on the curve of her breasts. Claire leaned forward and the soft fall of her freshly washed hair brushed his bare chest as she paused with their mouths inches apart. "Are you going to reject me again?" she whispered, a lilt of loving teasing in her voice.

And Nate was lost. Lost.

She was offering soul food to a starving man and he was powerless against his response. He stopped fighting it.

He loved her.

And though she knew his greatest regret, his greatest shame, she loved him. How could he resist such a gift? Tangling his hand around the silken strands tickling his pecs, Nate tugged her the final few inches and closed the gap. His lips touched hers, so warm, so pliant, and opened in a deep soul-searing kiss that held nothing back.

Claire broke free for breath, eyes wide, lips parted, maybe even a teeny bit afraid of the passion she'd unleashed. Nate smiled. Captivation worked both ways. "Okay," she breathed, up for the challenge.

"We should talk first." They'd had no privacy for his final confession.

"No second thoughts." She kissed him again, rolling into the tiny bed with him, and he lost his mind as her tongue teased his while her robe tangled around their limbs in an erotic slide of blood-warm satin.

Impatiently, Nate pulled the fabric loose and dropped the robe to the floor and at last they were body to body, skin to skin, her breasts pressed against his chest, his erection cradled against her soft belly.

Noses all but touching on the single pillow, he kissed her again. And again, each kiss deeper, more passionate, while he stroked her from nape to buttock, marveling over each new discovery, the silken softness of her skin, her finely boned shoulder blades and vertebrae, the sweet indent of her waist and the two dimples below it, the luscious flare of feminine hips and plump bottom. She was a miracle and he kept slowing himself down whenever hunger threatened to take over because he wanted time to absorb and savor every perfect inch of her.

Claire moaned as he fondled and suckled her breasts, shivered as he nipped her neck and chuckled as he nuzzled the ticklish point along the side of her ribs. He could tell by the way her lower body squirmed against his that she wanted his attention there. "Patience," he whispered. "Let's make this last."

With a groan, Claire caught his lower lip between her teeth and gently bit. "Maybe I don't want to."

"Yeah—" he bit lightly in return "—you do."

And he kept teasing. Until Claire punished him by teasing back, skimming her palm over his erection and dipping her tongue in his navel, across his ridged abs. "Oh, my God, Nate…" She chuckled deep in her throat. "Your body is incredible."

For the first time Nate was glad of the endless gym work with Zander that had sculpted his frame into a living work of art. Loving that it turned Claire on.

And between the kisses, through every caress, their gazes returned to each other, intimate and trusting. He'd never experienced such openness with a woman. So this was love. This ache, this intoxicating joy.

They grew hot and sweaty under the blankets and flung them off. Claire stretched, lissome and pale, in the moonlight, her white-gold hair falling to her shoulders, leaving her breasts bare. The shadowy glimpse tantalized; it wasn't enough. Nate switched on the bedside light and she became warm flesh and blood, her ethereal moon-silver limbs gilded and rosy, earthy and real.

He reached between her legs, finding her wet heat, stroking her until she was sobbing with need, until she climaxed and collapsed limply against him.

He cradled her until she came back. And said in a steely voice, "Now, Nate."

He laughed, but then reality hit him and he stared at her in dismay. "I have no condoms." They'd been the last things on his mind when he packed to leave L.A.

"I have." Claire rolled over him to reach her robe and pulled out a silver-foiled packet. "Jules gave me a couple," she murmured, and blushed.

"God bless her," Nate said fervently.

She ripped open the foil then hesitated. "I've

never used one of these. It just rolls down, right?"

The huskiness in her voice made his cock ache. "Right. Want me to do it?"

Claire smiled. "No." She flung the sheet aside, her gaze hot as she looked at his erection. Which got even harder. Then she took her time, teasing him, until Nate groaned and covered her hand with his, helping her finish the job.

"Can I…?" She straddled him, waited for permission. She was going to kill him.

"Yes," he growled. "Please."

She lowered herself onto him and he suffered every torturously slow, tantalizing inch of union, watching her face lose its impish fun, watching her eyes darken.

Clasping her waist, he lifted her, in thrall to the silken strength of her thighs around his hips. She sank down on him again. They both took a shuddery breath and then smiled at each other. Planting her hands on his broad shoulders, she rose again, her face intent, concentrating, and Nate let her set the pace, losing himself in her blue eyes, in the sensual glide of sex.

Their breathing grew faster, his hold on her waist tightened, his hips lifted, driving up as she sank down. The build to orgasm became a surge, the surge a race, stronger and stronger until she cried out, "Come with me," and he gave himself up to her with a groan.

In the aftermath, they returned to earth with gentle caresses and murmured endearments. Claire traced his face—his brows, the column of his nose, his cheekbones.

"Hey, you," she said softly.

Wrapped in his arms, she fell asleep before he could turn off the light. Nate pressed his nose against her hair. *First thing in the morning I tell her.* The one decision he'd never regretted that terrible day.

Because this woman was his future and secrets weren't going to be part of it.

THE SLAM OF A CAR DOOR woke Nate the next morning. Untangling his forearm from her silky hair, he checked his watch: 8:30 a.m.

"The curtains are pulled." Ellie's voice penetrated his haze like bullets through fog. "Surely they can't still be in bed."

"Oh, hell." Falling out of bed, he scrambled into the only clothes he had available, the dark pants and dress shirt of the night before. "Claire, wake up!"

Opening sleepy eyes, she smiled at him, and even in his panic, Nate registered a moment of pure joy. "Incoming," he warned. "Lewis... Ellie."

"What!" On a squeak of panic, she jackknifed upright and he tossed over her satin robe.

"Save yourself. I'll keep them busy."

Another door slam, more cheery voices—Dan's, Jo's, Viv's and Ross's. The whole damn cavalry had arrived.

Nate hurried to the patio doors and opened them, angling his body to block entry and trying to look as if he hadn't had one of the most incredible nights of his life.

"Hi, everyone, great to see you." The way the breeze ruffled his hair suggested it was sticking up all over the place. "Is that a white heron on the point?"

"Where?" Lewis's gaze followed Nate's pointing finger, but the adults stared at his formal clothes with a dawning comprehension that made unexpected heat rise to his cheeks as he tamped down his cowlick. He felt as self-conscious as a teenager caught by his parents.

Ellie's lips tightened.

Shit. It wasn't supposed to happen this way. It was important to get Lewis's approval before going public. To break it to Ellie gently. "To the left of the pine," he said desperately.

"Where's Mum?" Lewis continued to search for the nonexistent bird.

"Sleeping in… You, um, know she's not a morning person."

"That's slander," Claire said behind him. "I've been up at least five minutes." Breathing a sigh of relief, Nate stepped onto the deck and turned around. His lover wore a bright smile, white jeans and a baggy pink sweatshirt. She'd also sensibly taken the time to tie her hair into a neat ponytail. It gave an excellent view of the beard burn on her neck.

Everyone stared. Ellie's hand crept to her mouth.

"I know it's shocking!" Claire misinterpreted their expressions. "No coffee made yet."

Nate coughed, but she refused to meet his eye. Lewis started to turn. "I can't see that bird."

Jo stepped forward to block his view of his mother. "What are we looking for again?"

"Yes," said Ellie. "Just what are we looking at here?"

Lewis answered. "A white heron." He pointed the direction for Jo.

Viv was the first person to swing into action, propelling a confused Claire backward into the bach. "Let's get that coffee started," she said cheerfully. "Ellie, you relax in the sun. Being the matriarch has to have some privileges. Guys, get Ellie a chair."

Dan pulled one forward with alacrity; Ross pressed on Ellie's shoulders to make her sit. "Looks like Viv will be marrying me in the very near future," he said, shooting a grin at Nate over her head.

Reluctantly, Ellie gave him her attention. "Congratulations."

While Ross kept her occupied, Nate glanced inside. Viv had pulled a powder compact out of her handbag and expertly covered the beard burn on Claire's neck. Tough job—his beloved's whole complexion flamed red.

"Speaking of flying away…" Ellie's tart tone dragged his attention to her. "You're still leaving tomorrow, aren't you, Nathan?"

Lewis pricked up his ears. "What, you're thinking of staying? Cool."

Nate opened his mouth, but Jo got in first. "How about you guys unpack the food from Dan's car?" she suggested. "I'm eating for two, all going to plan."

That distracted Ellie. "Are you pregnant?"

"Nearly," Jo said.

Claire reappeared at the open ranchslider, the beard burn hidden by concealer. "How are we all doing," she beamed. Without waiting for a reply she grabbed her son's elbow. "Lewis, help me fetch more deck chairs." And she steered him down the side of the building, where a small door gave access to a dugout under the bach.

Ellie stood to follow. Gently, Ross pressed her

down again. "I want you to talk to Viv about honeymoon lingerie," he told her. "Viv, hon, come out here, will you?" He helped Dan shepherd Nate toward the ute. "I'm totally reliant on your judgment," he called earnestly to Ellie over his shoulder. "But FYI, I do have a soft spot for corsetry."

THE MAKESHIFT BASEMENT under the bach was a rough-hewn storage space cut out of the earth, not quite deep enough for a six-foot man to stand upright without ducking under the overhead joists supporting the building's floor.

It smelled of dry dirt and mustiness, and spiderwebs draped from the beams like post-party streamers. Reaching into one of the crevices, Claire pulled out a couple of folded deck chairs, the jaunty blue-and-white-striped canvas brightening the gloom. It wasn't really the place to ask her son's permission to bring Nate into their small family, but Ellie's expression suggested she had no choice. Claire had to get in first.

"Sit down a minute," she said, unfolding a deck chair. "We need to talk."

"In here." Lewis looked at her, clearly puzzled. "Seriously?"

"Seriously." She waited until he'd lowered himself into the canvas sling. "How would you feel about Nate staying…living with us? For good."

"As your boyfriend?" he said. "I mean, I can see how much you like each other."

Claire blushed. "Probably more serious than that."

"You mean, your husband?"

She took a deep breath. "Probably…yes." Wryly, she hoped she was speaking for Nate. But she was absolutely certain he was the man she wanted to spend the rest of her life with. And equally convinced he felt the same about her. Must be love. "Which would make him your stepfather. So lots to consid—"

"I'd like it," he interrupted, "but Nana won't." So he'd picked up Ellie's hostility. "She'll be worried that he'll try to replace Dad."

Claire crouched beside the deck chair. "Does that worry you, son?"

"Nah, Nate wouldn't do that." He paused, trying to find the right words. "He loved Dad, too. So we don't have to worry about hurting his feelings when we talk about him."

"I need you to be happy about this, Lewie, so if you want more time to think about it—"

"Mum, I never got why he was going back anyway," he said impatiently. "Not when it was obvious you liked each other." Lewis shrugged. "You guys were the ones who couldn't decide."

"Oh." Put in her place, Claire sat back on her heels.

"'Course, he'll find it lame living here after working for a rock star in Hollywood." He looked at her doubtfully. "But I guess he thinks you're worth it."

Her lips twitched. "Maybe I should marry him quick before he realizes he's got the bum end of the deal."

His eyes lit up. "We could move to Hollywood."

Claire laughed.

"Mum," Lewis said, "seriously, we have to talk about this."

Exit, stage right. "C'mon, let's get these chairs to the others." Later she'd remind him she had a new business to run. First, there was Ellie to appease.

Lewis picked up a couple of folded deck chairs. "And until we move to Hollywood, Nate can help on the boat charters." The kid had a one-track mind. "I know you keep saying I don't have to, but now I don't have to feel guilty about it."

The pragmatism of a young teenage male. "You are all heart," she marveled.

"At least I feel guilty," he pointed out.

She ruffled his hair. "And I appreciate it, honey."

Outside he stopped her. "I'm sorry for giving you such a hard time earlier this year." He shrugged, avoiding her gaze. "I don't even remember why I thought it was cool—all that stuff. Or why I even liked those guys. Now I think they're idiots."

"You never know." Claire put down the deck chairs, caught his face between her hands and kissed his forehead despite his disgusted protest. "They might grow out of it."

CHAPTER TWENTY-THREE

NATE FOLLOWED THE GUYS to Dan's four-wheel drive. The fragrance of fresh-baked bread and cinnamon rolls wafted from a couple of shopping bags as Ross opened the trunk.

"So you're staying?" As usual, Ice didn't bother with preamble.

"That depends on whether Lewis is happy about it," Nate replied. Ellie clearly wasn't. He felt a pang of annoyance at himself for sleeping in. She shouldn't have found out this way, but nothing he or Claire could do about it now.

"And are you happy?" Trust Dan to ask the hard question.

"I'm all over the place," Nate admitted. "Last night wasn't meant to happen. I wanted to give Claire more time. Hell, we only talked about the ambush a few days ago. And I didn't cover everything." He glanced toward the dugout where Claire had taken Lewis. They still had challenges ahead.

"When are you going to tell us?" Ross's quiet

inquiry refocused Nate's attention. He looked at his friends, his buddies, his brothers.

"I guess—" he swallowed "—I'm ready to tell you now."

Ross picked up the shopping bags. "Let me give these to the girls.… I'll offer to do the dishes if they cook breakfast. We'll take a walk."

"Lewis will want to come," said Nate.

"I'll call it a jog, then."

He returned within a couple of minutes. "Dishes and coffee is the deal. Claire and Lewis walked by with deck chairs as I left. She gave me a thumbs-up. I think you can read that as a good sign. Ellie, on the other hand, is scowling. She'll need some nurturing when we get back."

Nate and Dan stared at him. "Nurturing?" said Dan.

"Amazing how far using that word gets me with your sister," Ross replied cheerfully.

"Thank God," said Nate. "The world has tilted on its axis enough as it is." But his part in the banter was perfunctory. The three men walked along the beach while he struggled for a starting point. He still wasn't ready for this conversation, but today marked a new beginning.

"If it helps…" Picking up a piece of driftwood, Ross used it as a walking stick over the soft sand. "We're aware Steve wasn't killed instantly."

"How?"

Dan answered. "The call for backup. Even distorted, it's Steve's voice, not yours."

"The C.O. knows," Nate said. He'd told him as soon as he found out that he'd been cited for a heroism medal. And been absolved of culpability. The C.O. had insisted Nate receive recognition for saving Ross; his only compromise had been allowing Nate to accept the highest civilian award instead of a military one.

Nate looked at Ross, limping beside him. "Steve and I worked together to stem the bleeding and save your life." He told the story slowly and the telling was no easier. When he'd finished, they were all sitting at the base of the dune and Dan was leaning forward, his face buried against his drawn-up knees.

"Did you expect us to ostracize you?" Ross said hoarsely. He was picking up fistfuls of sand, and then letting it slide through his fingers.

"I was afraid you wouldn't." Nate laid an arm across Dan's shoulders. "I needed Claire to forgive me before I could forgive myself. She said guilt only undermines Steve's courage in sending me away. He saved both our lives," he said to Ross.

"Don't underestimate your contribution." Dan lifted his head and his eyes were wet. "You fended off a dozen insurgents for twenty minutes before backup arrived."

"I had to." Nate gave a ghost of a smile. "Steve kicked me in the ribs and told me to save Ross's life. Yelled 'That's an order, soldier!'"

The other men smiled. "He had faith in you," Ross croaked. "His faith made staying alive an obligation." He stopped sifting sand. "I just had a flashback to the ambush. You saying we were the Indestructibles."

"We're still the Indestructibles," Dan said. "Lee's optimism and Steve's altruism can live on through us." He wiped his face dry on his T-shirt. "We live big for them and we make the rest of our lives count. The prospect of Jo's cancer recurring has only reinforced that philosophy for me." He punched Nate's arm. Hard. "And we don't shut each other out again."

"Okay." Massaging feeling into his biceps, Nate gazed out to sea where an unwieldy trawler crawled across the horizon, its funnel puffing black smoke. "There's one more thing I need to tell Claire," he said. "It's not something I regret, but she needs to know everything.… So do you."

"Hey!" They all glanced up at the shout.

Lewis jogged up, panting. "You have to come for breakfast."

The teenager's presence precluded further conversation. They started back, Lewis slipping into step alongside Nate. "Mum said you're getting married."

Nate laughed; he couldn't help it. A little ahead of herself, his love. He matched the boy's casualness. "That's my hope." Understatement. Out of the corner of his eye, he caught Dan and Ross exchanging startled grins. "If you're okay with it," he added.

"You mean, because of Dad? I'll always miss him, but at least now I don't have to miss you, too."

And just like that, Nate's vision blurred. Without a word, Dan pulled a pair of sunglasses out of the breast pocket of his shirt and passed them over. Ross offered Lewis his makeshift walking stick. "How far can you throw it?"

Nate jammed on the sunglasses and struggled for control. He wanted to cry like a baby for this second chance; instead, he wrestled his emotions under control and surreptitiously wiped away the few tears trickling under the sunglasses. Fortunately, Lewis was too absorbed in lining up his shot to notice. With a whoop, the teen hurled the stick like a javelin.

The sunglasses had fogged up, Nate didn't

see where it landed—hell, he could barely see where he was walking. He laughed suddenly, an old rusty chuckle. Somewhere Steve was probably laughing, too. *Are you okay with all this, mate? Give me a sign...something, anything.* His left foot kicked the remnants of a kid's sandcastle and his friends threw out a hand to steady him. *Okay,* he thought. *Yeah. I'll take that.*

WHAT WERE THEY TALKING ABOUT?

Clearing plates after breakfast, Claire noticed Lewis having an earnest conversation with his grandmother on the beach below the deck. In the flurry of organizing the meal, there'd been no opportunity for their own private showdown and she was feeling the strain of Ellie's martyred silence and wounded pride.

She picked up her mother-in-law's scraped plate. Though it hadn't affected Ellie's appetite. A good sign?

The sound of raised voices returned her attention to the estuary. Lewis had his arms folded; Ellie was frowning. Please, not an argument now. Her son's expression changed, grew pleading. His grandmother's frown softened, though it didn't disappear. Good, they were sorting it out.

"Let me take those, the guys are on dishes,

remember?" Nate's arms encircled her from behind. "And since the coast is clear." He nuzzled her neck, and Claire closed her eyes briefly in a delicious shiver. Momentarily she leaned into his solid warmth then stepped out of his embrace.

"Not quite clear." Handing over the stacked plates, she pointed to the two figures on the beach. "I thought you were a covert operator."

"Turns out I'm a 'shout it from the rooftop' kind of guy when it comes to love." Oh, God, she lost the power of thought when he smiled at her like that. Nate looked beyond her to Lewis and Ellie and sobered. "Sure you don't want me to talk to her first?"

"No, she needs to hear this from me.… But thanks." One step closer and she could kiss him. He must have read her thoughts, because his eyes darkened to the color of cognac. Oh. Wow.

"So, let's check out this boat of yours." Jo walked through the patio doors, applying a last dab of sunblock to her pale skin, followed by Viv who'd borrowed one of Lewis's caps and still managed to look New York chic.

"Nate, my brother is looking for a kitchen hand," she said.

"I'm on it." One last smile at Claire to weaken her knees—that was going to help walking—and he disappeared inside.

Claire blinked to refocus and saw two women grinning at her. She grinned back. "Ellie and Lewis are already on the beach," she said. "And I need you two to help me out."

Ten minutes later, her friends had drawn a tactful distance ahead with Lewis, and Claire was waiting at the bottom of the path while Ellie fetched a sunhat.

Ellie glanced along the shore to the others when she reappeared but made no comment. They started their stroll to the boat shed in silence. "So what were you and Lewis talking about?" Claire began by way of opener.

"He told me I was acting like a sulky brat."

"What?" She gaped at her mother-in-law. "Oh, my goodness, I'll make him apologize right now." She picked up her pace to catch the other walkers, but Ellie caught her arm.

"He said, 'That's what you tell me, Nana, when you think I'm giving Mum a hard time.'"

Okay. "He's still wrong," she said. "Ellie, your reaction is completely understandable. This was a terrible way to find out about me and Nate." They resumed their walk. "It only happened last night and we slept in.... I'm sorry."

Ellie adjusted her sunhat. "You've done a good job with Lewis," she said.

It wasn't the direction Claire expected and it took her a moment to respond. "We had our concerns for a while, didn't we?" she replied cautiously. "But he seems to be settling down again."

"And you did a good job of raising him when Steve was deployed, too," Ellie said. "I also appreciate that you were always there for me when Steve couldn't be. Never once have you treated me as a pain-in-the-ass mother-in-law."

"Well, you've always been there for me." She wasn't quite sure where this was heading, but instinct told her to follow. "Mum and Dad can only visit so often from Australia."

"About Nathan…" Ellie paused.

Claire steeled herself. "Yes?"

"It's going to take some getting used to." Ellie stared straight ahead. "But as Lewis said, he and I already share you with each other—we can make room for one more."

Awed, Claire stared after her son. "And perhaps," Ellie admitted in a tremulous voice, "I'm not jealous for Steve's sake, perhaps I'm also jealous for my own."

Moved, Claire hooked her arm in her mother-in-law's. "You're my family," she said. "That will never change. Up until the ambush you were Nate's family, too."

"And he walked away," Ellie reminded her. "From everyone. I don't want you getting hurt again. You've had enough heartache losing Steve."

Appreciating her concern, Claire squeezed her soft forearm. "Nate had some healing to do. We all did. But he won't leave me, Ellie. Or hurt me—at least not intentionally." Wanting to alleviate the older woman's anxiety, she added lightly, "Only Robert was perfect."

Her mother-in-law sighed. "We both know Bob was a grump and our marriage wasn't as idyllic as I'd have everyone believe. But—" her voice wavered again "—yours and Steve's was."

Claire thought about the hard times she and Steve had gone through as young marrieds, then about the many happy years they'd spent together before he broke his word and died in Afghanistan. "Yes," she agreed. "It was."

"And I think you and Nathan will be very happy, too," Ellie said bravely.

"Your acceptance means a lot, Ellie. Thank you."

Lewis glanced over his shoulder, saw them arm in arm and grinned. His grandmother frowned.

"Now he's smug." She raised her voice. "Lewis Langford, have you still got those new shoes on? I told him salt water ruins suede." Ellie hollered again. "I'll have your guts for garters if they get wet!"

Her grandson stopped and hastily stripped them off his feet, then ran to catch up Jo and Viv.

Claire laughed. "Where did that expression come from?"

"No idea," said Ellie. "My English mother used it. I think it's probably got something to do with disembowelment in the Middle Ages." She said it with the same relish her grandson used to describe docking lambs' tails.

Genetics was a wonderful thing. "So I take it," said Ellie, "Nate's not leaving?"

"No," Claire said, feeling joy ripple through her. Life was suddenly spectacularly good. Ellie turned to gaze across the estuary. "Now, why would someone be burning rubbish on a beautiful day like this?"

Claire shaded her eyes. "It's okay, it's in a drum." The flames blazed high, a plume of smoke painted a charcoal smear across the blue sky. Something tugged at Claire's consciousness, something critical.

"I thought I could smell smoke," Ellie commented as they resumed their walk. The acrid tang reached Claire's nostrils; she stopped dead.

Ellie looked at her in surprise.

"I... I forgot something," she stammered. "It's important." She dragged her gaze from the flames. "You go on ahead with the others. I'll catch you all up."

"Sure."

Claire hurried back, her anxiety spiking until she broke into a flat run. Shells crunched under her sneakers. By the time she'd sprinted up the steps to the bach she was gasping with fear.

Ross was on the deck, cleaning the barbecue. He glanced up, smiling. "What's the hurry?"

Ignoring him, she flew into the bach. Dan stood at the sink washing dishes. Holding a tea towel, Nate was drying a cup. "You lied to me," she panted.

"Calm down, tell me what's going on."

"You said Steve didn't suffer."

Nate put the cup and tea towel on the counter. "He didn't."

"But the Humvee burned. The rear was hit with another IED. Steve…" Her voice cracked. "Steve would have burned alive." In her mind's eye she watched cruel licks of flame blister and burn Steve's flesh while her trapped husband writhed, unable to escape. "No!" Claire covered her mouth against an involuntary gag.

"I swear he didn't suffer." Pinning her horrified gaze, Nate moved to take her arm, but she shook it off, hysteria rising.

"You lied to me!"

"Claire, listen to me." His voice was slow,

very deliberate. "I didn't let him suffer," he repeated.

Her brain scrambled to make sense of conflicting facts.

"Jesus," said Dan. "Oh, God, Nate."

Behind her, Ross sucked in a breath.

Nate didn't take his eyes from her face. "As a soldier, the thing you're most scared of isn't dying. It's failing your brother when he needs you. Steve needed me, Claire. I couldn't let him down again."

Her stomach plummeted, her knees started to shake. "You shot him," she whispered.

"Yes." A grave statement of fact. She saw no remorse, no apology, no guilt. A soldier's eyes. Not Nate's. Stoic in their acceptance of the horror of war. It was unbearable, incomprehensible. Wrong.

Dan moved. Empathy in his face, he placed a hand on Nate's shoulder. His silent support enraged her. When Claire felt Ross's comforting touch, she spun away. "No! It's not right. It will never be right. Don't you dare accept this as normal."

"Claire." Nate only had focus for her. She took one step back, two. "I hate this," she cried. "I hate all of it. Don't any of you follow me!" Pivoting on her heel, she shoved past Ross and ran.

CHAPTER TWENTY-FOUR

THE REVULSION IN Claire's face stopped Nate in his tracks.

How could he have expected her to understand? How could any civilian? And yet there'd been no doubt as he'd raised his weapon and adjusted the sights, pain blossoming inside him until it obliterated everything but grief and love.

Knowing it would kill something of him to do this, he'd never hesitated. Hesitation meant agony for Steve.

After he pulled the trigger he'd gone into autopilot against the rebel attack, firing, reloading, moving like a robot between grenade launcher and his M4A1 semiautomatic. Changing magazines as they emptied with clinical precision. Feeling nothing, not even hatred.

He worked to save Ross's life because Steve had told him to, but at his core Nate waited for death with a calm fatalism. He barely heard the incoming American Apache gunship, barely registered the arrival of reinforcements or the counterattack. Certainly he felt no relief. Only when Dan peeled his fingers off the assault rifle did Nate grasp that it was over and returned from the dead himself. Only, part of him didn't. Part of him died with Steve.

Another part of him was dying now.

"It's over," he said. Over with Claire before it had begun.

Dan's fingers tightened on his shoulder. "You don't know that, she's in shock."

But he did. Her repugnance had made it clear. "Make sure she's okay," he said.

"Ross is on it."

Dazed, Nate tuned in. Ross paced the living room with his cell, his limp barely noticeable. "Viv? Send Jo after Claire. She's headed to the surf beach and she's upset. Keep Ellie and Lewis occupied until I phone." He stopped to listen and then rubbed a hand over his eyes. "I knew I could rely on you, babe."

"Was I wrong?" Nate asked when Ross ended the call. Horror, deeply buried, welled up and threatened to spill over.

"No," said Ross.

Dan's hand was still on his shoulder. "I hope I'd have had the guts to do it," he said hoarsely. "And I thank God I didn't have to."

Ross came up and hugged him. "We'll share your burden, soldier. You've carried it alone long enough."

THEY SENT JO after her. Claire couldn't have coped with a male right now. Her friend stopped a couple feet above the tidal edge where Claire stood, arms wrapped around her body like a straitjacket.

"You need to talk?"

"Men and testosterone, war and grief," she raged. "What about the women and children, Jo?" A bigger wave rolled through, water hissed across the sand and surged over her sneakers, soaking the hem of her white jeans. She didn't care.

"I have no answers," the redhead said. "Confronting death, overcoming cancer made me feel more alive. But choosing to put your life at risk as a professional soldier? I've never understood that.... What happened, Claire?"

"Your husband didn't tell you?"

"No."

Claire did. All of it. "Nate shot Steve," she finished wildly. "He shot my husband. He shot his best friend." A bigger wave surged against her shins, nearly knocking her off balance. "I want this to stop," she said. "The horror, the grief. I can't do this anymore, Jo."

Jo started wading through the tide. "Come here, honey."

"No, don't touch me." Her friend backed up. "But...don't go anywhere either."

"I won't."

"I made love to him," Claire said. In Nate's view he'd done what he had to do. He didn't see this as the barrier she did.

"What are you afraid of?" Jo asked.

"Of not being able to get past this with Nate." Claire hugged herself tighter. "Let's walk," she said. "I have to move."

"Okay," said Jo. "We'll walk." They trudged along the beach while Claire's thoughts whirled, shaken snowflakes in a globe. Whenever they settled, she'd think, *Nate shot Steve,* and raw emotion shook them up again. On their second circuit, she ran out of nervous adrenaline and gestured to the base of a sand dune. "Can we sit a few minutes?"

"Of course."

The tide had receded as they'd walked— Claire figured they must have been gone half an hour. She started. "Lewis and Ellie?"

"Don't worry, Viv is keeping them busy."

"I need more time to decide what I'm going to do."

"We have time," Jo soothed.

Claire pressed her throbbing temples. "Except I can't think," she cried. "It's too much." Too big, too terrible.

"And you're exhausted," Jo said softly. "Then rest a few minutes. Just sit."

"Yes." Next to her, the spinifex stirred softly in a light breeze. Claire cupped her hand over it, felt the caress on her palm as she stared out to sea, letting the sound of gulls and crash of rolling waves drown out the clamor in her head. On impulse she lay down on the warm sand and spread her arms wide, watching the grains spill across the sleeves of her pink sweatshirt in a glittering sparkle as the sun caught them.

Jo lay down too as if it was the most natural thing in the world for two thirty-something women to sprawl in the sand fully clothed. "I'm glad you're here," Claire said. When her friend's fingertips touched hers, she didn't pull away.

The sky stretched overhead, a limitless blue. It was easy to believe your dead watched over you from a sky like this. *Help me, Steve. Help me find my way.*

"I've never told you this," Jo said, "but I wouldn't have married Dan while I had cancer hanging over me without your insight. Do you remember? You said, even though you'd lost him, Steve was worth it."

At the time Claire had thought if she concentrated only on the good she'd never have to confront her deep sense of betrayal. "He was worth it," she said. It was even truer since Nate helped her own the anger and move beyond it. God, she was so confused.

"Now you have to decide whether Nate is worth it."

Claire said nothing. She fancied she could feel the pulse of the earth under her back and closed her eyes. Let her mind go blank under the hot sun. Rested.

Jo's cell rang. "It's Dan.... Honey? Yeah, she's coping.... Uh-huh. Well, can't you stop him?" Opening her eyes, Claire turned her head. "I'll tell her." Jo flipped her cell closed. "Nate's packing. He seems to think it's over, and that it's unfair for you to see him, as upset as you are. Dan can't talk him out of it. Ross has gone to help Viv hold off Ellie and Lewis."

Her grip tightened on Claire's. "That choice you need to make about whether Nate's worth it? I'm sorry, but you need to make it now."

THE INSTANT SHE SAW Nate, Claire knew her decision didn't matter. He was set on leaving.

She found him on *Heaven Sent* in the cabin, stuffing his belongings into his bag. He'd changed out of last night's clothes into jeans and a black leather jacket, worn over a forest-green T-shirt. Zipping the bag closed, he picked up the passport lying on the bed beside it—and saw her.

Instinctively, his dark gaze scanned her face, ascertaining she was okay. Then he dropped the passport into the pocket of his jacket, his expression shuttered. "I meant to be gone before you got back," he apologized gruffly. "But I had to wait for Ross to clear the coast first. He and Viv are walking Lewis and Ellie over to Stingray Bay South."

"No goodbye?"

Momentarily his expression was raw. "I didn't think you'd appreciate one."

Claire went and sat on the bed next to his bag. "Why didn't you tell me before we had sex?"

"Because I'm stupid." Nate raked a hand through his hair. "I said we needed to talk. You said no second thoughts, and I let it go without any myself. I honestly didn't think it would have anything like the same impact of telling you I left Steve. It was only when I saw your reaction—" he swallowed "—your revulsion, that I understood how badly I'd misjudged. I deeply regret that, Claire."

She searched his face; he didn't hide from her. "I believe you."

"Leaving Steve ate me up with guilt, but sparing him an agonizing death—I can't regret that."

She flinched.

"And that's why I'm leaving," he said, and went to pick up his bag.

Claire put her hand on it. "I don't condemn your choice."

"But you can't live with the man who shot your husband." There was neither a question nor a trace of self-pity in his voice.

"I don't know." And that was the God's honest truth. She loved him too much to leave this unresolved.

His mouth tightened, in a calm voice he said, "My bag, Claire."

Her fingers tightened on the strap. "What made you decide to tell me Steve's last words the other night? I mean, I get why you didn't. You hoped to protect me from the details of his death. But you'd kept the secret for eighteen months?"

"Because you wouldn't have forgiven him otherwise," Nate said. "Because no matter how awful his passing, I knew it would cut you up more to carry a grudge against him. Because you loved him and he loved you and in the end, Claire, that's all that really counted. Isn't it?"

"Yes." All her confusion lifted and she was left with one simple conviction, unadulterated by doubt. "I ran scared because I didn't know if I had the courage for this...for us," she admitted.

Two extraordinary men had made heroic sacrifices for each other in extraordinary circumstances. And she'd been loved by both of them. They must have seen something in her. Now Claire drew strength from that. "Stay, Nate."

She expected relief; she expected an embrace. Instead, he began restlessly tidying away every reminder of his presence—dumping a newspaper in the trash, putting away a cup left to dry on the galley counter.

"I keep going back to something you said about Steve when I refused to sign the sales agreement," he said, digging his hands in his jacket pocket. "'I want to forgive him, but all the good feelings are tangled up with the bad. There's no clarity anymore.'"

Feeling sick, Claire forced herself to ask. "Do you…want to go?"

"When I arrived, you said *Heaven Sent* and Stingray Bay represented a fresh start. I can never give you that. I kidded myself that it didn't matter, but it does—for both of us. I'll be a daily reminder of grief and pain.… There's too much that you'd have to forget to love me."

"I don't want to forget," she said. "Even if that were possible."

"And I don't want to question the decision that still feels like the most honorable thing I've ever done."

Nate scanned the cabin in a last check for any

belongings and that's when Claire glimpsed his old work clothes thrown in the trash can.

The sight hurt her. Only half conscious of what she was doing, she pulled them out, smoothed and folded them. "I thought I told you the next time you intended breaking someone's heart you had to run tactics by me first."

Nate removed the folded linen from her hands, his own cold, and returned them to the trash. "Claire, don't make this harder." There was an anguished plea in his tone.

Of course she was going to make this harder. She was fighting for her life. "How could I not fall for a man whose heart is so big he can put aside his own trauma to reconcile me to my dead husband?" she demanded. "How could I not fall for a man who always puts others before himself, regardless of the personal cost?"

Nate set his jaw. "So let me do the right thing by you now."

A horn tooted outside. She watched in disbelief as he shouldered his bag. "I don't understand."

"I ordered a cab," he said. "Tell Lewis… No, don't tell him anything. I'll phone him from the airport. I won't make things worse for you than I already have."

He glanced around the cabin with the blind gaze of someone who didn't wish to see.

Stunned, Claire followed him onto the deck. "We have to talk about this."

He shook his head. "You'll be glad I found the guts to do this when you're settled with a guy who has no scars on his soul, no shadows in his eyes and no blood on his hands."

He's leaving me. The certainty hit her like a blow. "What about the trust?" she said, because any words would do while she struggled for the ones that would stop him making the biggest mistake of his life.

"I don't know...." For the first time his face showed his exhaustion. "Courier any documents... I'll sign and send them right back. But there's nothing urgent in the short term. You have the sale money."

Bag over his shoulder, he descended the ladder, the iron clink of each step resonating through the boat shed. Numbly, Claire stood at the railing. She felt trapped in a horrible dream, because her limbs, her brain felt as sluggish and leaden as they did in nightmares when she tried to outrun monsters.

At the bottom Nate looked up and love burned in his eyes, bright as the eternal flame, unquenchable. Why couldn't he believe she felt the same way? Why couldn't he feel it?

"Goodbye, Claire." Abruptly, he started walking away.

She found her voice. "I gave you redemption," she said. "In forgiving Steve, I saved you, Nate. Now save me."

He paused. "Someday," he said without turning around, "you'll find another guy like Steve."

Her stomach clenched. "What if I want a guy like you?"

Shaking his head, he resumed walking, long strides that took him swiftly away.

"You know what I wish for?" she said through a tight throat. "What I really need? A man who loves me enough to stay."

Nate's steps slowed, and then stopped. Claire held her breath and it seemed she held it forever. She wouldn't beg, she wouldn't plead. She'd begged Steve and he'd placated her with words, with kisses and with promises.

This had to be Nate's choice. Commitment had to be freely given. He adjusted the strap over his shoulder. Her heart beat faster. Her future, her son's future, hung suspended on one held breath.

He turned around.

Claire gasped in air and then released it on a sob. Dropping his bag, Nate walked toward her, faster and faster. No shadows in his eyes now. No barriers, either. She scrambled down the ladder, jumping from halfway and he caught her, crushing her to his chest as he rained kisses on her brows, her eyelids and cheeks. "You have my heart," he said, and kissed her lips. "You always will."

This man didn't make vows he couldn't keep. Tears mingling with his, Claire silently made her own.

And I will hold yours safe.

* * * * *

LARGER-PRINT BOOKS!

GET 2 FREE LARGER-PRINT NOVELS PLUS
2 FREE GIFTS!

Harlequin

Super Romance

Exciting, emotional, unexpected!

YES! Please send me 2 FREE LARGER-PRINT Harlequin® Superromance® novels and my 2 FREE gifts (gifts are worth about $10). After receiving them, if I don't wish to receive any more books, I can return the shipping statement marked "cancel." If I don't cancel, I will receive 6 brand-new novels every month and be billed just $5.44 per book in the U.S. or $5.99 per book in Canada. That's a saving of at least 16% off the cover price! It's quite a bargain! Shipping and handling is just 50¢ per book in the U.S. or 75¢ per book in Canada.* I understand that accepting the 2 free books and gifts places me under no obligation to buy anything. I can always return a shipment and cancel at any time. Even if I never buy another book, the two free books and gifts are mine to keep forever.

139/339 HDN FEFF

Name _____ (PLEASE PRINT) _____

Address _____ Apt. # _____

City _____ State/Prov. _____ Zip/Postal Code _____

Signature (if under 18, a parent or guardian must sign) _____

Mail to the **Reader Service:**
IN U.S.A.: P.O. Box 1867, Buffalo, NY 14240-1867
IN CANADA: P.O. Box 609, Fort Erie, Ontario L2A 5X3

Not valid for current subscribers to Harlequin Superromance Larger-Print books.

**Are you a current subscriber to Harlequin Superromance books
and want to receive the larger-print edition?
Call 1-800-873-8635 today or visit www.ReaderService.com.**

* Terms and prices subject to change without notice. Prices do not include applicable taxes. Sales tax applicable in N.Y. Canadian residents will be charged applicable taxes. Offer not valid in Quebec. This offer is limited to one order per household. All orders subject to credit approval. Credit or debit balances in a customer's account(s) may be offset by any other outstanding balance owed by or to the customer. Please allow 4 to 6 weeks for delivery. Offer available while quantities last.

Your Privacy—The Reader Service is committed to protecting your privacy. Our Privacy Policy is available online at www.ReaderService.com or upon request from the Reader Service.

We make a portion of our mailing list available to reputable third parties that offer products we believe may interest you. If you prefer that we not exchange your name with third parties, or if you wish to clarify or modify your communication preferences, please visit us at www.ReaderService.com/consumerschoice or write to us at Reader Service Preference Service, P.O. Box 9062, Buffalo, NY 14269. Include your complete name and address.

HSRLP11B

The series you love are now available in

LARGER PRINT!

The books are complete and unabridged—
printed in a larger type size to make it
easier on your eyes.

Harlequin
Romance

From the Heart, For the Heart

Harlequin
INTRIGUE
BREATHTAKING ROMANTIC SUSPENSE

Harlequin
Presents

Seduction and Passion Guaranteed!

Harlequin
Super Romance

Exciting, emotional, unexpected!

Try **LARGER PRINT** today!

Visit: www.ReaderService.com
Call: 1-800-873-8635

Harlequin

A *Romance* FOR EVERY MOOD™

www.ReaderService.com

HLPDIR11

Reader Service.com

You can now manage your account online!

- Review your order history
- Manage your payments
- Update your address

We've redesigned the Reader Service website just for you.

Now you can:

- Read excerpts
- Respond to mailings and special monthly offers
- Learn about new series available to you

Visit us today:
www.ReaderService.com

RS10